R0201085305

03/2020

Rumpel's Redemption

Twisted Ever After: Book 3

Tamara Grantham

RUMPEL'S REDEMPTION
Copyright ©2019 Tamara Grantham
All rights reserved.
Printed in the United States of America
First Edition: January 2020

CLEAN TEEN PUBLISHING
WWW.CLEANTEENPUBLISHING.COM

Summary: Kardiya Von Fiddlestrum, a dark elf, yearns for adventure. But when she gets kidnapped by Rumpel Stiltskin and taken to a foreign magical realm, she realizes not all adventures are created equal.

ISBN: 978-1-63422-371-3 (paperback)
ISBN: 978-1-63422-372-0 (e-book)
Cover Design by: Marya Heidel
Typography by: Courtney Knight
Editing by: Kelly Risser

Young Adult Fiction / Fairy Tales and Folklore / Adaptations
Young Adult Fiction / Fairy Tales and Folklore / General
Young Adult Fiction / Fantasy / Wizards and Witches
Young Adult Fiction / Legends, Myths, Fables / General

For more information about our content disclosure, please utilize the QR code above with your smart phone or visit us at www.CleanTeenPublishing.com

"All that is gold does not glitter.
Not all those who wander are lost;
The old that is strong does not wither.
Deep roots are not reached by the frost.
From the ashes a fire shall be woken.
A light from the shadows shall spring.
Renewed shall be blade that was broken.
The crownless again shall be king."

- J.R.R. Tolkien

For my dad.

One

I PULLED BACK THE ARROW and aimed for the man under the tree. As I edged along the branch, a twig snapped.

The man—Rumpel—looked up, his shrewd eyes focused on me.

"Come down, Kardiya," he said, his deep voice laced with warning.

"Sure. After I shoot you, I'll be happy to."

Even from up here, I heard his growl. I'd been nothing but a pain in his side since he'd captured me. I didn't plan to break the habit.

"I won't hurt you. I told you that," he said.

"I don't believe you. I tend to distrust people who *capture* me."

He stood beneath the bramble of branches. If I let the arrow fly now, it would stick in the wood or bounce back and hit me. I had to keep him moving until I got a clean shot.

"I had my reasons for taking you," he said.

"I don't care."

"Even if you'll be saving my people by helping me?"

"By saving *goblins*, you mean? So more of your people can trick mine and take us prisoner. No, thank you."

1

Keeping the bowstring held taut made my muscles burn. He needed to move an inch to the right, and I'd have a clean shot.

"Come down so we can talk about this like civilized people," he said.

"Never. First, you tell me where I am and how I get home."

"I would love to—if you come down out of that tree. Unfortunately, should you shoot me, I may have trouble telling you anything useful, as I'll be dead."

He had a point.

I lowered the bow, the arrow's shaft itching under my fingertips. I'd been so close to putting it through his chest. But what good would killing him have done me? I still had no way of getting home. I needed him alive—at least for now.

After capturing me in my bedroom, he'd used a magical key, put it in my closet door, and opened it to an unfamiliar world. Then he'd dragged me through. When he'd shut the door behind us, it had disappeared. I was trapped in an unknown land—*the goblin realm*—and I didn't know how to get out. Aside from stealing the bow and arrow from the passing caravan, I had no advantages.

I slung the bow over my shoulder and clamped the arrow between my teeth, and then I grabbed the branch and climbed down. When my feet touched ground, I pulled the weapon out of my mouth and pointed the tip at Rumpel's chest.

He was taller than most men. As a goblin, he hardly looked like the gnarled creatures I'd read about in the story books. He looked like a barbarian from the wilds, his hair shaven on the sides, leaving a strip of blond down the middle. A swirling tattoo covered half his cheek and streaked down his neck. His leather tunic moved with suppleness over a well-muscled torso. He looked male in every sense of the word, though why I noticed such a thing was inexplicable.

He took a step toward me when I thrust the arrow's tip under his chin. His icy blue eyes narrowed.

"Not another step." I sank as much grit into my voice as I could muster.

A slight smile curved around his mouth as he glanced at my flimsy arrow. Crossing his arms, he stood defiantly, feet planted on the dirt-packed path.

He grasped the golden key hanging around his neck. The metal glinted, tempting me to pull it off and discover how its magic worked.

"Tell me how I get home," I said.

"Awfully demanding, aren't you?"

"Tell me," I repeated.

"Very well. You don't. Not without my help. This key is fueled by goblin magic, meaning you won't be able to use it. If you want to go home, you'll play by my rules. I need your help restoring my kingdom. Once you do, I'll gladly use the key to escort you back to your world."

"Why can't you restore your own world?"

"Because I've tried. I can't. Not without the help of the dark elf child who wears the magical pendant of Malestasia. That pendant." He pointed to my necklace. I clutched the metal disc, my grandmother's magic warming my hand. "Do you know what that is?"

I didn't answer. It was my grandmother's pendant. It contained her magic, but I suspected that wasn't the answer he was seeking.

"It's the pendant spoken of in prophecy. Your grandmother wore it. Now it's yours. You'll be the one to save my people."

"What?"

"It's true. It wasn't as if I enjoyed having to bargain with your grandmother." His voice turned soft. "But my people are desperate to save their home." His tone, for once not full of venom, gave me pause. He was trying to save his people?

"I've waited a very long time to find you." He took a step toward me. "Help me save my people from the Shadow Lords—the Sai-hadov. They took my world more than a half century ago. Now it's time I take it back. Help me."

Half a century ago? He barely looked eighteen. Nineteen at most.

"But you captured me! How can you possibly expect me to help you with anything when I'm your prisoner?"

He clamped my wrist, squeezing painfully tight. I gasped, and the arrow fell to the ground, hitting the dirt with a thud.

Drat. There went my chances of escape. I knew I should've shot him.

"Because," he growled in my ear, his breath warm on my cheek. "I tried before. It didn't work. This time, I won't fail."

"Tried before? I never met you until now."

"With your grandmother," he said. "I made a deal to possess her firstborn, but she tricked me, turned me into a shifter dwarf with no name and no memories, and took my leg and eye for good measure. I've lived for years as a pathetic creature. I won't fail again now that I've got my identity back."

His story made me pause. Grandmother's tale of the wizard came back to me. The way she'd described it, she'd made him sound as if he were a vile goblin bent on thieving her firstborn. She'd never mentioned a bargain.

Even so, I couldn't allow him to be my captor.

I stomped on his foot. He grunted but didn't release me. Magical bands encased me, tightening around my wrists and ankles.

"I wanted to avoid this, but you've given me no choice." He picked me up and slung me over his shoulder as if I were a sack of flour. I screamed and hit his back with my entwined fists, but it was like hitting a rock wall.

He would regret this.

I called on my magic, but he'd used an enchantment to steal my powers when we'd entered his land, leaving me empty and cold inside. Panic settled inside me as I stared down the road stretching behind us, the bow and single arrow lying uselessly on the ground. Rows of trees overshadowed us, their branches thick and covered with rough bark that reminded me of dragon hide.

"Let me go, you stupid oaf! Or I'll stab you through—" The magic bands covered my mouth, muffling my words.

Anger fueled me as I pounded on his back, but he didn't react. He only continued walking down the forest path with me slung over his shoulder. Blood rushed to my head.

I would kill him. It would be a slow, excruciating death, and I would enjoy every minute of it.

His footsteps echoed as we entered a cavern. A dome of rock shaded us from the sun, the shadows cooling my overheated skin. My fists ached as I punched the man's back. He didn't stop.

Deeper into the cavern, torchlights flickered. Eyes reflected the light. Several people wearing rags and dirt-smudged faces emerged. They followed us with guarded faces and quiet footsteps, stalking like wisps of shadows.

Most had leathery skin, wrinkled and shrunken, and their haggard gazes reminded me of starving wolves. The cave widened. Dome-shaped huts made of mud and straw rose from the ground like mushroom tops.

We entered a large area, footsteps echoing up toward the curving rock structure encasing us. Sunlight peeked through holes in the rock above, revealing snaking roots that hung like tentacles from the ceiling.

Rumpel dumped me on the floor. Not gently, I noted. Curse him.

"I've come with the child of the dark elves—the one who wears the pendant of Malestasia." His booming voice echoed through the domed chamber.

A crowd of people gathered around. Beneath the dirt covering their faces, swirling tattoos appeared. For some, the inked patterns covered their entire face. For others, only cheeks or chins were marked. Their eyes shone yellow in the dim lights, reminding me of the were-jaguars infesting our jungles back home.

I wasn't sure if these people were any less dangerous.

Whispers filled the air, some I couldn't discern, and others I could. *"He's returned." "Is she the one?" "Another failure?"*

Chills prickled my skin as the people gathered around. Lean, hungry gazes fixated on me. I swallowed my fear. I wouldn't let them intimidate me. I sat up straight. The magical bands tightened as I moved.

A few children stood hugging the skirts of their mothers. A girl—perhaps four—took a step toward me. Cornsilk yellow hair crowned her head and fell to her shoulders, a bright spot in the darkness of the cavern. She eyed me shyly, her gaze lingering on my pointed ears, when her mother grabbed her and pulled her back.

Rumpel moved in front of me, blocking my view of the girl. His smug, satisfied smile made anger burn through my blood.

He wouldn't get away with this.

A commotion came from the far side of the cavern. Raised voices echoed as the crowd parted.

An ancient woman shuffled over the uneven ground, her walking stick clicking with each step. Her face was so wrinkled that it was hard to make out her eyes—twin raisin orbs stuck in sundried leather. Tattered robes in colors of red and blue hung from her stooped shoulders. The tatty ends dragged on the floor, sweeping the dirt behind her.

She stopped walking when she reached us, straightening as best as she could.

"Rumpel." Her voice cracked as she spoke, like stones grating together. "You've returned. We thought you were dead."

"I'm alive, Mistress Baelem." He nodded respectfully.

"You've brought the child of the dark elves?"

"Yes." He stepped aside and pointed to me. I must've looked a sight, with my fiery red hair disheveled, the tiny braids most likely sticking up in every direction and knotted with briars, dirt smudging my freckled face, and my hunting garb littered with leaves and brambles. What a gift I made.

The woman hobbled forward, her raisin eyes squinted as she examined me. With the magical bands covering my mouth, I couldn't make a sound.

"She's too *old*!" the woman croaked.

Old?

"No, she won't do," the woman said. "Not at all. You were supposed to bring us a baby, Rumpel. This is a grown woman. Bah!" She spat at my feet.

Grown? I'm only seventeen, I wanted to argue.

"I'm sorry, but time passes differently in the human realm. The baby of the miller's daughter grew up and gave birth to her own children. This is her youngest. And she's wearing the pendant of her grandmother. That means she's the one we seek."

The woman—Baelem—stuck a gnarled finger in Rumpel's face. "We wanted the firstborn, so we could raise her as a goblin, so she'd do what we asked her when the time came. This girl is grown. She'll never cooperate with us."

"She will if I tell her. She's quite docile and obedient."

"Hmph," I groaned through the bands covering my mouth, my eyes boring a hole through his. *Liar*, I wanted to shout. Docile? Obedient? Really?

"She'll obtain the three objects of Elevatia for us?" the woman asked. "She'll do it without complaint? She'll give them to us when the time comes?"

"Yes. I swear it. She won't fail us."

"Uh-umm," I said through the bands.

The woman eyed me. "Is she trying to speak?"

"Umm!" I grunted. *Yes!*

She stooped nearer to me. "Perhaps we'll let her tell us if she'll help us willingly."

"I'm sure that's not necessary," Rumpel said. "I give you my word. She will be the one to restore our kingdom."

Baelem laughed. The crowd shifted around us, distrustful, whispering voices echoing. "I see you haven't forgotten the ways of a goblin—deceit and trickery. If she's so willing to help us, why have you bound her mouth? You took her from her home. She'll escape when she gets a chance. No. She won't do. Take her back. Wait for her to have her firstborn, and then steal it from the cradle. We can wait."

"No, we can't." He spoke with passion, his hands fisted, steely determination in his eyes. "The longer we wait, the closer the Sai-hadov come to taking all our lands from us. We'll not even have the caves to call home."

"You're confident you can coerce her?"

"Yes." He puffed out his chest. "I promise. She will restore our kingdom."

"Mmm!" I muttered. *No, I won't!*

"What's she saying?" the woman asked.

"She'd be happy to help us," he answered.

I wish I knew what was going on. Who were the Sai-hadov? Why was I supposed to stop them? Why couldn't *they* stop them?

A man walked forward, stopping behind Baelem. Gray streaked his wiry black beard. Dark green tattoos swirled around his forehead and down his cheek. His stocky frame was accentuated by a broad barrel chest. An axe hung from a loop at his waist. Distrust clouded his eyes as he glanced my way.

He spoke quietly to Baelem. I couldn't hear his words, but with the look he gave me, I could only imagine what he was saying. Was he suggesting they kill me and be done with it?

When the man stepped away, she turned a shrewd

gaze on me. She struck the floor with her walking cane, its loud click reverberating.

"We've come to a crossroads," she shouted, her croaking voice louder than I thought possible. "Rumpel, you have not redeemed yourself. You have not brought us a babe, but a grown elf. Your failure continues."

"It's no failure. I've brought the child spoken of in prophecy. She will save us!"

Shouts and jeers erupted from the crowd. She pounded her stick on the ground until the noise decreased.

"So you say. But what does she say? Remove her bonds. Let her speak."

Rumpel's eyes clouded with fear for a half-second. He turned to me, then crossed slowly to my side. As he knelt by me, he hesitated before removing the bands covering my mouth.

He gave me a stern stare, fidgeting with the key around his neck, as if reminding me of my way home. But there was more to his glance than that. Pain. Heartache. *We need you*, he seemed to say. He reached for my mouth, touched the band, and it disappeared. I breathed deeply, working my jaw back and forth.

"Well?" the old woman called. "What say you, elf? Will you choose to help us?"

I stared from Baelem to Rumpel. He'd captured me. He'd snuck into my room, took me by force, and stranded me in the goblin realm. How could I possibly help him?

But if I refused, what then?

Would they demand my firstborn as payment for Grandmother's debt?

Good luck with that.

There wasn't a dark elven man I had the slightest interest in. I would never get married, least of all have children.

Plus, if I said no, I would completely humiliate Rumpel. Seeing the look on his face was worth it for that.

The girl with the yellow hair peeked at me behind her mother's ragged skirt. A pang of sadness gripped me, tugging on my heartstrings, blast it all.

I didn't know what I was supposed to do for these people. Save them? How? I'd spent my entire life secluded in Malestasia—the home of the dark elves. I'd only left once to go to the Outerlands. They weren't much to look at, nothing but sand and ruined buildings, and I'd only been there for a day. A magical realm like this was completely foreign to me.

I'd had wild plans of traveling to the mainland and having adventures—not getting captured by goblins and doing their bidding, with the threat of never returning home looming over my head.

What was I supposed to do?

Accept them and somehow save them? Or deny them and fight my way home—and most likely get killed in the process?

I looked from the girl to Rumpel. The intensity of his eyes caught me off guard, the icy blue brightness drawing me in. He knelt in front of me with his hands clasped, unspeaking, and his lips pursed. He didn't challenge me. He only sat with a look of desperate pleading.

Something horrible had happened to his people. Somehow, I was the key to saving them.

I had no idea what I was getting into. But I supposed I was about to find out.

"Fine," I said, sitting straight. "Tell me how I'm supposed to help you."

Two

"YOU'VE GOT SOME GALL COMING back here." The black-bearded man planted his meaty fists on his hips as he faced Rumpel.

I sat in the cavern's corner as I watched the two men face-off. It wasn't that I didn't enjoy watching Rumpel being humiliated… Actually, I did. I very much enjoyed it. With giddy anticipation.

"You should have never come back," the man said. Rumpel only stood with his arms crossed over his chest, as if allowing the other man to have his say and get it out of his system. "We didn't need you. We could've found the three objects ourselves. We didn't need some dark elf to do it for us."

"Is that so?"

"It is."

"Then, by all means, be my guest. You've had more than enough time to find the objects yourself. Where are they, Malleus?"

The man—Malleus, I assumed—grunted.

"Where are they?" Rumpel repeated.

"I would've had them myself if you'd never come back. You know very well where they are."

"So… you can't get them?"

"He's tried," another man said who entered the cavern behind us. The man walked with an air of confidence. He resembled Rumpel, with the same blue eyes and well-proportioned lips, though he stood shorter, and wrinkles lined the creases of his eyes and around his mouth. He wore clothes unlike the others in the cavern. For one thing, they weren't covered in dirt. A purple cape flowed behind him as he strode toward us, smiling with a broad grin to reveal neatly-spaced white teeth. He clapped Rumpel on the shoulder. "I'm glad you've returned, nephew."

"That's one person," Rumpel said.

Malleus sneered. "Dex, imagine seeing you here in these caverns. I thought the mud was too much for you—didn't want to soil those fancy clothes."

The blond man—Dex—straightened his golden-embroidered lapels. "Why would you say a thing like that, Malleus? You know I love to visit the caverns whenever my schedule allows it. I came as soon as I heard my nephew had returned." He turned to Rumpel. "You've done it, have you? You've found the child of the dark elves?"

"Yes." He pointed to me.

I sat up defiantly as their eyes focused on me. I still hadn't gotten a chance to change my clothes or pick the briars out of my hair. Not that I was trying to make a good impression on my goblin captors.

"Goddess be praised," Dex said, his voice hushed, eyes wide as he stepped to me, focusing on the pendant hanging from my neck. "It's really her?"

"Yes, it's her."

Dex knelt in front of me and stuck out his hand. "Pleased to make your acquaintance," he said formally.

"My name is Dex Stiltskin. I'm Rumpel's uncle."

"I'm Kardiya." I took his hand and shook it, holding firmly to his fingers. I refused to appear weak.

"Kardiya. Beautiful name. Let me guess, no one has troubled to tell you what we need you for, have they?"

"No, actually, they haven't." I cast a dark look at Rumpel.

"Ah. As I suspected. You'll have to excuse my nephew. He's under a bit of strain. Let me guess, he captured you against your will and demanded you help us with the threat of death or some such punishment?"

"That's pretty close."

"Yes, typical. Goblins have never understood the art of tactfulness."

"I can hear you," Rumpel said as he stood a few paces from us.

Dex only smiled.

"Will you tell me what I'm here for?" I asked. "What I was *captured* for?" I sank as much venom into that word as I could.

"Of course, but I'm afraid it's a bit of a long tale, and it looks as if you're in need of some refreshment first. Come, I'll show you to the inner hall where we'll get you more comfortable." He stood and held out his hand. I decided to play along.

I took his hand and stood, then followed him out of the main cavern. Most of the people had left when Baelem had, and only a few goblins lingered. They kept up with their incessant staring, scrutinizing me like I were from another world—which I supposed I was.

We walked through a narrow tunnel, Dex in front of me and Rumpel trailing behind. When we reached another cave, we stopped. It was smaller than the first area, and the scent of cooking food wafted.

A bubbling pot sat on a bed of coals at the center of the room. Several people milled about, some stirring the soup, others filling earthenware bowls. Woven mats had been placed on the stone floor, and Dex motioned for me to sit beside him. I glanced back at the passageway, hoping to see a glimpse outside, but Rumpel blocked my view, which seemed nearly poetic.

I sat beside Dex, folding my legs under me. A woman came forward and offered me a bowl. When her wide, brown eyes met mine, I saw the look of hope in their depths.

No one had ever given me such a look before, as if I were a heroine. But I hadn't done anything. I wasn't even sure what I was supposed to do.

I took the warm bowl from her. My stomach rumbled. Steam rose from the broth, smelling of salted meat. The swirling soup stirred a strange emotion in me. It felt as if taking their food meant I was fully committing to the goblins—that I was accepting them and agreeing to help them.

I'd already told Baelem I would help them, but I'd only done that because I felt I had no other choice. If I hadn't, I wouldn't go home. But this—taking their food, allowing them to become part of me, felt as if I would be fully committing, that once I did this, I could never go back.

Swallowing the lump in my throat, I shoved my fear aside. It was just food. Nothing more. I took a sip of the soup, its broth salted and tasting of mushrooms and tender meat. The liquid warmed me as I swallowed.

At least one good thing had come from the situation. I couldn't deny the goblins were talented at cooking, although the meal was scanty and hardly filling. I suspected they'd given me their best. What was everyone else eating? Dex also sipped his broth, though Rumpel hovered around us, stalking back and forth, a dark cloud as usual.

"Tell me," I said to Dex. "Why have I been brought here?"

He adjusted his cloak. "The short answer is that we need you. The old woman you met earlier—Baelem—is our seer. When our people were first attacked by the Saihadov a decade ago, our king and queen killed, and our people driven from our home in the city of Elevatia, she had a vision of a child of a dark elf saving us—a child wearing a pendant like yours.

"We sent our prince, Rumpel, to find her. He failed us when he allowed your grandmother to curse him and keep him from returning to us with her child."

Rumpel paused his pacing to frown at his uncle, who held his gaze.

"It wasn't like that," Rumpel said.

Curious, I glanced at him. "Then what was it like?"

"I'd entered into a bargain with your grandmother. She was the miller's daughter, pregnant with the prince's son, a situation which could've ruined them both. She agreed to allow me to take the child in exchange for my help in turning the king's straw to gold. I helped her every night, using my magic to change the straw, but on the third night, she refused to give up the child.

"She cursed me instead. Tricked me into revealing my true name, used it to take my eye and leg, then transformed me into a shifter dwarf. She took my memories, because she didn't want me to reveal the truth of her child's father.

"But after years living in a pitiful state, I learned my name and broke the curse. Then I found you."

My mind reeled. How could Grandmother have been so selfish? "She really did that to you?" I asked quietly.

Rumpel nodded, and my heart squeezed with pity. On the other hand, how could I believe such a thing? "That can't possibly be true. The story is decades old. Rumpel appears only a little older than me."

Dex straightened. "Ah, but he was transformed for many years, meaning his true self never aged. When he regained his actual form, he became as he was when he was first cursed. Also, we measure time differently than yours. What seems like half a century to you is ten years to us."

Rumpel's footsteps echoed behind me. His story shouldn't have surprised me. Grandmother had always had her secrets. We'd known she'd married the prince, my grandfather, shortly before giving birth to my mom. They'd avoided scandal by claiming Mother was born early.

Was it possible Rumpel told the truth?

My grandmother's betrayal stung. What else had she lied to us about? Still, Rumpel had kidnapped me, and I wasn't sure I could trust him either, much less help him. But if I could, wouldn't I be righting my grandmother's wrongs?

I crossed my arms. "No one has told me how I'm supposed to help your people. Why can't *you* defeat the Sai… whatever they're called?"

"The Sai-had-ov," Rumpel enunciated. "Because they're the immortal spirits of goblins who sold their souls for power but became cursed instead. They were sent to a place called the Shadow Realm, but they escaped. Now, they want to make our world like theirs. Their ruler sits on my father's throne, a mockery of his name."

"And *I'm* supposed to stop him?"

"No," Dex said, clasping his hands. "You're here for another reason. Before the king died, he knew that for the Sai-hadov to take full control of our lands, they would need the three objects of power—the ring, the scepter, and the crown. If a person were to obtain them, they'd be able to destroy the Sai-hadov and chase them from our lands. Before the king died, he scattered the objects to the three corners of our land—Shigoshi, Volgrave, and Elevatia. He encased them in magical riddles and traps—ones that can't be broken by goblin magic.

"You, Kardiya, are the only one who can obtain the three objects."

"Why me?"

He pointed to my pendant. "Because of the magic contained in your necklace."

I grasped the metal disc, the three wire bands connecting to form a rosette. Its magic pulsed, giving me strength. My head spun with everything they'd told me— but one thing I couldn't understand—if my necklace had the magic to find the three objects, why hadn't Rumpel just stolen it from me?

"Have you told me everything?" I asked.

A look passed between the men. I wasn't sure what to make of it.

"Only this," Rumpel said, kneeling beside me. He opened his hands, face-up. A mist of gray gathered until three images shone in the fog—a ring with a glittering sapphire, a scepter topped with a similar blue jewel, and a wire-wrought, golden crown. The three objects fell on the ground in front of him. "Pick them up."

I hesitated before reaching out and touching the crown. When I lifted it off the ground, the metal was cold. I looked up at him, confused, as I picked up the ring. The sapphire's facets refracted the light.

As I held it, the gray fog gathered once again, and the three objects disappeared.

"That's goblin magic," Rumpel said. "We deal in illusions, but nothing is real. We can do nothing with our own magic. For us to repel the Sai-hadov, we can't use our own magic. We need magic that can travel from your realm to ours, the kind that can reveal truth. That's why I sought you out. That's why you're here now."

"I'm here now because you took me against my will."

He frowned. "You've reminded me."

I wasn't going to stop reminding him, either. "So why not just take my necklace and be done with it?"

"Because the prophecy says we need you. And that's the only reason," Rumpel answered.

I crossed my arms. My opinion of him had sunk even lower, and I hadn't thought it possible.

"So, I'm supposed to somehow find these three objects and then chase these shadow goblins out of the city? I'll have you know, I'm terrible at finding anything."

"You don't have to find them," Dex said. "We know where they are. The trouble is getting them free." He reached into his inner vest pocket and pulled out a piece of vellum. He unfolded it, then smoothed his hand over the hand-drawn map. The image was detailed with mountains, rivers, and cities. A city labeled Elevatia sat in the east. To the north lay the Volgrave Mountains, and on the western side lay a land labeled Shigoshi. In each location, a drawing of an object had been inked onto the parchment—a ring in Volgrave, a scepter in Shigoshi, and a crown in Elevatia.

"The objects are here. We've tried for many years to get them free, but we've learned the hard way that we'll never succeed with goblin magic."

I studied the map, and the unfamiliar land I had no business being in.

But I'd already given my word to help them. They believed in me. Maybe somewhere along the way, I'd believe it, too.

THREE

UNABLE TO SLEEP, I LAY on the woven pallet, staring up at the beams of moonlight shining through the holes in the cavern's ceiling. Hugging the thin blanket around me did little to thaw my chills.

What was I doing here?

I was so accustomed to looking up at the sturdy oak-beamed ceiling in my bedroom at home in Malestasia, where the warm, humid air never made me shake with chills. It felt different here—cold and stagnant.

All I'd wanted for the longest time was to leave my home and go on an adventure. Now I'd gotten my wish, and all I wanted was to go back.

Could nothing work out the way it was supposed to?

Scuffling came from a hallway to my left. I sat up, imagining some crazed goblin coming after me. I reached for my boot where I'd once kept my knife, only to remember that the inner sheath was empty.

That was a problem. If the goblins wanted me to go on this quest, I'd have to do it armed. I didn't know what creatures lurked in these lands, but if they were anything like home, I'd be smart to arm myself.

Footsteps treading quietly filled the hallway, followed

by the sound of someone sobbing.

I stood, tiptoeing toward the hallway as I followed the source of the sound. In a dark room at the end of the corridor, I could make out the forms of two people—dark silhouettes outlined in moonlight.

Rumpel sat next to a boy with thin limbs and a misshapen face, his forehead broad and flat, and his jaw hanging open, as if he'd been deformed at birth. Tears streamed down the boy's face as he sat next to Rumpel.

Rage burned in my chest for a half-second. Was Rumpel hurting him? But the movement of Rumpel's hand caught my attention. He patted the boy's back in a gentle gesture. The boy smiled through his tears and hugged Rumpel's neck.

What was happening?

Rumpel glanced at me, though he didn't speak, and I didn't question him.

I backed away. When I returned to my sleeping pallet, I lay down, but closing my eyes wasn't easy. Who was the boy? What was he to Rumpel? Better yet, why was Rumpel treating him kindly? I didn't know the man was capable of compassion.

Rolling over, I rubbed my eyes, but the image of Rumpel sitting beside the boy wouldn't disappear.

I wasn't sure what to think of Rumpel. How could anyone respect a person who'd taken them from their home? He had no need to capture me. He should've just asked me to help him like a civilized person. But he wasn't a person. He was a goblin.

I was here now. I had to help them if I wanted to get home. If I couldn't help them and died trying, I doubted they would care.

My thoughts turned to my family. Did my mother and my brother Drekken realize I was missing? Or did they suppose I'd already set sail on the ship I told them I was leaving on? It might've been months before they even realized I was gone—not that they'd ever be able to find me here anyway.

I wished I'd never planned to leave. In truth, I'd wanted to find someone other than an elven man to court me. I'd never been in love, though I couldn't deny I wondered what it might be like. The boys from my home had only ever sought me out for my status. They'd never looked at me as a genuine person. I'd had vain dreams of traveling to the mainland where my title of princess wouldn't follow, where I could be myself and fall in love with someone who saw me as a person, not a means to power.

Sounds of footsteps, quiet voices, and the frigid air kept me from sleeping. I was too accustomed to my goose down bed at home. Shivering, I huddled under the thin blanket that smelled of the outdoors and forced my mind to be calm.

I flexed my fingers, willing my magic to surface, but an empty void settled where my powers had once been. Since Rumpel had wrapped me in the enchanted cords, my magic hadn't returned.

When sunlight finally streamed through the holes in the cavern's roof, illuminating the tendrils of tree roots that dangled like spider webs, I wasn't sure I'd gotten more than a few hours of sleep. Booted feet approached me. Sitting up, my stomach churned as I focused on Rumpel's smug face and piercing blue eyes. He knelt beside me, wearing a different leather vest that fitted to his lean, muscular torso. The scent of oiled leather drifted. He was entirely too handsome to be trusted.

"We're leaving today," he said, his voice gruff as usual.

"Where?"

"To the Volgrave Mountains. They're closest. From there, assuming we've obtained the ring, we go to Shigoshi, then Elevatia. It's more than a day's journey to Volgrave. I hope you're ready to travel."

"I'll be ready once I have a weapon. I need a knife."

He arched an eyebrow. "After what you did with the bow and arrow you snatched from the caravan? You'd have to be dreaming before I gave you a splintered piece of wood, let alone a blade."

Frustrated, I crossed my arms. I'd only just woken, and it was already looking to be a foul day.

"You expect me to go on this quest with you unarmed?"

"I'll be armed, as will my uncle and brother who will be joining us. You have no need to fear."

"If you won't let me have a weapon, then I demand you return my magic to me."

He glanced away, as if seeing who else was in the room before turning back to me. "Listen, *elf*, don't forget your place. You're my prisoner. My uncle may see you as an invited guest, but not me. I remember what your grandmother did to me—transforming me into a pathetic, dimwitted creature, which is why I captured you rather than begging for your help. You are my prisoner, and you always will be. Whether or not I choose to return your magic to you depends on how well you cooperate. I won't risk being cursed again. Is that understood?"

Cursing him, yes. That wasn't a bad idea. What would I transform him to? A donkey might be fitting.

"Get ready. Eat your morning meal. We leave in an

hour." He stood and tromped away.

"*Ass*," I muttered under my breath.

I stood, smoothed my leather vest, and attempted to pick the remaining briars from my hair. I needed a bath and a change of clothes, but I doubted I would get either. The smell of bread wafted from the room I'd eaten in last evening, and I wandered until I found the entrance leading to the common area.

The somber stone-gray walls were made a little brighter by the sunlight peeking through the domed roof. The air still held a chill, but after spending most of my night shivering, I was beginning to get used to it.

Steam rose from loaves on flat stones. Only a few goblins sat in the room.

Goblins. I had trouble realizing I was surrounded by the creatures from Grandmother's stories. Except for the tattoos on their faces, they looked no different from ordinary elves.

Rumpel and his uncle sat in the corner, along with the boy I'd seen last night. An elderly woman handed me a loaf of bread and a dish of goat cheese. I took them and wandered to the three men, not sure what else I was supposed to do with myself. It wasn't like I knew anyone else in this place.

Plus, I was a tad curious about the boy. Who was he?

"Good morning, Kardiya," Dex said, smiling. "Please, sit. We've an extra mat."

I sat on the woven reeds, crossing my legs under me, keeping my gaze averted from Rumpel's annoying stares.

"I trust you slept well?" Dex asked.

"Hmph," I said between bites of bread. "I would've slept better had I not been kidnapped."

"It's a pity you see it that way. I would hardly use the word kidnapped. You're a heroine to us. You shouldn't think of yourself as a prisoner."

I cast a dark glance at Rumpel, who still insisted on staring at me. "There are some who disagree with that line of thought."

Dex shrugged. "Well, the good news is that we should have excellent weather for traveling. The sky didn't have a single cloud when I checked earlier. I, for one, would rather not have to tramp through the mud."

"Mud," the boy sitting by Rumpel said. He smiled, his mouth hanging open as if he couldn't close it properly. "Mud, mud! Mud is fun!"

He was a few years younger than me. Now that I could see him in the light, it was clear he'd been born with a deformity to his face.

"This is Orlane," Rumpel said. "My younger brother. He's traveling with us."

"He is?" I asked, slightly shocked. "Is that a good idea?"

"Why wouldn't it be?"

"Well… can he keep up with us?"

"He gets around just as well as you or me."

"Yes, but…"

"But what?"

"Nothing." I sighed. "I'm sure he's very brave."

Orlane smiled. "Brave. I'm brave. Very brave."

"You are," Rumpel said, giving me a dark glare. What was Rumpel thinking taking his brother with us? What if he wandered off and lost his way? What would he do if we were attacked? But I didn't dare question the almighty Rumpel.

"Rumpel tells me you're skilled with a bow," Dex said.

I shot Rumpel a questioning glance. "He did?"

"Yes. That's a handy skill for a young woman such as yourself to have. I've always thought every young lady ought to have some skill in self-defense."

"I agree. Unfortunately, I'll be going on this quest unarmed."

"Yes, so Rumpel tells me. Well, never fear. We'll crack him at some point." Dex winked at me.

"No," Rumpel snapped. "We've already had this conversation. She's not to have weapons of any sort."

I shared a look with Dex. Yes, I would have them eventually.

"I'm finished," Rumpel said, standing. He held out his hand to his brother. "Come, Orlane."

Orlane took Rumpel's hand and stood, limping behind as Rumpel led the way out of the room.

"He's being brave to take his brother with us," I said to Dex, hoping he'd shed a little light on the reason Rumpel chose to put his brother's life in danger, although why I decided to try to figure out what went on in Rumpel's head was a mystery to me.

"Regret," Dex said. "He abandoned his brother for many years while he was stuck in the human realm. Now, he feels responsible for him. I suppose you might call it brotherly duty."

"It seems reckless to me. Wouldn't his brother be safer here?"

"Perhaps, but then Rumpel couldn't keep an eye on him. He's nothing if not controlling, which I'm sure you're starting to learn."

"Yes, that's a lesson I'm learning too well." I finished my bread and cheese. Dex helped me find a knapsack to keep a few extra loaves in, a change of clothes, and a comb for my hair. It wasn't much, but it was more than I had now.

As I slung the knapsack over my shoulder, it made me think of all the things I'd left back home. My favorite green gown and matching jeweled comb, my hairbrushes and rosewater perfume. It all seemed so trite now that the only things I owned were strapped to my back.

I followed Dex out of the cavern. The sunshine came as a shock. I squinted against the brightness. The scent of green plants and soil filled the air, reminding me of home. Rumpel and his brother stood in the shadow of the forest canopy, and we walked to them.

Rumpel's face was unreadable, though he seemed fixated on my hair. I picked at the braided strands. Had I left a stray bramble in it?

Behind us, raised voices came from the cavern's entrance. We turned, facing a mob of goblins led by Baelem and the man with the wiry black beard. What was his name again?

"Malleus," Rumpel said.

Yes, Malleus. That was it.

"Stop right there, Rumpel. You'll not be taking the elf unless I come along."

"Says who?" Rumpel demanded.

"I do," Baelem said, her voice commanding as she stepped forward. "If you wish to survive this quest, Malleus must go with you. The bones have foretold this."

"Perhaps the bones were wrong this time, Baelem. I can assure you, his presence isn't needed," Rumpel said. "We've got this under control."

"Don't argue with the bones, child. He must come."

Rumpel's eyes darkened.

"I'm coming," Malleus said, straightening the battle axe strapped to his belt loop. With the furs he wore over his bulky frame and the swirling tattoos covering his face, he looked like a barbarian ready for war, not a man merely helping us to go on a quest.

What exactly did he plan to use that axe for?

"Fine," Rumpel bit out. "Don't slow us down."

Malleus laughed. "I think I ought to be the one saying that." He marched ahead, his buckles jangling as he strutted down the dirt path and into the forest.

I flexed my hands, itching to have my magic back. A weapon of any sort would've been nice.

"Let's go," Rumpel grumbled, following behind Malleus, his brother trotting along at his side.

Dex fell into step with me. He'd worn his purple cape and a deep red vest, his bright colors standing out in the dark greens and earthy browns of the forest. His tall boots shone, as if they'd been recently polished. Unlike Malleus, he looked ready for a day at court.

Dex made small talk about the weather and the various villages we would be passing through—goblin customs and the latest in clothing fashions. None of it was of interest to me, so I smiled and nodded when appropriate, all the while keeping my eyes on Rumpel who walked ahead of us.

"…little more than an hour's walk to the next village," Dex said. "Rosenthorne is a quaint place to be sure, but you can never be too careful in a place such as that. When the Sai-hadov wander the land so freely after darkness falls—"

"They wander the land?" I asked, his conversation finally drawing my attention. "I thought they were locked inside the city and couldn't get out?"

"Yes, the ones who take a mortal form. But there are others who can't. They're wanderers, weaker than those in the city, to be sure. They'll do little more than give you a fright, but there are rumors…"

"Rumors?"

"Ahh… yes." He cleared his throat, and then he glanced away, his face brightening. "Would you look there? I believe those are apple trees. Do you think we've been so lucky as to come upon an orchard?"

I looked in the direction he pointed, but I saw only spindly needles of pine trees overshadowing us. "I don't see anything."

"Ah well, perhaps my eyes were only playing tricks. What I wouldn't give for a fresh apple or a baked tart. Now that would be a treat. I've been eating nothing but bread and cheese for too long. I think the lack of fresh food is getting to me."

"Dex, what were you saying about the Sai-hadov? Some of them can wander the land? Can they hurt us?"

"No, of course not." He laughed, a forced sound. "Harm you? I wouldn't be the one to put such notions in your head. That's the job of nursemaids, isn't it? To spin such tales of dark shadows standing over the little ones' beds at night. It's all myth, anyway. Why look there, wild strawberries. Perhaps I will have something fresh to eat after all. Pardon me." He gave me a polite nod and strode away, his purple cape flapping in the breeze.

I stared after him as he went to the patch of red bulbous berries growing in the moss. What was his game? Why did he keep avoiding talking about the Sai-hadov?

Perhaps he feared them, but he didn't care to show it.

Not wanting to waste time waiting for Dex to forage, I caught up with Rumpel and Orlane instead.

The boy gave me a smile that showed his crooked teeth. "Kard-ee," he said. "That's your name?"

"Kar-dee-ya," I enunciated. "But you were pretty close."

"Kard-ee," he said again.

"That's a good try." I smiled.

Rumpel gave me an odd glance. Not quite a smile, but a quirking of his lips. It was the closest thing I'd seen to a genuine smile since I'd met him.

"My name is Orlane," the boy said, his words choppy, as if he had trouble putting them together.

"Yes, so I hear. You're very brave to come on this quest with us."

"Brave, brave. You hear that, Rumpel? Brave."

"Yes, so she says." Rumpel's glance held a hint of warmth, which made butterflies flit through my stomach. Confused, I looked to the forest path, not wanting to meet his gaze again.

The trees thinned, allowing sunlight to shine down. A cart passed us, hitched to two horses who snorted as they trotted, their hoofbeats clomping until they disappeared.

"Dex says we're only an hour's walk from the next village," I said, wanting to think of something to break up the silence.

"Rosenthorne," Rumpel said. "We'll take our noonday meal there, then, the goddess willing, I'd like to hire a few horses. If so, we'll be able to make it to the foothills of the Volgrave Mountains before nightfall."

Orlane laughed. "Horses!"

"Would you like to ride a horse, Orlane?" I asked.

31

He clapped. "Yes, horses!"

"He also mentioned something about the Sai-hadov," I said. "But he wouldn't say much. Only something about rumors. Do you know what he meant?"

"About the villages, yes. It's why my people live in the caves. We're safer underground. The spirits wander through the villages at night."

"Can they harm us?"

Rumpel's shoulders stiffened. "Not physically."

"What does that mean?"

"Most claim they're harmless, but recently, rumors have been surfacing." He voice grew quiet. "They say the Sai-hadov spirits have been attacking people in their sleep, leaving them with their eyes gouged out but alive."

He cast a protective glance at his brother.

"Shadow. Bad," Orlane said.

"Yes, very bad. But we'll stop them soon, and then we'll never have to worry about that. Kardiya is helping us now." We exchanged glances, and I couldn't be sure, but I detected a hint of admiration.

"Hold up!" Malleus shouted in front of us, holding up a fist. He pulled his battle axe off his belt loop.

Behind us, Dex approached, holding a handful of red berries. "What's he going on about?" Dex asked, popping a berry in his mouth.

We walked to Malleus, but he rounded on us, holding a finger to his lips.

"Woodwraiths," he said.

"I didn't hear anything," Rumpel said.

"You would've if you'd been paying attention."

Howls, like those of wolves, came from the trees. Reflexively, I reached for my knife, only to ball my fists, my hands empty.

"Rumpel," I said. "I need a weapon."

He gave me a sharp glance. "No."

"Yes!"

"Stay out of the way, and you'll be fine."

I balled my fists, anger making my blood run hot. The bushes along the path rustled. The howling drew closer. I had no idea what a woodwraith was—or how to kill one. Without a weapon, I supposed I'd never have a chance.

A form emerged on the path ahead. A humanoid form wearing a tatty brown cloak flapped in the breeze. A muzzle peeked from the cowl, though the rest of its face was hidden. It snapped its jaws, revealing black fangs.

Yellow eyes glowed under the hood as it focused on us. Fear skittered down my spine as I flexed my empty hands. I willed my magic to surface, but nothing came.

Malleus charged the beast, his battle axe raised. The creature moved lightning fast, darting out of the way of the blade. It rounded, raising its hands, which were tipped in scythe-like black nails.

It struck at Malleus, its nails gouging the man's back. With a loud cry, the warrior rounded and swung his axe, though again, the beast escaped the blade.

Growling came from behind us.

I spun around. Two creatures stood behind us. I backed toward the forest, searching for anything I could use as a weapon. A large stick lay not far from where I stood, and I grabbed it, the bark rough under my hands, but it was better than nothing.

One of the beasts charged me. I swung the stick, though it evaded the blow. It struck at me with its claws. I spun around, attempting to flee. Pain exploded in a jagged, searing line down my back, as if I'd been flayed by a scorching hot knife.

The pain turned to bloodlust as I spun around to face the demon creature. Holding the stick with sweaty palms, I struck the beast's head.

It howled and darted back. Its yellow eyes narrowed, and it lunged at me. I fell to the ground. Breath escaped my lungs. The beast pinned me, snapping its massive jaws, its sickly black teeth filling my vision.

I thrust my knee into the soft tissue of its stomach. It jerked away, just enough to allow me to scoot backward.

Rumpel charged the creature. He stabbed it through the chest. With a shriek, it fell to the ground. Placing his foot on the beast's chest, he leveraged his blade from the limp body.

It fell, giving a final gasp.

Around us, two other creatures lay dead. Dex and Orlane stood uninjured, as far as I could tell. Malleus stood straight, though he grimaced at the wound on his back. Rumpel, breathing heavily, reached for me, but I slapped his hand away, making pain shoot down my back.

Gritting my teeth, I stood, though the movement only made the pain worse.

Rumpel smirked. Heat rushed through me. I slapped his cheek, hard enough to make my hand sting.

"You oaf!" I said. "If you'd let me have a weapon, I wouldn't have been injured."

I expected him to retaliate, to rant and yell and bind me in cords the way he'd done when he'd first brought me here. Instead, he kept his face turned away. Slowly, he turned to look at me, his eyes flat and emotionless. "We're going to the village," he said in a quiet, dangerous voice.

"You'll need a healer."

Staring after him, I couldn't make sense of his reaction. I'd slapped him. He should've come after me and attacked me—at least tried to defend himself. But maybe he didn't view me as a threat, and that bothered me even more.

Or perhaps he realized he deserved it.

FOUR

WHEN WE MADE IT TO the inn, I collapsed onto a wooden bench, unable to take another step. My skin had grown clammy, and the cut on my back burned down my spine.

People bustled around me as I sat staring at a large, empty hearth, nothing but a few blackened coals sitting inside. Rumpel appeared in the crowd, holding a small vial filled with purple liquid.

The wooden bench creaked as he sat beside me. He placed the vial on the table. "I was lucky enough to purchase this from a healer. This is water purified from the touch of a unicorn's horn, plus some other healing herbs. This should cleanse the poison from your blood and heal your wound quickly enough."

I glared at him. "Why are you helping me? Why don't you just let me die?"

He gave me a smug grin. I hated that stupid expression. "Let you die? Why would you say that? There's no need to be so negative."

"I'm not negative. I'm realistic. If I wasn't here to save your people, you wouldn't care if I lived or died."

"That's not completely true."

"Not *completely* true?" I snatched the vial away from

him, pulled off the cork, and held it to my lips.

"Drink it slow—"

I emptied it. Bitter liquid trailed down my throat. When it hit my stomach, I breathed deeply to keep from heaving. If I didn't know better, I would've accused Rumpel of poisoning me.

"Oh, dear goddess, that's awful."

"I tried to warn you, but you didn't listen, as usual."

The burning sensation in my wound immediately stopped tingling, and I was left with a dull ache.

"Here," Rumpel said, removing a jar of salve from his bag. "You can apply this to cover the wound. The wood-wraiths carry venom in their claws. The good news is that we have an easy remedy for it with the potion and salve combined. You should be good as new in a day or two."

I took the earthenware jar and sniffed the salve. The white paste held the soothing scent of rosewood.

"I'll apply it," he stated matter-of-factly as he took the jar from me.

My heart stopped. Apply it? What did he mean? That he would be touching me?

"No," I said, taking it back from him. "I'll do it myself."

He raised an eyebrow as I scooped up a small amount of salve and attempted to reach behind me and thread my fingers through the cut in my shirt. My shoulder twisted uncomfortably. As I touched my fingers to the open wound, I winced.

I did a poor job of spreading it on the gash, and when I handed the jar back to him, I wasn't sure I'd made it any better.

"If you weren't so stubborn, I could've done that for you."

"If I'd had a weapon, I wouldn't have been in this situation to begin with."

"Yes, you've mentioned it. Many times. Which is why I'm giving you this." He pulled a sheathed knife from his bag and placed it on the table.

I stared at it suspiciously. "Is this a trick?"

"No. It's yours."

I crossed my arms, not sure if I should take it. There had to be a catch. "What happens if I accept it?"

"You'll get what you want. Why are you resisting?"

"Because I don't trust you."

"Fine. If you don't want it, I'll take it back." He picked up the knife, but I grabbed his arm, stopping him.

That was a mistake. Hardened biceps flexed under my hands beneath the layer of his tunic's fabric. My heart fluttered inexplicably.

"Do you want it?" he asked. I took a deep breath to slow my pattering heartbeat, though it didn't help much. What was happening to me? I couldn't be attracted to him. He'd *abducted* me!

"Do you?" he repeated.

"Yes," I said slowly, hoping to control my voice. "Let me look at it first."

He handed it to me. I took the blade from him, careful not to let my fingers brush his. The leather sheath was worn around the edges. The scent of tanning oil brought back memories of times spent in combat training with my brother. He'd always been better than me, as I'd relied on my magic, but I'd learned to hold my own.

The hilt was wrapped in leather cord. I gripped it and pulled the blade free of the sheath. The polished metal reflected my face. Only a little tarnish marred the base of the blade, but that could be cleaned. It was a decent weapon. I felt no enchantments surrounding it. At least it was real, which was a bit shocking.

"You're really trusting me with a weapon?" I asked.

"Yes."

"Why?"

"Because I can't defend you at all times." His voice softened. "I realize you may've been right. I can't afford for you to be killed."

"How touching," I muttered. I held up the blade in his face. "What if I try to stab you in your sleep and steal that key from you?"

"Then you'd be doing yourself a great disservice."

I looked pointedly at him. "But I might try it."

"No. You won't."

"How do you know that?"

His icy blue eyes seemed to pierce through me. I couldn't help but stare at the ruggedness of his features—the flat plane of his forehead, the fullness of his lips, and the stubble on his chin and cheeks. It wasn't hard to imagine that this man came from nobility, but he'd become disgraced, his good name gone, redemption his only path back to the life he once had.

"Because I know your type," he answered with a firm tone.

"My *type*?"

He squared his broad shoulders. "Naïve but quick to learn. Smart but stubborn. Loyal. Headstrong. You know better than to destroy your only chance of making it back home. You won't kill me."

"You sound confident about that."

He nodded. "I am."

"Why?"

He paused before answering. "Because I've known someone like you before."

Someone like me? "Who?"

"A girl. A long time ago." He shook his head, looking away, as if caught up in a memory.

"Who?"

He paused before answering. "Her name was Myrna."

"What happened to her?" I asked quietly.

He shrugged. "I was young. Barely sixteen. I thought I was in love, but I never told her how I felt. She left me because she thought I had no feelings for her." He glanced at his clasped hands resting on the table. "When I came back from my quest to the elven lands, I found her again. I'd told myself I wouldn't let the same mistake happen twice. I told her my feelings, but by then, she'd found someone else." He straightened his vest, his eyes roving the room, as if to erase the memories. "We need to eat our noonday meal, then I'll hire a few horses. The woodwraiths slowed us down. We'll have to ride hard if we want to make it to the Volgrave Mountains by nightfall. If we don't, the woodwraiths will have the advantage of the cover of darkness, which we can't afford."

He stood and strode away, his footsteps heavy thuds on the oaken floor. I watched him go, wondering at the girl he'd lost, and why it was I'd had such a strong reaction to him. I'd never had such a response to anyone. But I couldn't be attracted to him.

He'd kidnapped me. I'd never forget the fear I'd felt when he'd dragged me from one world to another—away from my home and everything I knew.

But he'd had his reasons. Were they good enough?

A woman bustled past and placed a bowl of pottage and two loaves of white fluffy bread in front of me.

"Barley lamb stew for you, my lady, and an extra loaf, fresh from the oven."

I eyed the bowl. Had I ordered the stew and forgotten? No, I was sure I hadn't. "I'm sorry, I can't take it. I have no way to pay for it."

The woman smoothed her hand over her grease-covered apron, which bulged over her protruding middle. "No need to pay. 'Tis taken care of. That handsome young gentleman there paid three silver already, enough for an extra loaf for you, me lady. And what a handsome sight he is, isn't he?"

"Yes. A sight," I answered drily.

The woman bustled away with a chuckle, leaving me with the food.

I grabbed the spoon and stirred the stew. The barley held a rich scent, and the tender bits of lamb fell apart under the tip of my spoon.

I took a small bite. The broth warmed me, and the bread held a rich, buttery flavor. I ate until I'd cleaned the bowl.

Glancing around the room, I spotted Rumpel and the others gathered at a table near the doorway. Had they eaten without me? I supposed I shouldn't have been surprised. I wasn't one of them. My lack of tattoos denoted me as an outsider.

It was just as well. I wanted nothing more than to go home and be done with these people.

I stood and walked across the room toward the others. They spoke with hushed voices.

"...don't tell her yet."

"She'll lose our trust."

"But she has to know."

Rumpel saw me approaching. His eyes narrowed, and the conversation stopped. He stood, and the others looked up.

He cleared his throat. "I've secured four horses for our journey, though we'll have to ride quickly." His gaze lingered on me, softening as he took me in, but it only lasted a moment before he sighed and turned away, looking at his brother. Rumpel walked away, and his brother followed at his heels. Dex and Malleus stayed behind.

"Well, I dare say I was right about the weather," Dex said. He took a long drink from his tankard of ale. "Not a cloud in the sky for our journey. I count that as a good omen."

Malleus grunted. "Wait till we get to the Volgrave Mountains. We'll have blizzards and snow beasts to contend with. You won't be so cheerful then." He stood and clomped away, following behind Rumpel and Orlane.

What had they been talking about?

"He's quite gloomy, that one," Dex said, staring after Malleus.

"Yes, I've noticed."

Dex finished his ale, then he stood, and we walked to the doorway. The others had already left, leaving me to make conversation with Dex yet again.

"Malleus has his reasons for his attitude," Dex said. "You can't blame him too harshly."

"What reasons?" I asked.

"You haven't heard?"

"No. I'm rather new to this world."

"Ah." He laughed. "Yes, I do forget. You'll have to forgive me. Malleus is lucky not to be imprisoned."

"Why?"

"Because, years ago, before the Sai-hadov infested our lands, there was a gateway keeping our kingdom and the Shadow Realm separated. Rumors surfaced. We heard the gateway was being breached. The king sent Malleus, who was the captain of his army, to secure it. But instead of doing it, Malleus betrayed us. He didn't defend it, he opened it."

"Opened it?" I asked, shocked.

"Yes. He claims it was an accident, but some of us have our doubts. Including me. He got away with it."

"How?"

Dex flicked a piece of lint from his coat. "Malleus had connections. He convinced the king to forgive him. I never knew why the king pardoned him so easily." He shook his head, his gaze wandering. "My brother paid the ultimate price for Malleus's treachery."

"But what reason would Malleus have for opening the gate?"

"For power, most likely. With the king dead, and the Sai-hadov infesting our lands, taking control of the goblins, in theory, could have been possible. If the king hadn't scattered the three items, he would've had it too."

"Do you think he still wants the three items for himself?"

Dex paused before speaking. When he did, he spoke with a hushed voice. "He's tried before. Many times, although he was never successful."

I stared at the inn's doors, which were partially propped open, revealing a sliver of sunlight that drifted inside, and a view of the front courtyard. People bustled past, though I couldn't see Malleus.

Did we have a traitor with us?

I'd have to talk to Rumpel about the man who traveled with us. Surely he would know more about the story.

"Should we go then?" Dex asked.

"Sure," I mumbled, following him. We walked outside the inn. Rumpel and the others stood with the horses. Most of the animals looked like little more than nags, with thin frames and their ribs visible. But I wouldn't complain. Riding beat walking.

I made my way to a sorrel mare with a crooked white stripe down her nose that covered her left nostril. I patted her nose and she sniffed my hand, her breath warm on my fingers, her soft muzzle like velvet. We'd had a few horses back home, and I wasn't as adept at riding as other elves, although I could hold my own, so long as the beast wasn't overly spirited.

"Are you riding that one?" Malleus said behind me, startling me.

I turned around to see him standing in his usual stance, hands on his hips, frowning, eyes narrowed with suspicion. The tattoos on his face had faded, his skin leather and wrinkled, half-hidden by his wiry beard.

"I suppose so."

Dex's tales of Malleus's betrayal piqued my curiosity. I couldn't help but wonder if they were true. The horse nudged me, and I patted her nose.

"Did they teach you to ride in the elven lands?" Malleus asked.

"I can ride well enough."

He grunted and turned away to his horse—a black one with white feathering surrounding his hooves. I watched as the big man awkwardly climbed atop his horse. What was his story? Had he really betrayed the king?

The other horses trotted around mine. Rumpel lithely mounted his steed, his brother sharing the saddle in front of him. He gripped the reins with firm hands, the look of an experienced rider. They rode a chestnut stallion, and I couldn't help but smile as I looked at Orlane's gleeful expression. He sat in front of his brother, his thin frame exposed against the horse's flanks. His malnourishment bothered me, and I was once again struck by the idea that this quest wasn't a safe place for him.

I stuck my foot in the stirrup and climbed atop the horse. She pranced as I mounted, and I grabbed the reins quickly, tightening them to keep the horse still, and to show the beast who was in charge.

Keeping my legs tight against her flanks, the horse held still, and Crooked Stripe and I seemed to come to a truce.

Do what I ask, and we'll survive this.

Rumpel turned his steed to the road crowded with carts and peasants. "We ride north," he called. I kicked my horse forward to follow him. We rode until we left the village. The thatched-roof homes and inns disappeared on the horizon behind us as we trotted down the narrow lane in a single-file line. Rumpel and Orlane at the front, me behind them, then Dex, and finally Malleus at the rear.

Thoughts of Malleus nagged me. If he'd opened the gateway to the Shadow Realm, that meant he should've been held responsible. Even if the king had forgiven him, he should've been tried for his actions at some point. Why wasn't he in prison? If he were in Malestasia, he would've never gotten away with it.

But I knew nothing of this kingdom or their laws. Perhaps with the king dead, law and order had ceased to exist, which is what Malleus had counted on. With the Sai-hadov on the verge of taking over their entire kingdom, he was in a position to rise to power.

Should I warn Rumpel? It seemed pointless. Surely, he already knew of Malleus's treachery.

Tree branches formed a canopy over us. As the day turned to evening, the waning sunlight drifted through the limbs, creating a patchwork pattern over the leaf-strewn path. The light faded, and the air turned chill.

I pulled my cloak around me. The wound on my back turned to a dull throbbing that was slowly fading. Whatever potion Rumpel had given me must've been laced with magic for it to work so quickly.

Howling came from the forest. My horse pranced nervously, and I tightened the reins to keep her steady. Chills prickled my neck as the cries grew louder.

We couldn't afford another attack from the wood-wraiths. Even with my new knife tucked inside my boot, I had no desire to battle them again.

"We've got to move faster," Rumpel shouted over his shoulder. I kicked my horse into a trot, then to a gallop as I followed behind the others. Thundering hoofbeats echoed in my ears. I kept my legs pinned to the horse's sides. Sweat lathered her neck as we continued riding down the twisting trail.

The howls followed us.

I glanced back. The silhouette of a creature loping on all fours appeared behind me. Elongated jaws protruded from its skeletally thin, wolf-like face. I turned to face the road, refusing to look behind me again. I kicked my horse, urging her to go faster. My heartbeat echoed the thundering hoofbeats.

Ahead, the jagged peaks of a mountain range cut across the horizon. Snow turned them white against the darkening sky. The others rode alongside me, the wailing howls following, my heart beating with fear and adrenaline.

We rode out of the forest onto an open field. The trail led to the mountains. Dark clouds gathered above us. The scent of rain lingered in the air. My hands burned as I held tightly to the reins. A chill made my skin prickle with goose bumps.

Growling came from behind. My horse kicked back, and a yelp followed. More growls came, until I finally dared to look behind me once again.

Half-a-dozen beasts chased us.

My horse breathed heavily, her sides heaving for air. How much longer could any of us keep up this pace? We raced closer to the mountains.

"Ride faster," Rumpel yelled behind him. I kicked my horse's flanks, driving her onward. The moon rose above us, casting milky light over the stone-strewn ground. The shapes of the other horses and riders stood out as silhouettes in front of me.

My horse shrieked. A wolf clamped her back leg. She kicked, trying to throw it off, but the monster held tight. Keeping my legs clamped to her sides, I pulled the knife from my boot. Gripping the handle, I aimed for the monster's throat, but the woodwraith pranced out of my reach.

I spun my horse around as best as I could, one hand clenching the reins, the other clamping my knife's hilt. The woodwraith jumped at me, so close its breath washed over me. Wicked teeth gleamed, aiming for my throat. I stabbed the knife in its neck, the blade embedding in the creature's flesh with a sickening thump, and the beast fell to the ground. My horse sprinted ahead toward the mountains.

The orange glow of firelight came from an open cave at the base of the mountain. I raced with the others toward the entrance, my blood running hot through my veins, both hands holding tightly to the reins.

Part of me wanted to go back and get my knife. Would Rumpel trust me with another one? But then, I also wanted to live, and that thought drove me forward, toward the cave, until my horse fled with the others into the maw of the mountain.

FIVE

THE MOUNTAIN BEGAN TO SEAL behind us, the rocks closing like a doorway. The shrieks of the woodwraiths pierced through the night until the rocks sealed with a boom that shook the ground under our horses' feet.

Rumpel jumped off his steed as Orlane sagged, his face ashen.

"Is he all right?" Dex asked, dismounting.

"His leg," Rumpel said, grabbing his brother around the waist and pulling him off the saddle.

Campfires burned around us. In their light, hunched shapes emerged from the tunnels.

"Help me," Rumpel called to them. "He's hurt."

My horse pranced as the creatures emerged from the shadows. Yellow eyes glowed from bat-like faces. Gray leathery skin contrasted their red and orange robes strung with beads that clinked softly as they stalked toward us.

I stiffened, flexing my empty hands. Blast it all, couldn't I have kept my weapon for a day at least?

The creatures gathered around Orlane and Rumpel. Blood stained the boy's ripped pant leg and dropped into a puddle on the ground.

"*Hois ulin*," one of the creatures said, its voice guttural.

"Follow." It motioned us forward with a clawed hand, its fingers webbed.

Our group trailed behind the creatures who led us into a tunnel. One of them held a torch. As the darkness enveloped us, I kept my eyes on the firelight to stay oriented. Our footsteps echoed through the hollow passageway.

Whispers filled the air. A chill seeped through my clothes. When we reached a wide room, we stopped. Torches lined the circular walls and sputtered from the rocky pillars. A few rugs of bright yellows and reds dotted the subterranean floors, and painted jars and pots lined the walls in neat rows.

Rumpel placed his brother on one of the rugs. Dex stood over them as the creatures gathered around. One held a clay jar with an ointment inside.

"The Volgrave," Malleus said, startling me as he stood beside me. "Mountain dwellers. Nasty beings if you ask me."

I hadn't asked.

"It seems they're helping Orlane."

"Only because they feel indebted to the once royals. They wouldn't hesitate to put a knife through our backs if it weren't for the prince and his brother with us."

"You sound as if you speak from experience."

He didn't answer.

I studied Malleus, dark brows shading his narrowed eyes, his bushy beard hiding most of his face. A scowl pulled at his lips.

"I guess we're lucky Rumpel and his brother are with us," I said.

"Luck." He barked a laugh. "That's one word to use." He marched away from me to stand at the edge of the room, arms crossed over his barrel chest.

I paced toward the others gathered at the room's center. Orlane lay on a pallet, a bloody gash splitting his thigh muscle. His eyes were wide with fear, and he whimpered quietly. Rumpel and Dex knelt at his side as a Volgrave woman cleaned the blood from the wound.

After applying a salve and wrapping the injury, she gave us a brief nod, then shuffled out of the room, leaving us alone.

Orlane continued his moaning, so I knelt beside him. Rumpel eyed me, but he didn't speak as I rested my hand on Orlane's chest. The boy's brows were knit with worry. Sweat slicked his pallid skin, and his breathing came in shallow gasps.

"You'll be all right," I said to him. "You're brave, remember?"

Orlane focused on me.

"You're a brave warrior, aren't you? Just like your brother."

"Brave," he whispered.

"Yes. You battled the woodwraiths and survived. Not many people can claim such a thing." I wasn't sure how true my statement was, but I supposed it didn't matter.

A hint of a smile crossed Orlane's face. His breathing evened out. "Brave," he said with a sigh.

Rumpel shifted beside me. I caught him looking at me with a softened expression, as if he recognized my concern for his brother, as if perhaps he didn't think of me as a prisoner, but a person—someone who had a heart. Was I reading too much into his glance?

The Volgrave woman hobbled into the room. She carried a tatty blanket that she laid on top of the boy. I helped her smooth the cloth over him.

"Rest now," Rumpel told his brother.

He nodded, giving his brother a slight smile. When he closed his eyes, we stepped away.

"Thank you," he said with a quiet, intimate voice.

I raised an eyebrow. "You're thanking me?"

"Thank you for treating Orlane with kindness. Not everyone does. There are some who think of him as less than a person. I appreciate your thoughtfulness toward him."

I wasn't sure how to answer, but settled on a simple, "You're welcome."

We moved to the edge of the room where Malleus stood, Dex trailing behind us.

"What now?" Malleus demanded. "We'll not be traveling anywhere with a wounded boy in our group."

"You won't have to. You've got nothing to worry about, Malleus," Rumpel said.

"What do you mean by that?"

"The talisman is on the other side of this mountain. There's no need for all of us to come. Someone should stay here to watch the boy. I elect you."

"Why not you? He's your brother."

"Because someone's got to make sure she doesn't escape." He nodded at me.

Dex stepped forward. "Then I must beg to stay here as well. No need for us all to go. You know the way to the stone circle as well as we do, don't you?"

Rumpel dipped his head. "I know my way."

Malleus crossed his arms. "I don't like this. What if you trick us—try to take the ring for yourself."

"What good would that do?" Rumpel asked. "The

ring's only useful if we find the next two talismans." Rumpel grabbed my arm. "Let's go." He moved me away from the other two. "Quickly," he whispered.

We moved past Orlane, and Rumpel gave him a brief goodbye and a promise to return, then made it into a tunnel, out of earshot from the other two.

"What was that about?" I asked.

"What do you mean?"

"Why were you trying to evade them?"

"I was trying to evade Malleus," he clarified. "I don't trust him."

Fire flickered from sconces in the cavern's curving walls as we walked through a narrow passage.

"You don't trust him because he opened the Sai-hadov gateway?" I asked.

"Who told you that?" Rumpel asked.

"Your uncle mentioned it."

"Ah." He focused on me, ice-blue eyes reflecting the firelight, illuminating the strong line of his jaw. I had to admit, he was attractive in a barbaric sort of way. If one liked savages with a questionable moral code.

"I don't understand why you allowed him to come with us in the first place," I said.

"Because I had no choice."

"You always have choices. Unless you've been kidnapped, which you haven't been."

He gave me a shrewd look. "Baelem demanded he come," he said, as if that settled the matter.

"So?"

"So, I do what she says. Everyone does. We respect our last living seer. If she wanted him to come, she must've had a good reason."

"Like what?"

He shrugged. "I don't know, but I don't argue with prophecy. Still, I don't trust him, and if I can keep him from the ring, then I will."

"Do you think it's true that he opened the gateway?"

"I know it's true. I watched him do it."

"You were there when it happened?"

"Yes. It was on the northern border. I was part of the patrol. I didn't realize what was happening until it was too late. Malleus was my commander, so I didn't question him when he stuck the key into the gateway. He'd said he only meant to protect us. That he never meant to open it. But I don't know what to believe. His actions brought shame to not only him, but to me as well. I could've stopped him. I didn't. Which is why I was sent to Malestasia to right my wrongs. Something I'm still trying to accomplish."

"I don't understand. Why is he allowed to be free? Why isn't he locked up?"

"My father pardoned him."

"That seems like a lousy reason. Couldn't you un-pardon him?"

He gave me a slight smile that didn't touch his eyes. "If I were king, then perhaps yes. But I'm nothing anymore, nothing but a disgraced man without a name or country to call home."

We made it to another passageway where the air turned chill. A brisk, icy wind came from an opening at the tunnel's end.

"Where did the Volgrave creatures go?" I asked.

"Into the inner mountain. Most of them live as recluses and hardly ever come into contact with anyone in the outside world. But they guard the stone circle. We'll see a few of them again soon." He pointed ahead, to the opening, where the snow created a canvas of white in the outside world. Two Volgrave creatures stood at either side of the opening. Both wore furs that covered everything but their bulging yellow eyes.

One of them handed a fur-trimmed cloak to me. I took it and put in on, the soft, sealskin-lining warming me.

Rumpel spoke to one of the Volgrave in their language. They pointed to the edge of the mountain, sharp jagged lines spreading across the horizon. Rumpel said something in their language, and the two Volgraves led us down a trail leading away from the cave.

Ice particles whipped through the air, stinging my cheeks as I followed the others. I focused on walking on the icy ground, keeping a sure footing to prevent slipping. When we reached a precipice, we stopped.

The Volgraves pointed to a trail that wound precariously up the mountain.

"We've got to climb to the top of the mountain," Rumpel yelled over the wind. "That's where we'll find the stone circle."

"Is the ring at the circle?"

"Yes. It's trapped in the ice. No one's been able to solve the circle's mystery. That's why I've brought you." He turned to march up the trail, but I grabbed his arm, stopping him.

"Rumpel, I lost my knife to the woodwraiths. I'd appreciate an extra weapon." I felt sheepish admitting I'd lost it, but I wouldn't let my pride stand in the way of my safety.

"Lost it?"

I nodded.

"How many weapons do you think I can spare?"

I balled my fists. "You're the one who got me into this situation. If you want me to travel up that mountain with you, full of who-knows-what kind of creatures, then I demand another weapon. Please," I added for good measure. It never hurt to be polite, even if it was to a barbarian.

"I haven't got another weapon to spare."

"Surely you've got something."

He seemed to ponder, working his jaw back and forth. He stood with the wind battering against his fur-lined cloak, and I couldn't help but notice how the sunlight brought out the turquoise green flecks in his eyes. Mystifying, in a way.

I stopped myself right there. No need to admire my captor's eyes.

"Why should I give you another weapon when you already lost one?" he asked.

"Because I need it."

"Is that your only reason?"

I stamped my foot. "I said please this time, didn't I?"

He gave me a tight-lipped smile, not quite a happy expression, but not hate-filled either. Maybe that meant he tolerated me.

He lifted his cloak, revealing his belt, where several hilts peeked from sheaths. I counted three knives hanging from his waist.

"Don't have any to spare, huh?" I asked.

He pulled one out and handed it to me. "These are all I have. Do *not* lose that one."

I took the blade from him, our gloved fingertips brushing. A surge of warmth spread from his touch, shooting from the top of my head straight to my toes.

Heavens no, I didn't need to be reacting to him in such a way.

I pulled my hand away from his and tucked the knife into my belt, ignoring the fluttering in my stomach. Being in an alien world, deprived of my magic, was addling my mind. I needed to escape this world as soon as I found the three objects, then I could be rid of this.

Be rid of *him*.

I followed Rumpel on a narrow trail of switchbacks leading up the mountain. Snow covered the dark granite rocks that stuck up like jagged spires around us. I kept my hands folded under the warmth of my coat, grateful the Volgraves had given it to me.

"Rumpel," I asked. "Why are the Volgraves helping us? Aren't they concerned that we're trying to take their ring?"

"Not at all. They're glad to help us, so long as we don't try to cross them. They want us to succeed as much as my people do. Plus, it's not their ring. They guard it, but they also know who it belongs to. If the royal family gets it once again, we rid the world of the Sai-hadov. It works in their favor."

"And if we tried to cross them? What then?"

"Better not to ask."

The path grew steeper until I had to climb up a rocky cliff. Though I wore gloves, the chill seeped through to my bones. When we reached the top, an open plateau spread out before us.

Crystal pillars rose like silent sentinels around us, as tall as three men, arranged in a wide circle.

We walked into the circle. My footsteps echoed on

the ground with hollow thuds, and beneath the patchy snow, ice spanned.

"Are we on a lake?" I asked.

"Yes. The ring is frozen inside." I followed him across the lake. Faint blue light glowed from its center. Rumpel knelt by the illuminated ice, brushing off the snow, until a sapphire blue jewel glinted beneath. He held his hand just above the surface. The glow grew brighter and encompassed his fingers.

"Spellcasted ice," he said. "Can't melt it. Can't break through it. Only thing to do is to rearrange those stones." He pointed to the crystals surrounding us. "Unfortunately, my people have been trying for years to arrange the stones in the right pattern, but they've never been successful."

I paced to one of the crystal pillars. Smooth and prism-like, it stood over me, casting a faint shadow on the ice. The wind picked up, blowing the snow in swirling eddies over the frozen lake.

Runes etched the pillar in a vertical line. I didn't recognize the characters. Rumpel stood behind me.

"Can you read that?" I asked.

"It's written in our old language. Some of the symbols I recognize." He pointed to a circular symbol on top. "That one means sun."

"Sun?"

"Yes, as in sunlight."

Hmm. Interesting. "You said the pillars can be rearranged?"

"Yes."

"How? They must weigh too much for a person to easily move them around."

"That's why we use our magic to move them."

"How does that work?"

"Like this." He reached toward the pillar. A silver glow ignited around his hand. He pushed his hand through the air. The pillar shifted. The lack of friction made it slide once it started moving.

Rumpel pushed another pillar until the two switched places.

"How do you know what pattern to arrange them in?" I asked.

"We don't know exactly, except that those runes on the pillars must have something to do with it. Most pillars have seven runes on each face, and there are twelve pillars total."

I walked around one, running my hand over it, the etched runes bumpy under my gloved fingertips.

Each pillar had four sides.

Four sides. Seven runes each. Twelve pillars total. The numbers had to mean something.

"You said only some have seven runes. Which ones don't?"

He led me around the circle. We reached one that stood taller than the others. This one has three extra runes. Here." He pointed to the top. "There are others like this. Though some only have two extra runes."

"And only one has a total of seven on each face." I pointed to the pillar where we started. "That one."

"Yes."

The wind gusted past as understanding hit me. "It's a calendar."

"A calendar, yes. We already knew that."

"You already knew?" I rounded on him. "Then why didn't you tell me?"

His blue eyes turned shrewd. "Do you want me to tell you everything?"

I placed my hands on my hips. "Why did you bother to bring me here if you won't tell me the information I need to know?"

"Because," he answered, his tone brusque. "If you're to help us solve the riddle, it's better for you to find things out for yourself."

Fine. I was wasting my breath arguing with him anyway. "So, it's a calendar."

"Yes. It's a calendar."

"I'm assuming you've arranged them in order of their months and seasons already?"

"Yes. Many times. In order of our calendar and the calendar of the ancients as well."

"Show me how they're arranged now."

We walked to the pillars on the western horizon. "These three represent the winter months." We moved to the next three. "These are the spring months, then the summer and autumn months are arranged there."

"They're arranged in order, yet the ring stays trapped in the ice."

"Yes."

"But you've been using your magic to arrange them."

"Again, yes. I don't know what other magic we would've used. The pillars only move with magic. They're too heavy to push."

I flexed my fingers. The place tingled with an aura of magic. It filled the air and surrounded the pillars. The strongest magic came from the ring trapped beneath the ice. It called to me in a quiet whisper, pulling me to the lake's center.

I stood over the ring. The sapphire jewel glittered, so close within reach, but untouchable.

Kneeling over it, I pressed my hand to the ice, willing it to tell me its secrets.

How do I free you?

Rumpel stood over me, his tall frame casting a shadow. His words came back to me, nagging me. Something he'd said about goblin magic…

I faced Rumpel.

"It's your magic."

"What?"

"Your magic is hiding the truth. You said goblins deal in illusions. You need to take away all the spells. Then you have to return my magic to me."

"Return it?"

"If you want me to get the ring for you, then yes."

He ground his molars as he stood unmoving.

"Rumpel, return my magic to me. If you want that ring, you have to."

"I don't trust magic of the dark elves."

"I know you don't. I know what my grandmother did to you. Believe me when I say I'm not like her. I gave you my word to help you, and I will."

His piercing gaze lingered on me. "You mean that?"

"Yes." I put as much steel in my voice that I could muster.

"Very well." He flexed his gloved hands. "I will return your magic, but if you trick me, you will sorely regret it."

SIX

"ARE YOU SURE THIS WILL work?" Rumpel asked as he faced me. Snow blew past, creating swirling patterns over the frozen lake's glassy surface.

"No. I'm not sure, but I have to try something."

I flexed my fingers. If he returned my magic, then what? I could use it to beat him and steal the key he wore around his neck. I could try to escape, but to what end? I would leave these people to become victims of the Saihadov.

Plus, I'd given Rumpel my word not to use the magic against him. No matter how much I loathed him, I wouldn't break a promise.

The blue jewel of the ring glittered beneath the lake's surface, tempting me to free it.

"You won't trick me?" Rumpel asked, suspicion in his icy eyes.

"No."

His chest rose and fell as he took a deep breath.

"Take off your gloves," he said. "Give me your hands."

"What?" I asked.

"I need your hands. You want me to return your magic, don't you?"

"Yes." I sighed, took off one glove, then the other. Icy wind bit at my fingers as I held out my hands.

He removed his glove and took my hands in his.

My breath stuttered at the feel of his warm skin surrounding mine. I planted my feet firmly, doing my best not to flinch. He'd used some sort of goblin spell to cause me to have such a reaction. I was sure of it.

"Relax," he said, his voice deep and entirely too seductive. Power tingled from his hands into mine.

Whorls of silver glittered around our hands. Magic filled my chest, entering the empty spaces where it had once been. For the first time since I'd come to this realm, I could breathe again.

I kept my hands in his.

"You've got your magic?" Rumpel asked.

"Yes." But I didn't move.

He pinned me with his gaze. His eyes were the ice-blue of a mountain lake, so deep, I could've gotten lost in their depths.

Wind gusted, chilling my exposed fingers, and I finally found the motivation to take a step back. I replaced my gloves, not meeting his gaze as I did.

I walked toward a crystal pillar, its surface transparent, reflecting the sunlight. I tried to ignore Rumpel's presence behind me. He was nothing but a distraction.

Now that I had my magic back, I reached for the pillar. Its enchantment whispered to me, layers of a spell keeping things hidden.

I'd have to remove the magic first before doing anything else.

I pressed my hand to the column, closed my eyes, and concentrated on the spell. Web-like tendrils wrapped the stone in a network leading from one to another. The spell pulsed with a golden glow, only perceptible through magic.

The prickle of goblin magic called to my senses.

Something wasn't right.

I kept my hand pressed to the pillar as I conjured the word to undo the enchantment. It had been so long since I'd thought of my spell books back home. Another lifetime. But the word came to me easily, as if it had only been yesterday that I'd sat in the university classes.

"*Ulilo*," I whispered.

My voice carried on the wind, taking the spell word with it. Tendrils of enchantment disappeared, untangling with the shift in magic. The powers of the dark elves were foreign in this land, and goblin magic was no match against them.

The spell unraveled until the stones were left barren.

Runes glowed with golden light as the enchantment disappeared completely.

"What did you do?" Rumpel asked.

"Took the spell away. I don't know what's making the runes glow. That shouldn't be happening."

"You removed the goblin's spell?"

"Yes."

"Then the glowing runes aren't powered by goblin magic. There's another force at play here."

"If that's so, what's powering them?" I asked.

"I don't know."

I walked through the stones, staring up at the towering pillars. Their magic brushed against me. It was a dark power, reminding me of the jungles back home. An old, ancient enchantment.

"It's the magic of the dark elves. It's a very old spell. Centuries old, possibly."

"How is that possible?"

"Perhaps my people came to these lands once, long ago."

"There's no record of them being here."

"Then how do you explain the magic?"

He shrugged, offering no explanation.

I paced through the stones, my boots echoing on the frozen lake and muffled by patches of powdery snow.

The glow of the runes caught my attention. The markings had changed. Some of the symbols I recognized as the old language of the dark elves.

"That symbol." I pointed to an oval-shaped glyph on a pillar taller than the others. "It means new leaf in the language of the dark elves. And this one. The square one with the line through it. It means three."

"Three. As in the third month, perhaps?" Rumpel said. "The new leaf meaning spring?"

"Yes." I circled the other pillars, cataloging each one, scanning the numerals. "These are in the wrong place, the six and nine."

I used my magic to push the two stones, switching places. Crystals glided over ice until they reached their spots on the outer edge of the circle.

"What about this one?" Rumpel asked. "Does this symbol mean twelve?"

I inspected the glyph. Four squares with lines through the middle. "Yes. It's also in the wrong place." Magic sprang from my fingertips as I pushed on the stone. It gathered momentum until I stopped it between the eleven and one.

"Are they in order now?" Rumpel asked.

I moved around the ring of stones, observing the symbols as I went. "One, two, three…" When I reached the twelfth pillar, I stopped.

"They're in order."

"Then why is the ring still trapped in the ice?"

"I don't know." I bit my lip, deep in thought as I scanned the ring of crystals. "It must have something to do with the symbols. Have any of the runes stayed in your language since I removed the spell?"

He examined the stones. "This one." Rumpel pointed. "The sun shape. It stayed the same. I don't see any others that didn't change. So, what does it mean?"

"The sun." I shielded my eyes as I glanced up at the round orb above us. Soupy clouds blocked it out, making it appear to be a hazy white circle in the sky.

Sunlight. Light. The crystals reflected the light.

"I'm going to try something. We'll have to stand outside the circle."

Rumpel raised an eyebrow, but he didn't question me as we walked to stand outside the ring of stones.

Cupping my hands, I took a deep breath. The spell would take most of my energy, but I didn't have a better idea, and I wasn't going to leave this place until we had the ring in our possession.

I pulled on the energy within me. Heat filled my open hands. Golden magic created an orb. It grew until it rose from my fingertips and hovered above me. The orb spun slowly, golden light spilling around us.

I used my magic to push the orb upward until it floated above the lake's center. Light pulsed.

The runes glowed brighter.

The light refracted from each of the pillars. Beams shone from each one, reaching out to shine over the middle of the lake. With the light concentrated on the lake's center, the ice cracked. Hairline fractures split the surface.

Rumpel and I backed away until we stood on the snowy shoreline.

I pulled more of my energy from my body, fueling the spell as the light glowed brighter.

A fissure split the ice open, spraying water into the air. Freezing droplets splashed my face. We jumped back as the ice exploded. The twelve pillars fell until they floated on the lake of broken ice.

"Where's the ring?" I asked.

We knelt by the shore. "There." Rumpel pointed. I followed his line of sight to a glittering blue jewel sinking to the lake's bottom.

"I've got it," he said.

I eyed him. "You're not jumping in there, are you?"

He gave me a smile, one that nearly looked genuine as it touched his eyes. His teeth were bright and white, evenly spaced, not that I cared to notice such a thing.

He reached out. With a glow of silver magic, an enchantment shone from his fingertips. The water rippled, then the ring broke from the surface. Encased in glowing magic, it floated toward us.

"Hold out your hand," Rumpel said.

I did as he said. The ring glided toward me until it landed soundlessly atop my open palm. The silver glow of Rumpel's magic brushed against me, a strong power that stole my breath, something intense and full of life, reminding me of the magic running through the roots and leaves of the jungle trees back home.

My breath stuttered.

He was looking at me.

I couldn't look away, as if his spell possessed me. Goblin magic, of course. He'd placed a curse on the ring. That or I was indeed attracted to him, which I refused to admit, no matter how much my stomach flitted with blasted butterflies in his presence.

Clearing his throat, he looked away, breaking the spell.

The ring sat on my open hand, and only the layer of fabric from my gloves kept the metal and sapphire from touching my skin.

"You did it," he said.

"We did it."

"I can't believe we've finally got it. The first talisman. I wasn't sure it was possible." He picked it up, gripping it between his thumb and forefinger. The ring looked so small compared to his large hands.

I sat back on the snowy embankment as Rumpel placed the ring in his pocket. With my magic drained, my energy was quick to follow. A dull headache throbbed behind my eyes. The wind froze the exposed skin of my face.

"You okay?" he asked.

"I'm fine. Tired. I used up all my magic. It'll come back eventually."

"We should get back to the Volgrave's mountain."

"Yes." But I couldn't find the strength to move from my spot. "In a minute."

My magic had returned, only for me to lose it again. At least this time, I knew it would come back, as long as Rumpel trusted me with it. Since I'd gotten the ring for him, he'd better.

The sun sank toward the horizon. Rumpel stood. He held his hand out to me. I eyed it and considered not taking it. What help had he been anyway? But he'd given my magic back, which showed some amount of trust. Maybe it was time I returned the courtesy.

With numb fingers, I grabbed his hand and stood. Refusing to meet his gaze helped control the butterflies.

We set off for the Volgrave caverns. As the sunlight drained from the world, the cold increased. I kept the furs wrapped tightly around me, focusing on putting one foot in front of the other. How far away was the entrance?

The slope grew steeper, and I treaded carefully on the icy, rock-strewn ground. Numbness blanked my thoughts. Nothing mattered but getting back to the warmth again. I'd never been exposed to cold like this before. In my jungle home, it never grew this frigid. How could anyone stand to live in such a place?

We arrived at the cave's entrance. I was a shivering block of ice, and I wasn't sure I'd ever feel warm again.

Our footsteps echoed through the tunnel of stone.

The light of a fire shone ahead. I found myself sitting in front of the orange glowing warmth, hoping to thaw at some point, too numb and exhausted to care about anything else.

Someone handed me a bowl of pottage of some sort. The oats and barley warmed me, even if the taste was bland. Conversations filled the cavern, though I couldn't focus on anything.

I'd gotten the first talisman. I was one step closer to home.

Home. A place I thought I'd be happy leaving behind. Now, all I wanted to do was go back. To Mother. After losing her husband and a son, she'd never handle losing me, too. Once again, I wondered, did she realize I was missing? Or did she assume I'd escaped on a ship to the mainland without saying goodbye?

It wasn't uncharacteristic for me to do such a thing, and what other conclusion could she have come to? I was the ungrateful, spoiled daughter of a king and queen. A princess, even if I was one of the most talented magic users in Malestasia.

Tears stung my eyes. I blinked to keep them from falling.

I would return to her. I couldn't let my thoughts go down a darker path—one where I died in this land, and Mother was left to assume I'd abandoned her.

Holding the half-eaten bowl of stew, I watched the flames flicker. The feeling in my toes and fingers started to return with the sensation of needles prickling my skin. I realized Rumpel sat beside me, hands clasped casually atop his knees, his skin turned brown by the sun, tendons and veins standing out, hinting at a life of hard labor.

What would it be like to hold his hand, to feel his skin against mine again? Would it feel the same as I remembered, his skin calloused on his fingertips? Would his hands be warmer than mine? My hands had been in a constant state of cold since I'd entered this world, even as I sat here by the fire, my bones felt frozen through to the core.

"You're quiet," Rumpel said.

"I'm thinking about home."

"You miss it?"

I paused before answering. Was it wise for me to divulge such a personal piece of information? "Yes," I answered quietly.

"What was it like living in Malestasia?" he asked.

"Warmer. More comfortable. Predictable. I wanted to leave."

"You did?"

"Yes. I was packing to leave on a ship to the mainland when you took me. I couldn't wait to get away. There was nothing left for me in Malestasia. At least, that's what I thought."

"Why were you leaving? You were the princess, weren't you? Surely your parents expected you to stay in your land. Become a leader. Marry a dark elf."

"My mother expected it, yes. My father and brother were killed by ogres, but I suspect he would've wanted the same thing."

"I'm sorry you lost them. The death of loved ones isn't an easy thing to go through."

I only nodded. Perhaps he understood. "I had another brother. Drekken. He'd returned only a few weeks ago. I miss him."

Rumpel didn't answer, and his eyes darted a guilty look at me. Was he starting to realize the gravity of his actions? He'd taken me to restore his lands, but perhaps now, he understood that he'd taken me from a family who loved me. Who missed me.

"It was hard being without Orlane for all those years I spent on the mainland," he said. "Family is a bond not meant to be broken."

Then why did you take me from mine? I wanted to ask. But now wasn't the time. We'd mended what little we could in a situation such as ours, and I had no desire to go back to that place where I wanted nothing more than to see him dead.

I held the bowl of pottage as it grew cold.

"You need to rest," he said. "Tomorrow, we travel to Shigoshi for the scepter. The Volgrave have arranged a place for us to sleep. If you'll excuse me, I need to check on my brother."

I only nodded. He stood, and I watched him go. Confusion plagued me. The hate I'd felt for him had lessened. I wasn't sure that was a good thing.

SEVEN

I LAY ON A PALLET in the Volgrave caverns. Despite the furs stacked atop me, I shivered. When I closed my eyes, all I saw was Rumpel, his chiseled face, that faraway look he got, the determination in the hard set of his jaw, the love he held for his people and his brother, putting their needs above his own.

I rolled over, hoping a different position would help me get to sleep, but no such luck.

Whispers came from somewhere. Was it my imagination? Now the lack of sleep was really getting to me.

The whispering grew louder. Opening my eyes, the coals left over from the fire gave a little light to the room. My companions lay on pallets across the room. Only their silhouettes were visible in the light.

Something brushed my ear.

I sat up and gripped Rumpel's knife from beneath the blankets. My cold fingers felt stiff as I held the blade. A little of my magic had returned, and I held it at the ready, a warm glow inside.

Spinning around, I searched for the source of the whispers. Across from me, a pair of silver reflective eyes met mine. I couldn't make out the shape of the body.

Was it a Volgrave?

No, Volgraves had yellow eyes, large and round, and these eyes were slit-like. My heart pounded at the sight of the eyes looming over me. Wisps of a semi-transparent white robe fanned out around the being. A chill prickled the back of my neck.

Malice exuded from the phantom as it focused on me.

I got to my knees when the creature disappeared.

What kind of gods-forsaken land had I come to?

As I knelt facing the empty stone wall, Dex's reference to the Sai-hadov surfaced in my memory.

I remained upright a few moments longer, making sure the creature—whatever it was—didn't return.

I kept the knife, tucking my hand and blade beneath the pillow. Sleep escaped me. When the others rose, I was sure I'd only gotten a few hours of rest. It didn't matter. I had no choice but to follow them to the next talisman. To Shigoshi, wherever that was.

I gathered my things, arranged the blankets, and stood. A headache pounded behind my eyes. What I would give for a bath, or a strip of leather and some soda powder for my teeth. Surely there was some to be found somewhere.

"You look unwell," Rumpel said behind me.

I spun around. "How long have you been standing there?"

"Long enough."

"A little warning would be nice next time." I rubbed my eyes. "I feel like I've been bludgeoned."

"You didn't sleep well?"

"I didn't sleep." I pointed at the wall with the tip of my blade. "I saw something there. I think it was a Sai-hadov."

His eyebrows rose. "Are you sure?"

"I think so. Silver eyes. It disappeared before I could tell anything else about it."

"Silver eyes?"

I nodded.

"And you're sure it disappeared?" he asked.

"Yes. I was close enough I would've heard its footsteps if it had walked away."

Rumpel cursed. "Sai-hadov. They're the only beings who could disappear that way."

"It didn't attack me, but I could tell it wasn't fond of me. How did it find me here? What did it want?"

"I don't know." The way Rumpel stared daggers at the blank wall told me the sighting of the creature bothered him, perhaps more than it bothered me. "Let's get moving," he said. "There's nothing to be done about the Sai-hadov right now. You can't fight them unless they take a physical form."

I followed him and the others. Orlane fell into step beside his brother. Though he walked with a slight limp, a clean bandage wrapped his leg, and his smile had returned.

Several Volgrave led us through the maze of winding tunnels. We stepped out of the tunnels and into a canyon. Steep rock walls rose around us. Wind howled, and the air tasted of ice as it filled my lungs.

"Where are we?" I asked.

"The road to Shigoshi," Rumpel answered. "A two-day ride west. Luckily, we saved ourselves a day of traveling by going through the mountain."

Our horses stood outside the cavern, saddled and waiting for us.

"No time to waste," Malleus called, his voice loud and booming, making my headache pound and teeth rattle. As he mounted his horse, he glanced my way, and I couldn't mistake the malice in his eyes, the same look I'd seen in the eyes of the Sai-hadov.

Crooked Stripe nudged me, and I patted her nose. A bandage wrapped her back leg where she'd been bitten by the woodwraith, though she walked without limping.

"It's good to see you, too," I whispered before mounting. At least I had one friend in this land, even if it was just a horse. I'd take what I could get.

Dex rode alongside me as we set off through the canyon. Our horses trudged down the pathway cutting through the gorge, their bridles jangling and feet clipping over ice and stones. Clouds blanketed the sky as the sun rose.

After crossing the gorge, we traveled down a muddy path pocked with wagon wheel ruts. I hugged the furs around me, unable to shake my fear from the chill in the eyes I'd seen last night, as if the creature followed me.

The sensation of the thing brushing my cheek had been most disturbing of all. Even now, I felt as if it followed me. I glanced over my shoulder. Nothing but the barren landscape of snow stretched across the horizon to the canyon and mountains, yet the invisible presence of the Sai-hadov lingered.

"Is something the matter?" Dex asked.

"Nothing."

"If you're worried about the woodwraiths, don't be. They live in the forests to the east, well away from where we travel."

"That's good to know."

He cocked his head. His easy smile and bright eyes brought a little cheer to the otherwise dreary world. It caught me off guard how much his nephew resembled him, the high cheekbones, strong jaw line, and the wide set of his blue eyes.

"I take it you weren't concerned about the wood-wraiths?" he asked.

"Not particularly."

"Something else, then?"

I shrugged. "This is a different land. I never know what to expect."

"Yes, I understand. When I first traveled to the southern lands, I was taken aback to be sure. I was so used to living in the capital city, everywhere else seemed completely alien to me. It's a shame we lost the capital. You would've been impressed by it, I think. Gardens made entirely of glass. Food so delicate it melted in your mouth."

"It sounds amazing." I tried to put enthusiasm in my voice, but the only place I wanted to go was home.

"It was. Very much so. I hear the king of the Sai-hadov has completely transformed it."

"Transformed it how?" Black smoke belching from chimneys, burnt structures, and soot covering everything came to mind. Wasn't that what happened when shadowy evil forces took over?

"I hear it's quite incredible."

"Incredible?"

"Yes. The palace, you see. The Sai-hadov king is too frightening for most mortals to behold, so he covered the walls in enchanted mirrors. Their magic masks his true reflection, you see."

"Is that so?"

"It is, so I hear. You may get a chance to find out if you find the three talismans."

"What do you mean?"

"The talismans," he repeated, as if that explained it. "In order to defeat the Sai-hadov, you'll have to go into the capital and confront the Inshadov—the king of the Sai-hadov."

"Why me?"

"You freed the ring from the ice, which means you've started the prophecy in motion. The one who frees the talismans will be the one to destroy the Sai-hadov—or die trying. Either way, your path is set."

"Die trying? Does the prophecy really say that?"

"Indeed. It does."

Die trying. Of course. Why wasn't I surprised?

Rumpel had failed to mention that tidbit, hadn't he? It seemed a rather big piece of information to omit. I glared at the form of his tall figure riding ahead of me. What else had he failed to tell me?

I'd have to confront him about the prophecy. Not that he'd care enough to give me straight answers, yet why had I expected something more? It seemed I was finally getting along with him, but perhaps that was all an illusion.

The day dragged by. When we stopped for a midday meal, I had trouble keeping my eyes open, and my legs felt stiff and sore from sitting too long in the saddle. Rumpel and Orlane kept to themselves. When Rumpel finally dared talk to me, I ignored him. He eyed me but didn't question my silence. I wasn't ready to broach the subject of the prophecy yet, though I would demand answers from him whenever I felt ready, and not before then.

We set off once again. The sky cleared, allowing the sun to shine and take the chill from the air. Ahead rose the treetops of a forest. We entered as the afternoon sun melted the snow, leaving a road full of mud and ruts. Gold and brown leaves clung to the towering trees, and the air tasted of autumn. I pulled off a layer of furs as sweat clung to my brow. I would be happy never being cold again.

When evening approached, we stopped in a forest glade and dismounted our horses. Crooked Stripe snorted as I unsaddled her. I fed her a handful of oats that the Volgraves had packed in the saddle bags for us. She ate them with loud smacks, nodding her big head, then tromped away from me to be with the other horses as they grazed in the green meadow.

The last of the sunrays painted the sky in pinks and lavenders. Spire-like trees with gold and red leaves surrounded the edge of the clearing. I stood admiring the beauty of the horses as they grazed in the forest field, not so different from home, the green grass swaying in the wind, the air soft on my cheeks.

I closed my eyes, the wind carrying the scent of lavender growing in patches. I was closest to home when I spent time in places like this.

"What... you doing?" Orlane asked.

I opened my eyes to find him standing beside me. "I suppose I'm thinking of home."

"Home."

"Yes. A place very far away." A place I may never return to.

"Home." He looked at the open field, as if he, too, were searching for the same thing I was.

I supposed he'd never really had a place to call home. He would've been too young to remember life at the palace.

"Orlane," Rumpel called from the forest. Smoke

trailed toward the forest's canopy from a campfire where the others gathered. The boy gave me a toothy smile before turning away and shuffling toward the campsite.

I stayed where I was, content to stand and watch the horses. My thoughts inexplicably turned toward Rumpel and the aching sense of disappointment his omission caused me. I didn't know why I expected him to have been honest. He'd kidnapped me. He was capable of treachery, and he was a goblin, after all. Weren't they known for dealing in illusions? Weren't they masters of deceit?

My stomach growled. The lunch of nuts and cheese hadn't stuck with me. The scent of cooked meat came from the fire. I couldn't stand here forever. With a sigh, I turned away from the field and trekked toward the campfire.

Rumpel's gaze followed me as I moved toward a fallen tree and sat on the trunk.

Self-consciously, I pushed back the tiny braids of red hair that had fallen across my face. Someday, I'd have to do something about this hair and these clothes, which fit poorly, the too baggy pants and loose-fitting peasant's shirt. If it weren't for the rope I used as a belt holding it all together, I'd be out of luck.

It didn't matter anyway. I wasn't trying to impress anyone. Least of all Rumpel.

He rose, holding a tin plate piled with meat and nuts, and carried it toward me.

"For you," he said, handing me the platter of food. "Braised rabbit. A few pine nuts."

"Thanks," I mumbled, taking it from him and not meeting his eyes. My fingers brushed his thumb. His warmth stuttered my breathing. How was I supposed to hate him when I kept reacting that way?

He returned to his spot beside his brother. His uncle made small talk with them. Malleus stood behind them holding a plate and eating cautiously, his dark eyes roving the campsite as he searched for threats.

I was left alone with my thoughts, though why Rumpel's gaze kept wandering toward me, I hadn't a clue. Perhaps he felt guilty for keeping important information from me—things like, *oh, by the way, there's a strong possibility you'll be dead by the end of this quest.*

By the time we finished our scanty meal, the others cleaned the platters and prepared the bedrolls. I stalked toward Rumpel, unable to keep from confronting him a second longer.

He knelt over his sleeping pallet and placed a blanket atop the ground, chatting with his brother who sat at his side.

"Rumpel." I placed my hands on my hips as I stood over him. "May I have a word with you?"

"About what?" He didn't bother to look up at me.

"The prophecy."

That got his attention. He gave me a sharp glare. "What about it?"

I glanced at Orlane. "Could we speak in private, please?"

"Now?"

"Yes." I narrowed my eyes at him. "Now."

"Fine," he sighed, smoothing the blanket, then stood to face me. I led him away from the campsite, to the edge of the tree line where the horses grazed in the twilight.

"What's this about?" he asked.

I crossed my arms over my chest. "You tell me. Your uncle happened to let it slip about the prophecy—about *all* of the prophecy."

Rumpel cursed. "That block-headed knave. I should've known he wouldn't keep his mouth shut."

"You have some explaining to do. Apparently, if I don't stop the king of the Sai-hadov, I die. Seems a rather important fact you left out."

"It wasn't important."

My mouth gaped. "Not important? Are you serious?"

"It wouldn't have mattered either way. We've no choice but to confront the Inshadov, which, given the history of people he's killed, we have no chance of winning, which is why we need the three talismans."

"So, it wasn't important."

"No."

"I fail to understand your definition of importance. Is anything important to you? Is my life important to you?"

"Of course it is."

"You're only saying that to appease me."

"Are you accusing me of being dishonest?"

I laughed, though it was a cheerless sound. "You've been nothing but dishonest from the beginning. You captured me, refused to arm me until I all but demanded a weapon, then lied to me about the prophecy."

"None of those things were dishonest, but I'm a goblin. We're not known for our integrity. But hear me now, not once have I lied to you, and I never will. I kept the entirety of the prophecy from you for your own protection. I don't intend for you to die when you confront the Inshadov. That I promise." He spoke with heated passion. I couldn't deny the look of earnestness I found in his eyes.

Still, I wasn't forgiving him that easily.

"Is there anything else I should know about before I

continue this quest?"

"Nothing." The steely determination in his eyes warned me from challenging him. He turned and stalked away.

Good riddance.

As soon as this quest was over—assuming I wasn't dead—I would be more than happy to leave him and this ridiculous land behind.

I grabbed my sleeping pallet and placed it away from his, on the edge of the tree line near the horses, where I could look up at the stars—the same constellations I studied in the university.

Although I was in another realm, I must've been on the same planet for the constellations to be unchanged. How far away was home? I had visions of setting off through the woods on my own, finding a map, crossing an ocean or continent or two, and making it back. It would take months. Years, probably. But wouldn't that be preferable to this?

Realistically, I knew the answer.

I had no choice but to keep going.

EIGHT

WE WOKE TO A GRAY sky. I'd slept better than I had the night before. Thankfully, I'd gotten no visits from specters. As we saddled our horses and ate a quick breakfast, I avoided Rumpel. Orlane spoke cheerfully to his brother. At least someone was in good spirits.

By the time we set off, my mood had grown worse. I didn't like the feeling of being unable to trust Rumpel. I'd almost thought we'd been getting along, that I didn't hate him as much as I had when he'd first taken me. But I was wrong. I could never trust him.

My horse's plodding footsteps echoed down the forest path as I followed behind the others. Rumpel and his brother rode ahead of me. Rumpel's cloak flapped behind him, his hair turned golden in the morning light. The sound of his voice carried through the dense woods as he spoke softly to his brother, telling some tale of their people, how a prince fought an evil sorcerer to save his princess.

What ridiculousness.

Where I came from, men didn't save princesses. The princess defeated the sorcerer herself and laughed at the prince when he showed up.

Even so, the sound of Rumpel's deep voice lulled me. I could easily imagine him telling the same stories to his children. He had a soft, gentle nature he didn't show much, except times like these spent with his brother. He'd make a good father, though I was loath to admit it. He'd make a good husband, too.

Why had I thought of that?

Clearly my mind had been compromised by this stupid quest.

No. He wouldn't make a good husband. He would be an awful husband, one who could never be trusted.

Right?

I rubbed my forehead, confusion clouding my mind. I could hardly make sense of my emotions.

The pathway sloped as we left the forest behind. Peaks of green mountains sculpted the horizon.

"Shee…Goshi…" Orlane said.

"That's right," Rumpel answered. "A few more hours and we'll be there. How's your leg?"

Orlane frowned. "Hurts. Sore."

"Don't worry. We'll be in Shigoshi soon, then we can set their healers to tending your leg. The dressings will need to be changed."

"Hungry, too," Orlane said.

"Yes, brother."

"And tired."

"I understand."

"And my bum. Hurting."

I stifled a laugh. "We all understand," I said to Orlane. I, for one, couldn't wait to be free of this saddle.

As the sun reached its zenith, we reached the foothills of the Shigoshi Mountains. The air turned warm and humid. Our horses' hooves clipped over a stone path that wound up switchbacks through the mountains. Evergreen trees overshadowed us, their scent of sap carried on the wind. As we gained altitude, the air turned chill once again, and I pulled my cloak to surround me.

Birds chirping and the sound of a waterfall filled the forest. Magic emanated from this place; I felt it as a tingle over my skin, the hair rising on the back of my neck, a calling to my spiritual senses.

At the top of a rise, stood a pagoda. Smoke rose from a bier of burning incense beneath the red-tiled roof, and a man stood beside it. He wore long robes and kept his hands folded inside the sleeves.

As we approached, he stepped out of the pagoda and held up his hand, stopping us. His thin mustache hung down his face like tentacles.

"Stop," he said, his voice carrying through the forest.

I pulled back my horse's reins. She pranced before stopping, and I kept my legs pinned to her sides to keep her steady.

"Who are you?" Malleus asked.

"I believe that is the question I should ask you. Why are you on this mountain? This is sacred ground."

"We're here for the scepter," Rumpel said. The forest stilled at his words.

"The scepter of the house of Stiltskin?" the man asked.

"Yes."

"What right have you to obtain it?"

"Because I'm the true king's son."

He raised his eyebrows, then pinched his lips, as if pondering. "You're the son of King Alendale Stiltskin?"

"I am."

"Hmm." He chewed his lip. "Not good enough." He turned away. "Leave this place. You are not welcome here."

"Wait," Rumpel called. The man turned, his eyebrows raised, suspicion written on his face. "I've brought the child spoken of in prophecy, daughter of the dark elves. Her." He pointed at me.

The man scrutinized me. "Is this true?"

"It is."

The man paced to me, his footsteps shuffling over the pine needles blanketing the forest floor. His eyes narrowed as he inspected me, his eyes going to my grandmother's pendant. "Dismount your steed," he said.

I glanced at Rumpel, not sure if I should comply. I had no idea who these people were. Would they try to take me prisoner? Rumpel gave me a nod. I took a deep breath, climbed off my horse, and stood to face the man. He was shorter than me, his back hunched, his slight frame hidden beneath his robes. Fingers bent with old age, he reached for the pendant and held it for his inspection.

"Interesting," he mumbled. "What is your name?" he asked.

"Kardiya Von Fiddlestrum," I answered.

He cocked his head as he studied my red hair and pointed ears. "A dark elf, yes. Indeed, you are, and you wear the pendant. But how do I know you're the one spoken of in prophecy?"

"Because she claimed the ring," Rumpel answered.

The man raised his eyebrows, and once again ran his fingers down his thin mustache. "Is this true?"

"It is," I answered.

"Hmm." He released my pendant. "Perhaps the time has come. Perhaps it has." He turned toward the pagoda.

"Very well. I shall allow you up the mountain, but first, you must be cleansed."

"Cleansed?"

"Yes. Down the path to the house. You'll see." He shuffled back to stand beneath the pagoda.

I mounted my horse and trailed behind the others as we continued up the mountain. Thin trails of mist obscured the path, and branches of dark trees overshadowed us. The air smelled of rain-soaked greenery.

Shapes of buildings appeared ahead, built in the same style as the pagoda, with roofs that curled up on the ends. As we drew closer, the reds and golds painted on the buildings and statues came into focus.

The area held a fragile stillness that wasn't meant to be broken.

We stopped our horses. Ornate buildings surrounded us, some with smoke rising from chimneys. The fog muffled the sounds of croaking frogs and chirping birds. Water trickled from a koi-shaped fountain sitting in the town's square.

As I dismounted my horse and stepped to the forest floor, the magic of the place came to my senses, resonating through me, making my skin prickle with goosebumps. The word *sacred* came to me.

I stood on holy ground.

We tied our horses to stone pillars supporting a building's portico. Several people, wearing red robes with golden-embroidered dragons, emerged from a doorway. They eyed us with suspicious gazes as we approached them.

"Who are you?" a woman with silver-white hair asked, her almond-shaped eyes dark, her voice cracking with age.

"We've come for the scepter of King Stiltskin," Rumpel explained. "We were given permission by the man in the forest to come here."

"I surmised as much, since he allowed you to pass. Either that, or you killed him to get here."

"We did no such thing," Malleus barked.

She eyed him, then her gaze went to the axe hanging from his belt. "Is that so?"

"We've got her." Dex's tone was calm. "The dark elf spoken of in prophecy."

"I shall make that determination for myself. Come here, child." She motioned me toward her.

I walked to her. If she didn't find me worthy, what then? We were sent away without a chance of retrieving the scepter?

I climbed a set of wooden steps and faced her. Sheltered under the portico, the scent of incense wafted through the building's open doors, which were inlaid with jade and gold, the metal worked into the shape of a dragon with a lion's head and a serpent's body.

The woman's head barely reached my chin as she reached up and clasped my face. Softened by age, her hands conjured images of my grandmother, whose pendant I wore around my neck.

"Yes," she mumbled, peering into my eyes. "Bravery, I see. Courage. Great strength." Her hands clasped my face with more strength than I thought possible from a woman of her size. Her dark eyes pierced mine, pricking me with a magical enchantment, as if she peered into my soul. "Pride. Defiance. Something else." She pursed her lips. "Stubbornness. Doubt. Suspicion. Never finding what she searches for, though it be within her reach."

She stepped back. "No. You cannot enter this place.

Be gone."

"What?"

"You will fail."

"Excuse me?"

"You will fail," she repeated, as if that explained it. She turned to the doors.

"Wait," I called to her, desperation fueling my actions as I grabbed her arm.

She rounded on me.

"Wait, please," I pleaded, releasing her arm.

"Why?" She took a step away from me.

I took a deep breath. "I admit I'm not perfect. If you'll give me a chance, I can prove myself to you. I'll show you I can change."

She narrowed her eyes. "Why would you do that?"

Because I wanted the scepter, so I could be one step closer to going home. Because I didn't want to fail. Because I didn't want to be a disappointment in Rumpel's eyes. None of those were answers she sought.

"Because the goblins will die without me."

"Why does that matter?"

The image of the girl in the cavern came to me in perfect clarity, her sunlight hair like a halo, her eyes shining with innocence. My heart tightened, and I knew how to answer her. "Love." I stood taller, boldness in my words. "My answer is love."

"What?"

"Love is the reason why I want to save the goblins. I have no children of my own, but if I did, I would do anything to protect them, and I would expect the same courtesy from others."

"Hmm." She stood without moving. I couldn't tell

what she was thinking. The breeze rustled her robes. Wisps of white hair got caught in the wind, and again I was reminded of my grandmother.

Please, I pleaded. Until now, I'd only felt coerced to help the goblins. It was never because I wanted to. I did it because it meant I got to go home. But perhaps now, my motivation had changed. Maybe I really did want to help them. Not for me. But for them.

The woman shuffled to me. "You are a lucky girl," she said. "Your ancestors are with you this day. It is them that allow you in. Not me." She glanced up, just above my head. I had an image of Grandmother dancing above me, chiding the woman for not letting me inside sooner. "Come," she said with a wave of her hand. "All of you, join us."

I gave a silent prayer as I entered, thanking the goddesses for softening the woman's heart. *And thanks to you, too, Grandmother.*

Maybe Grandmother was also trying to make amends for her past misdeeds.

Inside, we walked over a bamboo floor. A low stone table sat at the room's center, where vases filled with sticks of incense burned. The thick aroma clouded the space. Open walls overlooked an immense garden of bonsai trees.

Rugs were placed around the table. One of the men wearing the red and gold robes shuffled to us.

"Sit," he said with a friendly smile, revealing a toothless grin.

The five of us found spots on the rugs and sat. Though I was happy to be out of the saddle, nervousness twisted inside me. Would they make us wait long?

Rumpel stared at me, but as soon as I turned to him, he glanced away.

His lips quirked into a smile, as if he found me amusing, but he said nothing. Irritation gnawed at me. I would figure him out, and I would understand those disturbing glances.

There was a possibility—a *miniscule* one—that he was slightly attracted to me, which may have been another reason for the furtive looks. But I refused to believe it. No matter how much a part of me wanted it to be real. I exhaled and shoved the confusing thoughts aside.

The woman reentered. In her arms she carried a basket laden with drying cloths and jars of liquid mixed with flower petals. She motioned me toward her.

I stood, not arguing as I followed her out of the room and down a path leading through the bonsais. Her feet shuffled over the gravel. We walked around flower pots that resembled cauldrons, water fountains shaped as fish, and a stream that led to a lake.

Lily pads and lotus flowers floated on the water, and koi darted beneath the surface. A bridge spanned to the lake's center where a pagoda stood on an island, a hulking object in the mist.

"Here is where you must go to wash. We do not allow the unclean to the mountain's summit."

"Is the scepter at the mountain's summit?"

She bobbed her head. "It is."

"How am I supposed to get it?"

She gave me a shrewd gaze. "That's for you to determine, but you must take it from the dragon, and you must choose which to take it from. Only one dragon holds the truth you seek."

"What do you mean by that?"

"You'll see." She gave me a knowing smile, then handed me the basket of jars and drying cloths. "Take these to the pagoda across the bridge, which houses the bathing chamber. There, you must wash and put on the robe you find in the basket. When you arrive back at the main house, we will escort you to the path leading to the summit."

"My companions can't go with me?"

She cocked an eyebrow. "You desire for them to accompany you?"

"Yes. It would be safer with them. Especially if there are dragons to be confronted."

"Hmm. We will allow one to join you—the king's oldest son, but that is it. He is the only one I trust. Our mountain is sacred. It cannot be soiled by dirty feet. Now, go wash. Return quickly. I have duties to attend." She turned around.

"Wait," I said.

She stopped and glanced over her shoulder.

"I don't even know your name."

"Mae-Ling," she said with a slight bow. "Priestess of this mountain." She turned and hobbled down the path. I stared after her until she disappeared, leaving me alone.

Mae-Ling, priestess of the mountain, trusted Rumpel. That came as a shock. How could anyone trust him? Especially someone as important as the priestess?

I turned around and trudged over the bridge toward the pagoda, the basket held in my arms. Swans glided over the lake's mirror-like surface. Koi fish occasionally splashed as they nibbled on algae.

When I stepped inside the bath house, a sunken stone basin filled with steaming water greeted me. I stepped to the edge, peering inside. Smooth stones rested at the water's clear bottom. Lotus petals floated on the surface. The air held the calming aroma of the flowers.

I placed the basket on the ground and inspected the rest of the pagoda. The walls and floors were made of bamboo and shielded me from the outside. I untied the rope around my waist and removed the shirt and pants.

I stepped to the water, then dipped my toe under the surface. The liquid was warm, though not scalding, and I made quick work of submerging up to my neck. Safe in the water, I decided I never wanted to leave. Mae-Ling would have to drag me out kicking and screaming.

But I couldn't stay here forever, no matter how much I wanted, so I pulled the basket toward me and removed one of the jars.

Purple petals combined in the transparent mixture. I unstopped the cork, and the scent of lavender washed over me. I left the jar sitting beside the pool as I removed the braids from my hair, releasing each one into a wave of red curls. After taking out the last of the braids, I grabbed the glass jar and poured a generous amount of liquid into my hand. I worked the soap into my hair until it created a lather.

I washed my hair twice, hoping to get all the grime from the road off me, wishing I could erase my memories as I went.

Holding my breath, I submerged under water, allowing the soap to remove the last of the dirt. I scrubbed my skin next, rubbing until my skin grew red. When I finally got out, I left the past behind.

Whatever came next, I was ready.

Nine

I TIGHTENED THE SASH AROUND my waist, tying the two ends in a knot over the silk shirt and flowing pants. I could get used to clothing like this. Running my hands over the red-and golden-embroidered fabric, I stood tall.

The fog had cleared, revealing jagged mountains against the sky. We must've been in a valley. A mountain taller than the others stood against the eastern horizon. I had my suspicions that it must've been the place where I traveled.

To the summit.

I ran my fingers over the knife tucked into my sash. The blade and my magic were my only weapons. I prayed they would be enough.

When I entered the main house, Rumpel stood waiting for me, his hair slightly damp, wearing a red tunic made of leather, black pants, and boots that rose to his knees. With a sword strapped to his belt, he made an imposing figure, one who I would think twice about before challenging.

His mouth slacked when I stepped to him. I self-consciously pushed my braid over my shoulder, biting my lip, wanting to look at anything but him. He took a step toward me. The clean scent of spruce forests enveloped me. My stomach flipped, forcing me to glance away from him and focus on anything else. The others sat on benches in the corner near a bier, smoke trailing from a bed of coals.

"Are you ready?" Rumpel asked, his voice deep. Heat rose to my cheeks as he spoke. Why did I have to have such a reaction to him?

Nothing made sense. I took a deep breath to steady my thumping heart.

"I'm ready," I answered.

He gave a quick nod, then walked to his brother who sat on the end of a bench. Kneeling beside him, he spoke quietly. Orlane gave his brother a tight hug.

When Rumpel finally stepped away, Dex and Malleus stood. His uncle gave him a handshake and a smile, and a few words of advice I couldn't hear, though both their gazes went to me, and I could only imagine what they said.

Keep her in check, nephew.

Rumpel turned away from the others and made his way toward me when Malleus blocked his path.

The big man's hand went to his battle axe strapped to his waist. I crossed to the two men, eying Malleus. What was he up to now?

"...not safe," he said. "You're fools to go to the summit. No one survives."

"Then how else are we supposed to get the scepter?" Rumpel demanded.

"Take me with you."

"Not possible. Only Kardiya and I are permitted."

"Tell them I'm coming," Malleus demanded.

"It won't do any good. The summit is sacred. We're

lucky they're letting us travel to it."

Malleus's bushy eyebrows drew together over his dark eyes. "How do I know you didn't pay them to say such a thing?"

"Because I didn't," he snapped. "And I refuse to argue with you any longer. Now, let me pass."

Malleus stood defiantly, unmoving.

Dex adjusted his cloak as he stood beside Rumpel. "There's no use in arguing this, Malleus. Will you keep them from completing the quest to retrieve the scepter?"

"I'm attempting to make sure they don't bloody die on that cursed mountain. Don't you know how many have been killed by the dragons? They'll die too, and don't pretend they won't. They need my axe."

"Are you accusing me of not being capable?" Rumpel challenged, fists clenched at his sides.

"And what if I bloody am?"

I stepped between the two men. The last thing we needed was for them to come to blows.

"Malleus, Rumpel," I said calmly, "I'm sure there's no need for us to worry. I retrieved the first item, and if I'm really the one mentioned in prophecy—the one who will stop the Sai-hadov, then I'm sure defeating the dragons will be something I can accomplish. Besides, I've battled dragons before and survived."

Malleus raised an eyebrow. "You've battled the beasts before?"

"Yes. My people share an island with dragons. Believe it or not, my brother married one. If anyone can accomplish this, I can. Now, shall we go, Rumpel? I hate to keep a good dragon waiting."

Malleus looked at me with irritation written on his

face. Dex gave a heartwarming smile and clapped Malleus on the shoulder.

"You see?" Dex said. "She's full of confidence. They'll have no trouble at all."

"Bugger it all," Malleus mumbled, crossing his arms over his barrel-sized chest. "Don't blame me for not warning you. You're both fools for attempting this."

"Then we're brave fools," Rumpel said, grabbing my elbow and escorting me from the room.

When we stepped outside, his grip relaxed, yet I didn't pull my arm away. His skin held the wild scent of dark forests and a hint of cloves, an aroma completely masculine and alluring.

We paced down a forest path. Our horses were sheltered under a thatched-roof hovel, but Rumpel passed them by.

"We're not taking the horses?" I asked.

"No. The path is too steep for them."

"You said you've been here?"

"Yes. I came once with my father, which is why he probably chose this place to hide the scepter. He knew what a pain it was to get to the mountain's summit."

I eyed him. He still held my arm, and I still hadn't asked him to let go. "Do you miss your father?"

He glanced at me before answering, his eyes matching the sky, as if they were made from the same material. "Why do you ask?"

I shrugged. "I miss mine. I know what that kind of pain feels like, even to someone who puts on a brave face." *Someone like you.*

"I miss him," he admitted. "But not as much as Orlane. I don't think he'll ever heal from our parents' death. That's why I do my best to protect him. I never want him to suffer like that again."

Trees grew with gnarled trunks, their branches forming a canopy to block out the sunlight. Our boots snapped over twigs and brittle leaves. Boulders covered in soft green moss sat along our path as the scent of life and greenery hung in the air.

We approached a weathered stone archway overshadowing the path. Magic glowed from the symbols etched on it. As we stepped to it, I ran my hand over the surface pocked with age and dotted with lichen.

An enchantment washed over me. "There's magic here. Can you read this?"

"They're glyphs crafted in the Shigoshi language. They explain how to get the scepter." He pointed to a symbol with two horizontal lines through a vertical one. "One hundred," he said, then pointed to another group. "False. Only one is true. The unclean."

"What does that mean?"

He shrugged. "No idea. I guess we'll find out."

"Haven't you been here before?"

"Yes, but only to the outskirts. There's a wall surrounding the inner summit. Only my father went inside."

"How are we supposed to get inside?"

"I thought we'd figure that out once we got there."

"Hmm, sounds like a solid plan."

He gave me a lopsided smile, not the typical scowl he'd worn since I met him. Was it possible there was an easygoing side to him? Not one constantly surrounded by a dark cloud?

"What?" he asked.

"You're smiling. I didn't think you were capable of it."

"I smile all the time."

"Do you? When does that happen exactly?"

"When I'm in a good mood. When I'm not bothered by pesky transformation spells. When I'm with someone I like."

My mouth gaped. "Does that mean you like me?"

"That's questionable. When you're not trying to kill me is a plus."

"I never tried to kill you."

He raised an eyebrow. "The arrow incident in the tree?"

"Fine." I bit back a smile. "Maybe once, but I haven't attempted it since. You can't blame me. You did capture me."

"For good reason."

I scowled. "Let's not get on that topic again."

"Agreed."

The path ended at a wall of stone covered in thick vines.

"Well, we made it." Rumpel stared up to the top. "The trick will be climbing it."

"Climbing it? Surely there's an easier way."

"Unfortunately, no. I hope you're not afraid of getting your hands dirty."

I couldn't help but laugh. "Except for the bath in Shigoshi, my hands haven't been clean once on this trip. You should know better than to think I'm someone unused to dirt."

"Well, you are a princess, aren't you?"

"What does that have to do with it?" I cinched the sash around my waist, stepped to the wall, and grabbed a woody vine, careful to avoid the thorns.

Rumpel stepped beside me, and we climbed together.

We didn't speak. Concentrating on climbing took every ounce of my fortitude. The wind picked up the higher we went. I clung to the vines, straining to keep my grasp.

Sweat slicked my palms, which made grasping them harder. Wind battered my cheeks. Loose strands of hair came free of my braid and tickled my nose, but I didn't dare push them back. Rumpel grunted as he climbed higher, and I refused to let him reach the summit before me.

Taking a deep breath, I inched my way up, my fingers shaking, the muscles in my arms burning. With only a few feet to go, I grabbed a vine, and it snapped. I scrambled to seize a jutting rock, and as I clung to the cliff face, my heart raced.

"You okay?" Rumpel called down to me.

"I'm fine. I slipped." I hugged the stones, their sharp edges cutting into my fingertips. My breath came in frantic gasps. Something about falling to my death completely unnerved me.

Fear froze me in place. I managed to glance up at Rumpel who edged his way to the summit. I couldn't hold to these rocks forever, but how could I move another inch?

With a deep inhale, I shifted my grip to the stone above, leveraged up, and grasped another, deciding not to rely on the vines. My momentum went excruciatingly slow, but I didn't care. My only thought was to make it to the top, where I could be on solid ground once again.

Clumps of grass appeared at the top of the ridge. I climbed until Rumpel leaned over the side and reached for me.

Grumbling, I grabbed his hand, too spent to worry about him beating me.

He pulled me over the ledge. I collapsed onto dew-soaked grass, staring up at a sky with wispy clouds. Breathing heavily, the only thought I had was of how grateful I was to be alive.

Rumpel knelt over me. "You made it."

"Barely."

"Now we've just got to battle dragons and steal a scepter and we're good. Easy."

"Sure. Easy." I didn't move from where I lay. I could stay here and take a nap for an hour, maybe thirty.

"Look at that," Rumpel said, awe in his voice.

I sat up and followed his line of sight. Giant dragon statues stood lined up like soldiers. White marble reflected the sun from their lithe, snake-like bodies and heads resembling a lion.

"There's got to be at least a hundred," Rumpel said.

"A hundred. Like the riddle on the archway."

"Yes," he answered.

He stood and held out his hand. I took it, no longer bothered by the gesture, comfortable with the feel of his warm skin on mine.

He gave me an approving glance, making my stomach flutter with the sensation of flitting butterflies. I'd never had such a powerful reaction to anyone, one that drew me to him more than I cared to admit. The tattoos swirling along his jawline and down his neck tempted me to run my fingers along his skin, to see if he felt as supple as he looked.

He squeezed my hand, drawing me closer to him. My breath caught in my throat. The dizziness in my head made me wonder if I were swooning. Was I swooning? By the goddess, how could anyone feel so strongly toward such a rogue?

"Kardiya." His tone was deep and seductive. Goose-flesh rippled over my skin.

"Yes," I asked, my voice breathless. His eyes went to my mouth. Did he intend to kiss me?

Surely not. He was my captor, blast it all. But I couldn't pull away from him. Without thinking, I rested my free hand on his chest, his muscles taut beneath his layer of clothing.

He pulled me closer until our faces were so near, all I had to do was raise onto my tiptoes to kiss him.

A screeching wail came from above us. We split apart, our gazes drawn to the sky where a dragon soared.

TEN

A BLUE DRAGON SAILED ABOVE us, its wings stirring the air. It circled twice before landing. Its body morphed to that of a man wearing a long, ivory-colored robe. As he walked toward us, his form moved stiffly, his skin and stringy beard as pale as his clothing. Even his eyes were devoid of color, as if he were entirely hewn from marble, just like the dragons.

When he stopped, he scanned us with a penetrating gaze, one that sent a shiver of fear up my spine. He didn't just look hewn from marble, he *was* hewn from marble—a living statue.

"Who are you?" Rumpel demanded.

"My name is unimportant." He spoke with a gravelly voice, his words drawn out, as if he weren't used to speaking. "The question is, why are you on my mountain?"

I stepped forward. "We've come for the scepter."

He raised an eyebrow. "If you intend to retrieve the scepter, you must be worthy. If you are not, you will pay with your life."

He kept his hands folded in his sleeves, but he took another step forward and unlaced his fingers. He held a golden scepter with a sapphire jewel atop. "This is the talisman you seek, but to obtain it, you must first find it. Good luck." He gave a slight bow, hid the object in his sleeve, and took a step backward.

His body morphed. Wings grew from his back, his neck lengthened, and his head turned to the shape of a lion's, though it was covered in marble scales.

He flapped his massive wings, and then he leaped into the sky. Spiraling upward, he soared wave-like to the other stone dragons and landed amongst them.

Wind howled, and we were left alone to stare at the maze of dragon statues.

"What now?" I asked Rumpel.

He grunted. "We find the scepter." He marched toward the dragons, and I followed.

When we reached them, we wandered into perfectly spaced rows where identical faces and body shapes stood like clones.

"They look exactly the same," I said.

"Yes."

"I don't see any with the scepter."

"I suspect the scepter is hidden."

"How do we know which one is the right one?"

Rumpel sighed. "Keep looking."

As we wandered, marble blurred in my vision. Tentacles sprouted like mustaches from their oversized heads. Their lion-like mouths with pointed teeth and scaled, serpentine bodies looked as if they'd come from the same mold. Even their facial expressions matched, quirky smiles and eyes that seemed to follow me.

We passed by dozens upon dozens of statues until I was thoroughly lost in the maze. I passed one dragon after another, and not a single one stood out.

My magic didn't react to any of them.

I reached for one, but Rumpel grabbed my wrist, stopping me. "I wouldn't," he said.

"Why not?"

"They're most likely enchanted."

"I don't feel any magic."

"You don't feel it, but that doesn't mean it's not there."

I crossed my arms. "Do you have a better suggestion?"

He glanced around the maze as clouds grew low and gray overhead. The wind picked up, howling through the endless rows. Loneliness settled inside me, as if we were the only people in the world this high up on the mountain. A sudden pang of homesickness gripped me. I pressed my hands to my stomach, hoping to suppress the feeling.

Rumpel's eyes betrayed the same emotion. Was some sort of enchantment at play?

"Something's wrong here," he said.

"I feel it, too."

"Keep moving." He rubbed the back of his neck. "The sooner we find that scepter, the better."

We trudged until we reached the end of the maze, then turned and took another path through them. I couldn't help but imagining them as tombstones, but perhaps my mind was playing tricks. Or maybe the enchantment of this place was getting to me.

I rubbed my eyes. Bleariness made it hard to see straight. Moving forward, my heart grew so heavy, I found it difficult to walk.

I stopped.

Around me, only the faces of the dragons met mine, staring with their mocking smiles and razor-sharp teeth. Where was Rumpel?

"Rumpel?" I called.

My legs grew heavy, as if I trudged through sand. A headache pounded with a dull throbbing.

"Rumpel!" My voice echoed. I pinched the bridge of my nose. Magic clouded around me. I breathed deeply, trying to clear my head.

Dizziness made the world spin. I fell onto a statue, my shoulder taking the brunt of the impact. I managed to stay upright, keeping my hand on the cool stone of the dragon for balance.

Cold marble slithered under my hand. The stone warmed. Scales turned crimson as they moved over muscle. I snatched my hand away, but the dragon's head whipped around to gaze at me with enraged yellow eyes.

The dragon towered over me to block the sun. Hissing came from its mouth before it snapped its jaws inches from my face.

As if on instinct, I ripped the knife from my boot. But if I wanted to defeat a creature like this, I'd need magic in the weapon.

The creature flapped its wings and flew over me. It circled me, then barreled down, whipping me with its tail. I fell backward, nearly bumping into another dragon.

Getting to my feet, I faced the monster once again. Magic gathered in my chest and through my hands. When it lunged for me, I planted my feet, pointed with my knife, and blasted a wind spell through the blade.

The dragon fell back. It flailed, then whipped around and dove for me.

I shot another blast, but it dodged. As the air cleared, the dragon disappeared. I spun around, searching. A crimson dot appeared in the sky, and a stream of fire poured from its mouth. I ducked under a statue, careful not to touch it.

The fireball exploded around me. I held my hands over my head.

Curse that stupid beast. If only I could hit it with a spell—something other than wind. Fire? No. It was likely immune to fire.

Water, maybe?

It was worth a shot.

When the fire died down, with nothing but singed grass around me, I jumped from my hiding spot. Magic warmed my fists as I prepared the spell. The dragon soared close enough, and I released my power.

I focused a volley of water from the blade's tip and hit its flank. The beast roared, pumping its wings, failing to gain altitude. Its eyes widened. Its shriek of frustration pierced the air as the water weighed it down.

I hit it again, magic draining from me, but I didn't care. I would kill this beast before it killed me.

It thrashed back and forth, which only served to throw it off balance. The dragon crashed to the ground, smashing statues to bits. Clouds of dust rose from where it landed.

My knife clutched in my hands, I crept toward it. If I had to slit the beast's throat, I would.

When I reached it, the dragon lay in the debris of smashed statues, a beast made of stone once again, vacant marble eyes staring lifelessly up at me.

Breathing heavily, I sheathed my knife, wiped the moisture from my face, and backed away, continuing my search for Rumpel. Where had he gone?

As I walked, mist gathered, cloaking the statues in a

veil of cold fog. I was getting tired of these chills. Hugging my arms around me, I focused on the statues. One of them had to be the right one, but how did I know which was right? The real one must've been different than the others. It was the only thing that made sense.

It would've been a slight difference. My toe caught on something. I stumbled but caught myself, though I nearly toppled onto the prone form of Rumpel. He lay face down on the ground sleeping. Or dead.

Kneeling beside him, I shook his shoulder, but he didn't move. I leaned close to his face. His breath warmed my cheek.

At least he wasn't dead.

I rolled him over to his back, though he was heavier than he looked, a solid block of muscle hewn from pure steel. The chain around his neck glinted gold, and I pulled it from beneath his tunic to reveal his enchanted key.

With the metal talisman clutched in my hand, my head swam with possibilities.

Now was my chance. I could take it and find the nearest doorway, attempt to learn its secrets, and be done with this place. I could be back home by tonight, eating dinner with my mother by the hearth, warmed by the fire. I'd never have to be cold again. Never have to worry about quests or death or an unwanted attraction.

I fingered the key, its wire pattern similar to my necklace, its magic a foreign spell that made my stomach queasy.

No. I hadn't taken it before. I wouldn't take it now, not until I'd finished this quest and assured the goblins were free from the Sai-hadov.

"Rumpel." I cupped his cheek, drawn to the tattoos

inked on his flesh. Without thinking, I ran my finger over the swirling pattern.

Magic pulsed through the marks, glowing with the light of orange coal fire. I pulled my hand away, and the light faded, returning to normal.

Rumpel coughed, and his eyes fluttered open.

"Where…where am I?"

"On the mountain's summit in Shigoshi."

He rubbed his forehead, not speaking.

"Do you remember?" I asked.

"It's coming back to me. What happened?"

"You disappeared. I stumbled into a dragon and defeated it, then I found you."

"You defeated a dragon?"

"Yes."

A ghost of a smile pulled at his lips. "I can't say I'm surprised. I take it we're still searching for the scepter?"

"Unfortunately, yes. There's got to be a statue that looks different from the others, something that sets the real one apart."

"I agree." He closed his eyes, his breathing labored.

"What's the last thing you remember?" I asked.

He shook his head. "I was following you. I got disoriented, then hit with a headache and dizziness. Next thing I knew, you were here."

"Yes. I had the same symptoms. It's the magic in this place. It's making us sick."

He nodded, pain etching the lines around his eyes. "Trying to keep us from finding the scepter."

"Can we do anything to stop it?"

His eyes strayed from mine, distant and unfocused.

"Rumpel?"

He shook his head. "Sorry. I don't know…" His chest rose with a deep inhale. "This place."

"What if I use a spell? Something to keep the magic from touching us?"

"Maybe. It won't hurt to try."

I reached for the magic in me, but the spells I'd used had depleted my energy. A fraction of my magic glowed within, and I drew it to me.

"I'll try to block the magic around us. Hold on."

He didn't answer. I pulled on my magic, breathing evenly as it tugged on my life source, careful not to draw away too much energy.

My spell wrapped us. Magic drained from me, but my headache and dizziness faded instantly.

Rumpel blinked, focusing on me. "That's better."

"Yeah. Let's hope we find the scepter before my spell takes too much of my energy."

I stood and held out my hand for him. He grabbed it and got to his feet. The fog had grown thicker. Only the statues beside us were visible through the white mist.

We walked through the rows. Marble scales blended with the fog. Sheepish grinning faces fixated on me. My magic drained as I kept up the spell to repel the enchantment of this place. Weariness tugged at me.

I passed a dragon, its tentacles fanning behind it. One looked longer than the others. I stopped, staring at the marble.

"You see something?" Rumpel asked.

"Yes. Look at that." I pointed to the longer tentacle. "Does that look different than the others?"

We stepped closer to the dragon. Other than the tentacle, the statue was a complete copy of the others.

"Do you think this could be the one?" I asked.

"Possibly. To find out for sure, we'll have to touch it. Battle it, most likely."

"Battle it?"

He nodded.

"I'm not sure I'm up for battling another dragon."

"I don't think we'll have a choice."

We stood facing the beast. My magic slowed to a trickle. The spell grew weak. Wisps of fog glided past.

"Should I touch it?" Rumpel asked.

I pulled my knife from my boot. "Go ahead."

He placed his hand on the statute's back. The wind shifted, carrying the mist with it until the fog cleared.

The statue shifted. Blue scales replaced white marble. The beast's head turned to life, with golden tentacles flowing from its muzzle. One of its tentacles transformed into a scepter with a sapphire jewel.

It whipped around to stare at us. "You found me." The dragon's voice came as a deep rumble from its chest. "Now you'll have to catch me. Do not show fear, and my talisman will be yours."

The dragon leapt into the air, lithe body undulating like a wave as it sailed into the sky, to the horizon, and over the edge of the mountain until it disappeared.

"We have to catch it?" I huffed. My body ached. Every muscle protested as the weight of the spell came crashing down on me. I let the enchantment go before it sucked away my life's energy.

"Are you okay?" Rumpel asked. "You look pale."

"I'm…" I sagged to the ground.

Rumpel came to me, holding me to him. My heart pounded. Clammy sweat slicked my skin.

"You used too much magic." He smoothed a hand over my brow. I couldn't help but realize how right his nearness felt. "You know that can kill you."

"I know," I breathed. "But… we have to catch a dragon."

"We will. Soon enough." He picked me up, cradling me to his chest.

"What are you doing?"

"Getting you away from these statues, for one."

"I… can't rest long."

Whatever enchantment was in this place would continue draining us until we succumbed to its spell, but the thought was fleeting, and I drifted as sleep took me.

ELEVEN

Screaming woke me.

I bolted upright. The world had grown black. Only the stars and a half-moon appeared through a canopy of twisted tree branches. The outline of Rumpel lay beside me.

Where am I?

The last thing I remembered, we were surrounded by statues.

I touched Rumpel's shoulder to wake him, but he didn't move.

"Rumpel." I shook him. "Wake up."

He blinked, then opened his eyes. "What is it?" he asked, his voice hoarse.

"Where are we?"

He rubbed his eyes as he sat up. "Still on the mountaintop. I found some shelter in the trees and decided it was best our magic recovered before dragon hunting."

I nodded. "I heard something when I woke."

"Heard what?"

"Screaming," I answered.

Leaves rustled as he sat up, a shadowy outline in the dark of the forest. Quiet filled the air.

114

"Could it have been the dragon?" he asked.

I rubbed my forehead. "Maybe."

He stood, and I followed. The soreness in my muscles made me move slowly. My head throbbed after losing so much magic, yet warmth filled the spaces where an ounce of power filled me.

"We need to get off this mountain," Rumpel said. "Hopefully find that dragon in the process."

"Do you think we'll have any luck in the dark?"

"We'll have to try."

I followed behind Rumpel, a shadow against the outline of crooked trees. Our footsteps crunching over sticks sounded too loud.

We crept to the edge of the mountain where the wall dropped below us. The moonlight didn't illuminate the bottom.

"It's too dangerous to climb down in the dark," Rumpel said.

"Then what do we do?"

"Find somewhere less steep to climb down, if such a place exists."

A shriek pierced through the stillness of the night. Chills prickled the nape of my neck.

"What was that?" Rumpel asked.

"The same thing that woke me."

"It didn't sound like a dragon."

"What else could it be?"

Rumpel shook his head. "I don't know."

We hiked through the forest, avoiding the dark shapes of trees. Twigs crunched under our boots. I kept my hands in front of me to prevent running into anything. I debated on conjuring a light spell, but I'd only managed to regain a small portion of my magic. Using it for an enchantment would waste my energy.

A bauble of blue light flitted through the trees, then disappeared.

"That must've been the scepter." My voice was a quiet sound muffled by the trees.

"I believe the dragon is toying with us."

"How are we supposed to catch it?" I asked.

"Good question."

I flexed my fingers, which had grown stiff in the damp air. "Let's lure it out into the open. Catching anything in this forest is impossible."

"But here, we've got the cover of trees if it tries to attack."

"True." I sagged against a trunk, my muscles weak, my breath coming in labored gasps. I blinked to keep the forest from spinning. "You've got your sword, and I've got my knife," I said. "We'll have to confront it eventually. I say we move to the open."

"Very well," Rumpel agreed without a fight.

We trudged through the forest. The blue light appeared again, accompanied by laughter. A shiver of fear ran down my spine.

"It's moving toward the dragon statues," Rumpel said.

"If it makes it there, then what? It becomes stone again and we have to find it all over?"

"Hopefully not, but my guess is yes."

I balled my fists. "Curse that dragon."

"My thoughts too."

Wind stirred the tree limbs, howling with a wail that mimicked the dragon's cry. Something brushed my neck.

I spun around.

A pair of reflective silver eyes stood level with mine. The creature stood with a hunched body. Wispy white robes fanned around it.

"Rumpel, do you see this?" I hissed, my heart racing as it pounded against my ribcage. The goblin didn't answer. In my peripheral vision, only trees crowded around me.

"Rumpel." I spoke louder, standing straight as I faced the creature.

It lifted a hand. Sickle-like talons reached from hands with a transparent blue luster.

"*Your death is mine*," it whispered, its words an echo. One of its talons brushed my cheek. I batted it away when the creature disappeared.

A clammy sweat broke out over my skin. I took deep breaths to control my racing heart.

"Rumpel!" I repeated. I turned around. Where was he?

"Here," he called. I followed the sound of his voice.

"Where were you?" he asked.

"I was following you before a Sai-hadov appeared."

"A Sai-hadov? Are you sure?"

I nodded. "Yes. It spoke to me. Said it wanted my death."

Rumpel cursed.

"Rumpel, what's going on? Why are the Sai-hadov here?"

"I don't know, but it's not strong enough to hurt you, not in its shadow form. The only thing to do is gather the scepter and crown, then destroy the Inshadov before they make good on their threats. They know you're after the objects."

"How do they know that?"

"It's possible they've been spying on us, but to do that,

they'd need help from someone mortal."

"Someone mortal?"

"Yes, they would've needed help to follow us. They have little power in their spirit forms."

"That's troubling. Do you think someone has been helping them follow us?"

"If so, I don't know who."

"Don't you?"

"What do you mean? You think you know?"

"Malleus. He betrayed the king. It doesn't take a leap to think he's betraying us now. You know he hates you."

Rumpel sighed. "We can't discuss this now. We have to find the scepter."

"Why are you avoiding the subject? You know it has to be him."

"Kardiya," he spoke my name firmly. "We have to get that scepter. That's the only thing that matters."

I followed him through the trees until we entered the open plateau. Without the cover of the forest, the wind raged.

Laughter came from behind us. I grabbed my knife, holding it with numb fingers as I faced the sound.

The dragon flew lithely through the air, an undulating wave of blue against a backdrop of glittering stars.

"Come to us," I shouted.

Rumpel eyed me. "You're calling to it?"

"Yes. Either that or we kill it, and I suspect killing it would result in our own deaths."

"Why do you say that?"

"Because it hasn't attacked us, and I suspect it won't. It wanted us to catch it, not kill it. I intend to do that."

I held my knife in the air, blade glinting in the moonlight. "Come to us! We will not hurt you."

The dragon turned, its gaze fixed on my knife. When I caught its eye, I dropped the weapon. "We will not harm you," I repeated. "Come to us."

"I don't like this plan," Rumpel grumbled.

"You don't have to like it as long as it works."

The dragon spiraled, changing its course straight for us.

"Drop your sword," I said to Rumpel.

"What?"

"Drop it. We can't show fear."

He hesitated, his hand fisted around the pommel. "I don't know."

The dragon sailed close enough for me to spot the blue jewel of the scepter growing like a tentacle from its face.

"Do it!" I demanded.

"Fine." He tossed his sword to the ground.

The beast circled, its body stirring the air, then it landed in front of us. The scepter grew from its face like one of its tentacles. The beast reached up with its claw and plucked the talisman from its face as if it were a blade of grass. The blue jewel glowed over its scales.

"You don't fear me?" It growled, slithering closer until its face was inches from mine. I stood tall as I faced the beast.

Don't show fear.

"Will you not fight me?" the dragon asked.

"I will not. The scepter belongs to the true king, and I am the one who will retrieve the three talismans. If you are wise, you will give it to me. The prince and I will save your lands."

"Hmm." Steam rose from his nostrils. "Bold words for a being made of bones and blood."

The snakelike dragon's body coiled around us, slowly closing the gap between us and it.

"None have confronted the Sai-hadov and won. How will you be different?"

"Because of the prophecy—"

"No," he snapped. "Do not speak of prophecy. If you are to defeat them, you must stand bravely in the face of fear." Its face loomed before mine, curving teeth in a wicked face. "Do you stand bravely?"

Its breath smelled of sulphur, its looming eyes like burning coals. Fear raced through my blood.

Rumpel grabbed my hand, grasping my cold fingers in his warm ones. I let go of my pent-up breath.

"I do not fear you." I stood tall, meeting its eyes. "And I do not fear them."

It didn't move, as if it were a statue once again. When the wind gusted, the dragon placed the scepter on the ground.

Mist gathered. Its form faded into the fog, leaving us alone on top of the mountain.

I picked up the scepter, the metal cold in my hands. The jewel glowed, casting Rumpel's masculine face in azure light, highlighting the crystal blue depths of his eyes.

"You got it," he said quietly, his voice mingling with the wind.

"Maybe you should have more faith in me."

"I do have faith in you, Kardiya. I always have."

Our eyes met. He placed his hand atop mine where I held the scepter. My breath stuttered at the gentleness of his touch.

"I shouldn't have doubted you," he said.

No, you shouldn't have, I wanted to say, but the words wouldn't come.

His lashes shuttered sparkling eyes. Curse those eyes. His lips, too. Why couldn't I look away from him?

"We should get off this mountain now," I said. "We've been here too long."

"Yes," he answered, his voice deep and velvety. "Much too long."

The mountain's magic was tampering with my head worse than I thought.

Rumpel placed his hand on my back, pulling me closer to him. I couldn't stop looking at his lips. What was it that made him so mesmerizing?

"Kardiya," he whispered my name. "Will you let me kiss you?"

Everything inside screamed for me to push him away—this rogue who had stolen me from my home—yet I stood immobile.

"Yes," I answered. Where had that come from?

He brushed his lips over mine. Tingles ignited like wildfire through my body. He kissed slowly, his lips softer than I expected. With his hand on my back, he pressed me to him. Goose bumps rippled over my skin.

He pulled away, moving his hand from my back, leaving a cold spot where his flesh had been.

"I'm sorry. I shouldn't have done that."

"Oh." I didn't know what else to say. He shouldn't have done that? The most amazing experience of my life and he shouldn't have done it?

"We should go." He took the scepter from me and hid it in his bag.

He walked away from me, but I couldn't find the motivation to follow, too stunned from a kiss that had ended too soon.

I pushed the feeling of his lips from my mind and walked after him. When I caught up, we hiked to the edge of the cliff. The sun rose, streaking the sky in pink and gray, giving us enough light to see the wall. I climbed down without thought, focusing on anything but Rumpel who descended beside me.

Curse him.

He was right. He shouldn't have kissed me. What was he thinking? I was his captive, and now he'd made himself into a man who took liberties with those he enslaved. He was a scoundrel in every sense of the word.

But he didn't kiss like a scoundrel. He kissed as if he meant it, as if he'd make me happy and care for me if I gave him half the chance.

Which I wouldn't.

When we finally reached the ground, I wiped my dirty palms on my silk pants, hoping to leave the stains of the night behind. We continued down the trail without speaking.

Why had he pushed me away? I'd given him permission to kiss me. It wasn't like he'd forced himself on me. Did he not like me in the way I supposed he did? All his furtive glances and whispered words. Had I made up the whole romance?

Maybe so.

Maybe it was the mountain's magic that had driven him to kiss me. If that was so, then I would put him out of my mind. After this quest was over, I would go home to Malestasia and never think of him again.

An empty pit opened a hole in my stomach. Thinking of my life without him should've given me hope. I would be free again. But it didn't.

With sunrays splayed over our path, we made it to the pagoda. When we entered, the scent of seared fish filled the air. My stomach grumbled with hunger pains. It was only now I realized I was hungry.

Our companions stood from where they sat on pallets and walked to us. Orlane's broad smile was contagious, and I couldn't help but smile with him as he embraced his brother.

"You're alive!" Dex said, clapping his nephew on the shoulder. "As I knew you would be. I never doubted it for a moment."

Malleus stood in the corner, dark eyes focused on us, not muttering a word.

The word *traitor* came to mind, and I couldn't shake the feeling I'd gotten while in the Sai-hadov's presence.

"Come, we've got plenty of food to go around," Dex said. "You must tell us of your adventures."

"No," Malleus said from his spot in the corner. We stopped to look at the big man, his arms crossed over his barrel chest. "They'll not take another step until they tell us if they retrieved the scepter."

"Of course they retrieved it," Dex said. "They're alive, aren't they? They wouldn't have made it back if they didn't have it."

"I want to see it," Malleus demanded.

"Now?" Dex asked. "Good gracious, man, they've only just returned."

"I want to see it for myself."

Dex opened his mouth to argue, but Rumpel lifted

his hand. "It's fine, Uncle. If he wants proof, I have it." He opened his bag and pulled out the scepter. The jewel's blue glow radiated an aura of magic that warmed my skin.

"Satisfied?" Rumpel asked.

Malleus grunted. "That's really it?"

"It is."

He looked at it with shrewd eyes. "I don't believe it."

"Kardiya took it from the dragon herself. She obtained it, just as she obtained the ring, just as the prophecy said."

Malleus shifted his gaze to me. "Is this true?"

I placed my hands on my hips. I was sick of his distrust, and I couldn't put off the nagging feeling that he was a traitor. I had no proof, nor did I have any idea how to get it, but I would keep a close eye on him. "It's true, and you'd be wise to trust the prince. When this is over with, he'll be your king."

Malleus's jaw twitched. I'd hit a nerve. "Be careful with your words, girl. You have no idea the danger you've involved yourself in." He turned and stormed out of the hut, his boots thudding on the wood-planked floor. The door slammed behind him.

"I don't like him," Dex muttered. "He's had nothing but a sour attitude since we've started this journey."

"Bad. Man," Orlane said.

"He's not a bad man," Rumpel said. "But he has a guilty conscience. Any mention of me becoming king disturbs him. It reminds him of what he did to Father."

"Then why are we dragging him around with us?" I asked. "We should leave him here."

"I agree, but Baelem thought it wise to have him with us."

Then maybe Baelem, too, was a traitor, but I didn't say

it out loud. Not yet. I'd have to wait for a better opportunity to broach the topic, preferably when I got a chance to be alone with Rumpel.

"Come." Dex guided us toward the fire where fat lumps of fish sizzled over a grill. Tankards filled with watered wine sat atop a nearby bench. He picked up several earthenware trenchers and passed them to us.

We filled our plates, grabbed the tankards, and sat around the blaze. The heat warmed me, and the seasoned fish satisfied the emptiness in my belly, though my heart remained cold. After Rumpel kissed me, my lips still tingled, and the place where he'd touched my back had left a chill.

Why couldn't I stop thinking about that blasted kiss? It wasn't as if I'd never been kissed before. Plenty of noble snobs had left me with a kiss after a night of dancing at the balls—not that any of them had meant a thing to me. I'd forgotten them as quickly as I'd forgotten their arrogant smiles and fake endearments.

Perhaps that's why I couldn't forget Rumpel's kiss. Although goblins dealt in deceit and trickery, his passion had felt more real than anything I'd felt in my life.

"...to the pass through the Vallderwydth Mountains," Dex said, his words bringing me out of my thoughts. "It will take more time, but we'll avoid the woodwraiths."

"Then we'll have the mountain dwellers to deal with."

"True. Either way, it will be a treacherous path. The question is, what sort of treachery do you feel more comfortable with?"

"The mountain dwellers," Rumpel answered. "They're reclusive. They won't like our presence, but I'm hoping we can convince them to let us pass."

"Malleus will be disappointed. He's been itching to use that axe since we defeated the woodwraiths," Dex said.

"He'll get over it," Rumpel said. "He's done nothing but whine and moan this entire quest. It's time I had words with him." Rumpel finished off his last bite, took a drink from his tankard, and set it aside. He stood, then stalked away. A cold wind swept through the room as he opened the door and stepped outside.

I sat alone with Dex and Orlane. After a night spent on an enchanted mountain, weariness tugged on me. I glanced at our things sitting in the room's corner. My rolled pallet sat among our bags and blankets. Would I get a moment to rest?

"You look weary," Dex said.

"Do I?" I rubbed my eyes, hoping to erase the image of Rumpel that stayed as a constant visage in the back of my mind.

"Perhaps you could use a few hours of rest. We'll not leave until Rumpel convinces Malleus to take the pass through the mountains, which will take the better part of a day, in my estimation."

"Maybe resting would be a wise choice." After finishing off my food, I placed my trencher aside.

As I rolled out my pallet, the idea that Sai-hadov stalked me gave me a moment's pause. Would it be wise for me to rest when I knew they were so close? But the thought was a fleeting one. Lying down, I fell into a deep sleep without another worry.

Twelve

"KARDIYA."

My whispered name woke me. Rumpel knelt over me. My eyes bleary, I sat up. Outside the hut's only window, a dark evening sky loomed behind the evergreens.

"It's dark already?" I asked, surprised I'd slept the whole day away. That had been thoughtless of me. "Are we leaving?"

"Not until morning."

I rubbed the sleep from my eyes. My dreams lingered. Mother had been there, her eyes wet with tears, pleading for me to return to her. I'd tried to tell her I was coming, only to realize my mouth had been tied with a gag—the same one Rumpel had put in my mouth when he'd brought me to the cave. I hadn't been able to speak. She hadn't heard my answer.

"I need to talk to you," Rumpel said.

"Okay." I pushed the covers off and stood, muscles stiff and protesting as I followed him out of the pagoda.

We stepped outside, the cool evening helping to clear the cobwebs from my head. I smoothed a hand over my hair. Most of the braid had come undone. I couldn't image what a mess I looked. My hair always got so disheveled

127

after I slept. No wonder Rumpel had regretted kissing me. I'd looked like a vagabond since I'd arrived in this realm. At home, I wouldn't have shown my face until the servants had combed and braided my hair to perfection.

Some of the priests shuffled past, giving us nods and brief smiles as they went on their way. Rumpel rested his hand on the porch post, the muscles flexing in his arms.

"What do you need to talk to me about?" I asked.

"I convinced Malleus to travel through the Vallderwydth Mountains."

"How?"

A small smile creased his mouth. "A fair bit of negotiation and goblin trickery were involved."

"What do you mean by that?"

"Well, first he demanded we take the direct route through the forest infested with woodwraiths. I told him it would be unwise. Then he demanded to hold the first two objects for safekeeping."

Anger made heat burn my cheeks. "You can't be serious."

"I am."

"Please tell me you didn't give them to him."

"I told you there was goblin trickery involved, didn't I?"

I crossed my arms. "What did you do?"

"I gave them to him. At least, what he believes to be them."

"You gave him copies?"

Rumpel nodded.

"And he fell for it?" I asked.

"So far, yes."

I eyed him. "How did you manage to pull it off?"

"Let's just say I'm adept at goblin trickery."

I laughed. "I can't believe he fell for it."

"It won't last long before he realizes what I've done. When that happens, we'll have no choice but to confront him as a traitor."

"So, you do believe he's involved in betraying us?"

"I've no doubt of it."

"If that's so, we should confront him now."

A breeze whipped past, pulling the loose strands of my hair. I pushed them behind my ear, Rumpel's gaze lingering as I did.

"If we confront him now, he'll deny everything. He'll also say we have no proof, which we don't. We'll make him angry, and he'll most likely do us harm."

"Then what do you suggest we do?"

"We wait him out. At some point, he'll slip up. He'll try to give the false items to the Sai-hadov, and we'll catch him in the act, then we confront him."

"You think we'll be able to do that?"

"I believe we will. Malleus is too sure of himself. He'll slip up at some point. Overconfidence is his weakness."

I sighed. "I hope you're right."

The wind gusted, once again blowing those blasted strands in my eyes. I pushed the tangles back and unbraided my hair, letting it fall free. Red curls released from their bindings, and the mass of my hair spilled down my back and over my shoulders.

Rumpel reached up and grabbed the strands between his fingers, pushing them gently behind my ear, the pad of his thumb rubbing my cheek.

I took in a stuttered breath. My heart could've pounded through my ribcage. Why did his presence turn me into such a swooning mess?

"Kardiya." He spoke my name so softly and with such passion, a bolt of energy melted straight through me. His eyes went to my lips, as if he wanted to kiss me again.

I placed my hand on his chest, his warmth seeping through his skin to mine.

"Why can I think of nothing but you?" he asked. "Have you bewitched me?"

"No." I smiled, amused by the thought of me doing such a thing. And to him. "If I'd bewitched you, you would know it."

His lips lingered near mine. I inhaled the scent of spruce and wild amber.

"You are so beautiful," he said, his voice so quiet, it almost got lost in the gusting wind.

"You can't be serious. I've looked nothing but an untidy mess since we've arrived here."

"That's not true. There's something about you. Different. Why can't I resist you?"

"I don't know."

He pressed his lips to mine, with more passion than the kiss he'd given me atop the mountain. Warmth spread through me. He pulled me closer, his arms wrapping around me. With our bodies melded, he deepened the kiss.

With a gasp, I savored the taste of him, raw and laced with a hint of magic.

When he pulled away, his eyes sparkled.

"Now, that was a proper kiss," he said, cupping my face.

I didn't know how to answer. In truth, he'd left me speechless. His easygoing smile was something I wasn't used to, as if I were seeing the true man for the first time, not one saddled with the task of saving an entire nation.

Raised voices came from inside. Rumpel's smile disappeared, replaced with his usual look of worry.

We left the sanctuary of the outside world to enter the pagoda. My fluttering heart wouldn't be still. I had a feeling it never would while Rumpel was near. His kiss shouldn't have had such an effect on me, yet it had, and I couldn't think of anything but the way I'd felt—as if I could fly and never fall.

As if I was free.

But it was an illusion, of course, and Rumpel wasn't my path to freedom. He was my captor. That's what he would always be, no matter how euphoric I felt in his presence.

Inside, Orlane sat cowered in the corner, wide eyes focused on Dex and Malleus facing one another with clenched fists.

"…lying to us from the beginning," Malleus said to the smaller man.

"Someone has been lying, but it wasn't me."

Malleus took a step closer, poking his finger in Dex's chest.

"You're not to confront me," Malleus said, puffing out his chest. Dex paled, though the big warrior's overbearing presence was enough to make anyone shudder. "Understood?"

"What's going on here?" Rumpel demanded, stepping between the two men.

"My blade's gone missing," Malleus said, bushy eyebrows lowered over his dark eyes. "I think your uncle took it."

"Why on earth would I take *your* blade?" Dex said. "By the goddess, I've got my own, and it's a better one than yours, I'll wager."

"Someone took it," Malleus growled. "I doubt it was Orlane. It wasn't Rumpel or the elf as they were on the mountain when it went missing. That leaves you."

Dex threw his hands in the air. "You're delusional!"

"Malleus," I said, stepping beside Rumpel. "Is it possible one of the caretakers of Shighoshi could've taken it? Perhaps mistaken it for their own?"

"One of the holy priests or priestesses?" He barked a humorless laugh. "I doubt they're in the habit of thievery. Doubt they even know the meaning of it."

"I didn't call it thievery," I said. "It could've been taken by accident. Or you could've misplaced it. There are other alternatives."

"It was him." He pointed at Dex. "I'll bet my beard on it. Rotten, miserable thief." He turned and stormed out, slamming the door behind him.

"Mad, he is," Dex muttered, straightening his cloak's golden-embroidered lapels.

"He's certainly on edge," Rumpel said.

"Can you believe him?" Dex huffed. "Accusing me of thievery? I've never stolen a thing in my life, least of all his filthy blade. What on earth would I do with a blade like his? Run through the forest and scare the rabbits?"

Orlane chuckled from his spot in the corner. "Rabbits."

Rumpel went to Orlane. The boy stood as his brother approached.

"Time...to leave?" Orlane asked.

"Not yet. We'll set off first thing in the morning. We could all use a good night's rest before heading to Vallderwydth."

ALTHOUGH I'D SLEPT THE DAY away, I'd still managed to rest soundly through the night. My strength must've been drained more than I realized on top of Shigoshi's summit. With the rest, my magic had returned, and its presence spread through my chest, filling the empty spaces.

Morning sunlight dappled our path as we rode down the mountain. Crooked Stripe snorted as she followed the other horses, and I patted her neck. She was ready to go, and so was I.

Rumpel and Orlane rode at the front, followed by Dex, then me, and Malleus stayed at the rear. With the birds chirping in the branches, and the air with the scent of spring, I felt more hope than I had in a long time.

We'd retrieved the first two items. We only had to get the third, defeat the Inshadov, and I would be free to return home.

Home.

Imagining being there without Rumpel tugged at my heart, and a feeling of loneliness crept inside.

I shook my head. No time to ponder such things now.

We reached the base of the mountain and took a trail leading west. The blue, cloudless sky spanned overhead, allowing the sunlight to shine on us unhindered. I closed my eyes, letting the sun soak into my skin. It reminded me of happier days I'd spent on the seashore gathering coconuts, my bare feet warm in the sand.

I'd stood on the beach, looking out toward the horizon, wishing I could cross the sea and start my adventures.

How foolish of me to have such naïve thoughts, when I'd had a home surrounded by people who loved me and wanted what was best for me.

I couldn't say the same now. Not for anyone in our group. Rumpel may have shown me affection, yet I would never forget that he'd kidnapped me, nor that he'd failed to tell me that this journey could very well end in my death.

My stomach soured.

Despite the sunlight, I pulled my cloak around my shoulders.

When the sun reached its zenith, we rode over an open plain. Golden blades of grass reached the horse's withers and brushed past my feet in the stirrups. A breeze gusted, stirring the stalks.

Crooked Stripe grabbed mouthfuls of grass, chewing loudly as we went. Orlane and Rumpel slowed their horse to ride beside me.

"How far to Vallderwydth?" I asked.

"We'll be there tomorrow if all goes well. As long as this weather holds, we'll make good time."

"Noon-ing." Orlane said.

"When we reach the forest, we'll take our meal. You see the tree line just there?" Rumpel pointed ahead, and I craned my neck to see the shapes of shadowy trees on the horizon. "We can eat when we reach it."

"Noon-ing," Orlane repeated.

"Yes, brother. I know you're hungry."

Our horses trudged through the grass, and I took a moment to enjoy the sunlight and inhale the fresh air. I hadn't spoken to Rumpel much. My emotions were too tied up. Making sense of them was impossible.

"You've been quieter than usual," Rumpel said.

"I don't have anything to say."

He gave me a confused grin. "Nothing to say? That's a first."

I shrugged. What did he want to hear? *I might have feelings for you beyond friendship despite my better judgment. You're the worst possible match for me. I can think of nothing but you.*

No. I couldn't say any of those things, so I had no alternative but to hold my tongue. We rode down a gentle slope, and the tree line loomed closer. Oaks and pines rose tall toward the sky, reaching like spires to brush the wispy clouds.

As we entered the forest, our horses' hooves crunched over acorns and twigs. The shade cooled my skin. Somewhere up ahead came the trickle of a stream. Dex and Malleus trailed behind as we followed along a deer trail through the trees.

"When we find the river, we can follow it to Vallderwydth," Dex called from behind.

"Noon-ing," Orlane demanded.

"I think we'll have to look for the river after we've eaten," Rumpel said over his shoulder.

"Find a clearing, and we'll take our meal there," Dex called.

We rode through the dense trees until my stomach grumbled, and I had the urge to chime in with Orlane. We reached a clearing where the trees had fallen, rotting logs bleached by the sun taking up most of the space.

"Will this work?" I asked.

"It should do nicely," Rumpel answered.

I dismounted Crooked Stripe and tied her to a lead line, giving her enough slack to allow her to graze on the wildflowers growing between the stumps.

Rumpel and Orlane sat on a log; Rumpel opened his bag and passed strips of dried fish to his brother. Dex and I sat by the brothers, and Malleus kept to himself, brooding as he sat on a log opposite us.

Malleus opened his pack and reached inside.

"What the—" He pulled out a knife with a smooth black blade and a leather cord wrapping the handle. He looked up at us, his eyes wide.

"Is that your knife?" Rumpel asked. "The one you accused my uncle of stealing?"

"I—" Malleus muttered. "How did it get here?"

"Has it been in your bag this whole time?" Dex asked. "After you accused me of taking it?"

"Well…"

"It looks like you owe Dex an apology," I said.

"He won't get it," Malleus said, pointing his blade at us. "Tricked me, he did."

Dex snorted a laugh. "Absurd. What purpose would I have in tricking you? My life is plenty amusing as it is, thank you very much. I have no need of thieving knives."

"How do I know you weren't all in on this? The three of you are toying with me."

Orlane barked a wheezing laugh. "Funny."

Malleus cast the boy a dark glare. "This amuses you, does it? Even the boy is in on it?"

"Orlane had nothing to do with your knife," Rumpel said. "I can assure you of that."

"Bah." Malleus shoved the weapon in his bag, pulled out a strip of jerky, and ripped off a bite with his teeth.

We ate in silence, a rift dividing us. I wasn't sure how much longer we could go without confronting Malleus of betraying us. What if he tried to stab us in our sleep?

But something nagged me that we didn't know everything about Malleus, and that if we wanted to find out, we'd have to wait to know more.

A cloud passed over the sun, casting the clearing in shadow. We finished our meal, packed our things, and mounted our horses. Ahead, the roaring of a river echoed the chatter of squirrels and chirping birds.

We rode until we reached the river bank. White sand stretched to the dark churning water. We allowed our horses to drink. When they finished, we guided our mounts away from the water. I rode alongside Rumpel and Orlane along the river, our horses' hooves leaving prints in the sand.

We rounded a bend where the churning river grew to a slow-moving current. A group of swans glided along the glassy surface, their bodies mirrored in the water.

Orlane flapped his arms, grinning as he pointed to the birds. "Ducks! Ducks!"

"Yes, you see the swans, don't you?" Rumpel answered. "Ducks."

"Bugger it all," Malleus called from behind us. "They're swans. Not ducks. Why won't you straighten him out, Rumpel?"

Dex rounded. "Mind your own business."

"I'll do what I bloody want. He spoils that boy. It's time he teaches him right."

Crooked Stripe snorted and bobbed her head. Maybe she was just as annoyed with Malleus as I was. I patted her neck. We rode past the swans to a slope where the water moved swiftly over smooth rocks to create rapids.

As evening approached, we exited the shelter of the forest, keeping the river within our sights as we guided our horses over sand and pebbles. Scrub brush pocked the landscape. The only trees we passed were crooked and deformed, as if the wind hand beaten them down. Jagged rock formations stood as sentinels along our path. The trail grew steeper. Our horses breathed heavily as we trekked up the rise and fall of the land.

The sun descended toward the horizon, leaving an orange-streaked sky in its wake.

"Where shall we camp?" Dex asked Rumpel.

"I'm hopeful we'll find a cave in these cliffs somewhere. Keep an eye out. If we don't find shelter, we can camp outside, though only if we must."

"I'd rather not camp outside," I mumbled.

"Agreed." Dex laughed. "Any chance we'll find a nice tavern with a warm bath and hot meal along our way?"

"You're wishing," I said.

"Aye, yes, I am. It's a shame you should be subjected to such a journey, Kardiya," Dex said. "It's too bad you couldn't have seen our realm during the time of the king. The palaces were such a sight, the height of comfort. Now, our people are nothing but a band of vagrants unless we restore the true heir to the throne. It can't happen too soon. I hardly remember what life was like before." Dex sat up in his saddle, then pointed ahead. "Look there. Is that a cave?"

Against the face of a jagged cliff, a dark maw split into an opening.

"It might be," Rumpel said. "Let's check."

We urged our horses forward, and the idea of being out of the saddle to rest my legs kept me going. The dark cavern loomed ahead, the opening larger than it looked from a distance.

The others dismounted and I did the same, my feet sliding to the ground, my muscles like jelly cordial.

"I'll search inside and see if it's safe," Rumpel said, pulling a flint rock and unlit torch from his saddle bag. "Wait here."

"Are you sure about that?" Malleus asked. "Could be anything in there. Likely to kill you, those beasts who live in caves. Wolves and bears."

"I've got my sword."

"Arrogant, as usual. I see I've got no other choice but to come with you."

"I assure you, I can handle myself."

"Hardly." Malleus unstrapped his axe. "Not to worry, I'll come along."

"You really think it's that dangerous?" Dex asked, patting his horse's nose as the wind flapped his purple cloak.

"One can never be too careful," Malleus barked. "Now, I'm coming and that's that."

"Fine," Rumpel mumbled. He struck the flint rock against his blade until it sparked, and the kerosene-soaked rag ignited amber and blue flames. He walked into the cave as Malleus followed behind, his axe's blade catching the last rays of sunlight. Rumpel's torch flame disappeared inside, and the echoing sound of their footsteps faded.

The wind gusted, billowing the sand into clouds. I stood alone with Orlane and Dex as we peered into the cave but saw only its black depths.

"Rumpel," Orlane said, his face pinched with worry.

I went to him and placed my hand on his shoulder, his muscles stiff with anxiety.

"It's okay," I said. "He'll be all right."

"Rumpel. Gone."

"Yes, but he'll return shortly, won't he?"

"Wolves."

"Don't worry, Orlane. Rumpel is stronger than the wolves. He'll come back before you know it, and then we'll all be sitting around the fire and warming our hands. Won't that be nice?"

Orlane sniffed, his gaze fixed on the cave, but he didn't say anything else. The wind gusted again, and I pulled my cloak's cowl over my head to protect my face from the gusting sand.

"Well," Dex said, running a hand through his blond hair. "Let's hope they found a suitable place for us to sleep tonight. I, for one, need a break from that accursed saddle."

"Agreed," I answered.

Orlane whimpered. I didn't say it, but I also worried about Rumpel. Not because of bears or wolves, but because of the man who'd entered the cave with him.

THIRTEEN

WIND HOWLED THROUGH THE CAVE'S entrance. After what felt like hours, Rumpel and Malleus emerged from the opening.

"It checks out," Rumpel said, motioning us forward. We led our horses inside. Cavernous walls surrounded us, the horses' hoof steps echoing in the domed chamber. The air held a musty odor. Mushrooms grew in clusters along the damp floor. Water dripped in the distance. Only Rumpel's torch gave us any light.

"We found some wood and rusted utensils farther in," Rumpel called over his shoulder. "It looks as if we're not the first ones to make camp here."

"Caves," Dex mumbled as he sidestepped a puddle of inky water. "Seems our people only ever dwell in caves and tents. What a miserable lot we've become."

We reached a charred firepit. A few boulders had been arranged around it. Tin pots and kettles littered the ground.

"There's dry wood stacked back here," Rumpel said. "Should be enough to start a fire."

"And we've got this," Malleus said, lifting a string from under his cloak where three rabbits were strung. "Enough for a decent meal."

Dex clapped his hands. "Well, big fella. Looks like you're finally earning your keep."

"You keep your mouth shut." Malleus said, pointing at him with his string of rabbits dangling under his fist. "Why don't *you* earn *your* keep and clean these hares?"

"Me?" Dex guffawed. "You must be joking."

"I'm not."

"Then you'd be daft for asking me to do such a thing. I haven't got the faintest clue how to gut an animal. I'd spoil the meat for sure."

Malleus placed his fists on his hips. "There you go, then. My point exactly. It's you who's not earning his keep. Not me. Now, excuse me whilst I step outside to skin and gut these wee rodents, so we can have a morsel to eat." He stomped away toward the cave's exit.

"He's a testy one." Dex sighed, sitting on a rock and rubbing his shoulder.

Rumpel approached us with an armful of firewood. He placed it in the firepit and began arranging the smaller sticks into a cone-shaped formation. I knelt beside him and helped. He gave me a guarded smile, and I couldn't help but notice the twinkle in his cobalt eyes, a look that set my insides aflutter.

Dex chatted as we worked. Orlane sat on a flat stone beside us, his arms crossed over his chest, rocking back and forth as his eyes roved the cave. When we got the sticks and larger logs arranged, we worked to create a makeshift spit where we could roast the rabbits. When we finished, Rumpel used his flint to strike a spark, then ignited the wood.

He stood and held out his hand for me. I took it

without thought, as if I'd always given him my hand, as if there had never been a time when I'd pushed him away.

I sat beside him as Dex kept up his chattering, speaking of better times spent in the palace with feasts of roasted duck, caramelized onion puddings, chocolate-drizzled cakes and lemon-custard pies.

"…melt in your mouth. The chefs in the palace kitchens were unequalled. How well do you remember the palace, Rumpel?" Dex asked.

"I was a boy. I remember running through the hallways and getting scolded by the housekeeper for getting the floors muddy, hating the collared outfits Mother made me wear to royal functions. Wanting to escape and climb a tree. It was home to me. The finery meant nothing."

"Well, I can't blame you for not noticing such things. Children are prone to impulsiveness."

Heavy footsteps thudded through the cavern. Malleus entered the glow of firelight, his string of rabbits skinned and cleaned.

"You've arrived just in time," Rumpel said.

The big man handed off the rabbits to Rumpel, and he worked to skewer the meat. We took turns rotating the spit until the flesh cooked and the juices ran clear, dripping and hissing as they hit the fire.

Soon, we sat around the blaze and filled our bellies with the meat and sips of water from our flasks.

Malleus sat across from me. His dark eyes, shadowed by bushy eyebrows, locked on mine, and I couldn't ignore the malice I found in his gaze.

When we finished our meal, we unrolled our sleeping pallets. Listening to the wind howl outside the cave, I closed my eyes, homesickness settling like an anvil wedged deep in my heart.

I'll be home soon, Mother. Wait for me.

THE NEXT MORNING ARRIVED DREARY and gray. A cold freezing mist clung to the rocks and froze the breath in my lungs. I stood with my horse outside the cavern. She pawed the ground in a nervous gesture, her ears pinned, showing her annoyance with the world in general.

I couldn't blame her.

I ran my fingers down Crooked Stripe's muzzle, speaking quietly to calm her.

"We'll reach Vallderwydth today if all goes well," Rumpel called, mounting his horse behind his brother. Orlane sat with stooped shoulders and a vacant stare. He'd been quiet since we'd come here.

I mounted my horse as she pranced, and I patted her neck, trying to calm her. The other horses also stomped and pinned their ears.

"Testy this morning, aren't they?" Malleus said from atop his black stallion that pawed the ground.

"It's this place," I said. "Something's not right."

"Wait until we reach Vallderwydth. Whole place reeks of dark sorcery. There's a reason I didn't want us taking this path. As usual, no one listens to me."

"Dark sorcery?" I asked.

"Aye. It'll get worse. Trust me."

Why were we going somewhere with dark sorcery? And why hadn't Rumpel bothered to warn me? As usual, he was withholding the truth.

But maybe I was overthinking this. Who knew what dark sorcery meant in this land? I was a dark elf after all.

It could've been harmless herb potions for healing and love charms.

We set off down the trail leading through the rock formations. The mist hovered, freezing my fingers despite my gloves. White puffs of air exhaled from my mouth. I clenched the reins to keep Crooked Stripe at a walk.

As noon approached, the mist finally burned away, though the sky remained thick with clouds the color of iron. Our horses' hooves echoed through the stony cliffs. Trees with misshapen branches hunkered like beggars along our path. I kicked Crooked Stripe forward, moving from my place at the back to ride alongside Rumpel and Orlane.

"Tell me about this place we're going," I said. "Malleus says they use dark sorcery."

Rumpel's eyebrows rose. He rode tall in his saddle, his tattoos swirling around his high cheekbones, hidden in places by blond stubble which only served to make him more masculine.

"Malleus told you that?"

"Yes."

"That makes sense coming from him, as he thinks all magic comes from the dark arts. I think the people of Vallderwydth will surprise you."

"How so?"

"They're an outcast clan of goblins. Believe in the old ways—in nature magic and potions, that sort of thing. They follow an outdated code of conduct and chivalry. Some call it dark arts."

"I'll determine that when we reach their village. Which brings up a question. Why didn't you tell me more about them? I feel like you're keeping me in the dark on everything. After getting the first two objects, I thought you would have more trust in me."

He gave me a confused glance. "I never said I didn't trust you."

"But you told me nothing. A warning would've been nice."

"A warning of what? Goblins who practice old magic? Who'll add a dram of sleeping potion to your evening soup if you're not wary? Which we could all use, by the way." He scrubbed his knuckles down his face. Dark circles shadowed his eyes.

"Rumpel, do you really think you can't tell me everything? I thought you'd have more trust in me by now."

He shook his head. "I'm doing my best."

"Then why are you so keen to keep things from me?"

He heaved a frustrated sigh. "I'll never understand you."

No. He wouldn't. And maybe it was best that way.

I kicked my horse ahead, stirring a cloud of dust behind me. Why I'd come to trust him was a complete mystery. I'd been blinded by his charming looks, and I cursed myself for it.

As evening approached, the landscape grew more treacherous, with steep valleys and hills that rose with walls of sharp rust-colored rock.

We guided our horses down a slope of loose shale. Broken pieces slid down the cliff and shattered to pebbles as we descended into a valley. Walls of rock rose on either side of us. The gorge made the hoofbeats echo. The sun sank, and the sky turned a shade of crimson.

I trailed behind the others when Rumpel halted his horse. He held up his fist in a gesture to stop us.

"Keep quiet," Rumpel said. "The Vallderwydth will most likely have scouts posted. If they confront us, I'll do the talking."

"Of course you will."

He shot me a sharp look, but I turned away from him. He sighed. "Let's move quietly."

We kicked our horses forward. I stayed a few paces behind the group. I was coming to understand how Rumpel had become disgraced in the eyes of his people. He was too proud, too stubborn. He would never admit he was wrong, which was a dangerous trait to have.

Even so, it was hard for me to forget the kisses we'd shared. It had felt as if he had a soft side, that he cared for me. I knew he cared deeply for his brother. He protected him. Rumpel wasn't an evil person, but he had his flaws—ones that were hard for me to ignore.

Ahead of me, Dex gasped and pulled his horse to a stop.

"What's that?" He pointed ahead. The others also halted their horses. I caught my breath, fear running like ice through my veins.

Two men lay dead in the path. Wearing robes of dark feathers and beads, their clothing marked them as goblin.

Their skin was missing. Only muscle and tissue remained.

"Welcome to Vallderwydth," Malleus muttered.

FOURTEEN

THE SCENT OF DEATH HUNG heavy in the air. We dismounted our horses, and I gripped Crooked Stripe's reins in sweaty palms as she shifted nervously beside me.

"What happened?" Dex asked.

"I don't know. I've never seen anything like this." Rumpel crouched over the corpses.

Orlane moaned. "Rumpel. Don't."

"It's okay, brother. These men are dead. They can't harm us."

He picked up something from one of the men's cloaks, holding it between his fingers as he inspected it.

"What is that?" Malleus asked.

Rumpel stood and walked to us. In his hand, he held a yellowed, sickle-like claw. Dried blood clung to its tip.

"Could it have come from a woodwraith?" Dex asked.

"Don't they have black claws?" Malleus asked.

"Most of the time, yes. Perhaps this is a different breed?" Dex said.

"Maybe," Rumpel said. "Except I've never heard of a woodwraith skinning its prey like this. Whoever did this must've had quite a bit of intelligence to skin them so precisely."

My horse whickered nervously. I ran my hand over her neck. "Easy," I whispered.

"We should get away from this place," Malleus said. "Turn back and leave the way we came."

"We'd lose three days of travel," Dex said. "Plus, we'd have to travel back through the woodwraith forest, which is most likely just as dangerous, and the Vallderwydth village is just outside the valley. We're nearly there."

"But we have no idea what we're up against here," Malleus said. "What if we get skinned just like them?"

"You've brought your axe, haven't you?" I said drily, which earned me a dark glare from the big man, and a sly smile from Rumpel.

"We don't know enough about what happened here," Dex said. "It could've been a clan feud or some such nonsense."

"A clan feud?" Malleus placed his fists on his hips. "I've never heard of a skirmish ending like this."

"I agree," Rumpel said. "But I think it's best to learn more about what happened before turning around. I say we keep moving."

Malleus let out a lengthy sigh of frustration. "You're all ignoring my advice, as usual. Why am I not surprised?"

"We're not ignoring you, Malleus," I said. "We only said we needed to learn more. If it turns out we're in danger, I'm sure we'll reconsider and turn around."

He groaned. "When it's too late, you mean? When you're all dead and skinned, just like that bloody pair." He thrust his finger at the corpses.

"Hold your tongue, man," Dex said, straightening the clasp on his cloak. "We've got a lady present in our group, and she doesn't need to hear your vulgar language."

I bit my lip to keep from laughing. If only he had heard the language *I'd* used in my university days, but I decided not to bring it up.

"We'll keep moving," Rumpel said, turning to his horse. "Maybe we'll find an explanation along the way." He held out his hand and helped his brother climb on the saddle. I gave a sidelong glance at the skinned bodies before mounting my horse.

An aura of magic shrouded the corpses—a dark cloud that sent a shiver of fear down my spine.

I mounted Crooked Stripe, then nudged her after the others, giving the corpses a wide berth. Sand and stones shifted under her hooves.

We rode out of the valley. The fear I'd felt in the presence of the corpses lingered, a palpable entity that followed like a shadow.

Whoever—or whatever—had killed them in such a sickening way must've been evil. There was no other word to describe it.

The sky darkened as the sun set. We rode to the top of a ridge. Crooked Stripe's harness jangled as she shook her head. Below us, a forest of dark spruce and fir trees filled the valley. Fires from torches clustered in the heart of the forest, where the shapes of buildings and thatched-roof houses stood out from the steeple-tall trees.

Rumpel stopped his horse, and we paused alongside him.

"The village is there." Rumpel pointed to the center of the woods. "We'll have to ride quietly. Whatever you do, keep calm. We don't want our horses to spook."

"What do you think we'll find down there?" I asked.

He shook his head. "Food and shelter if all goes well."

We kicked our horses forward, taking a narrow trail leading down the slope and toward the forest. When we entered the cover of trees, I was taken aback by the muffled silence—no hoots from owls, no animals skittering, not even the chirping of crickets.

A sliver of a moon appeared through the gaps in the branches. With night approaching, the air had grown chill. A sheen of ice coated the spruce needles, turning them white. Leaves thick with frost crunched under our mounts' hooves.

The trail wound through the trees. Firelight flickered ahead. We rode into a clearing, where a collection of log-planked buildings with thatched roofs stood. Torches lined the trail leading up to the structures.

Though the fires had been lit, I saw no one. We wandered through the maze of buildings until we stopped at one with a wooden sign hanging above it, the words *Raven's Ransom Inn*. A painting of a hatchet and a raven above a crown decorated the sign in colors of gold, black, and red.

"Should we stop here?" Rumpel called to us.

"It's the only inn I've seen so far," Dex answered. "And I'm past ready for a warm bed and a decent meal."

"Agreed," I answered, rubbing my sore thighs, images of an actual bed and savory hot stew overriding any sound judgement I may've had. Even Malleus didn't argue.

We dismounted our horses without speaking and tied our lead ropes to a crudely-made split-rail fence.

I followed the others up the steps to the sprawling three-story building made of mud bricks and timber. A heavy wooden door with rusted metal clasps barred our way.

Rumpel knocked on the door, the banging sound too loud in the quiet of the forest. In the window, the curtain shifted, though I couldn't make out anything inside.

A moment later, the door cracked open.

The tip of a knife peeked through, held by a weathered brown hand. A goblin man with a tattooed face stood just inside.

"Who are you?" he demanded. His voice held a rough edge.

"Travelers," Rumpel answered. "We seek shelter for the night."

"Travelers from where?" the man asked.

"The caves near Rosenthorne, though none of us has a place to call home. Not anymore."

"What are you doing here?"

"We're traveling to Elevatia," Rumpel answered.

The man's eyes widened. "What would possess you to travel to such a place?"

"I'll let you guess."

His eyes narrowed. "You're the prince, aren't you? Yes, I know you. Rumpel Stiltskin."

Rumpel nodded.

"Still trying to restore your disgraced kingdom? A fool's quest, I call it."

"It won't be a fool's quest if we're successful, my friend."

The man tightened his grip on the blade. "I'm not your friend. No one in Vallderwydth is. Do you understand? We can give you shelter for the night and spare some food, but that's all. You must leave when the sun rises. And it'll cost you."

"We can pay."

"I thought you might say that." His gaze traveled to

Dex, who wore his purple cloak, and still managed to look dignified despite the wilds we'd traveled through. "Very well, come inside."

He shoved his knife in a sheath at his belt, then opened the door wide and ushered us in. A fire crackled in a hearth across the room. Flickering coals gave light to the wooden tables and chairs arranged in rows. The air held the greasy scent of lard that had stewed too long in the kettle. A few goblin men sat in clusters, holding tankards, speaking quietly until we walked inside. Their lean gazes drifted to us.

"My name's Kier Umgrad. Ask for me if you need anything." The man who had let us inside led us through the room. A chandelier made of antlers hung overhead, candles dripping with wax topped each curving horn. Stuffed deer heads and taxidermy swans in flight crowded the walls, along with antler displays. I even spotted a few unicorn horns among the antlers. At the top of a corkscrew staircase, an actual stuffed unicorn head was displayed on the log-planked wall.

My stomach twisted with unease. What kind of place was this? Where magical creatures were killed to become nothing more than tasteless decorations?

It would've never happened in Malestasia. No matter how snobby and self-centered my people had become, they knew enough to respect nature and leave unicorns alone.

The man—Kier—faced us. In the light of the room, I got a better look at him. His spindly arms and legs contrasted his flaccid middle, which protruded beneath his stained white shirt. Several of his teeth were made of gold, and his oily, dark hair was slicked backed from his forehead. His gaze lingered too long on me, and I gave him a stern glare.

Keep your eyes to yourself, knave.

He cleared his throat and ran a hand through his greasy hair. "If you'll wait here, I'll see what rooms are available, and I'll tell Cook you've arrived. He's made lamb stew for the evening. Don't know if he's got much left." He turned and strutted across the room to a door I assumed led to the kitchens.

I crossed my arms. "I don't like him."

"Agreed," Rumpel said. "But we don't have many other options right now. This is the only inn I spotted in the village."

"We could sleep outside. In the ice." I sighed. Maybe I could tolerate men with shifty eyes if it meant I got a warm bed.

"Food," Orlane said.

"It's coming soon." Rumpel placed his hand on his sword's hilt, jaw clenched in his usual look of anxiousness. "We'll sit until the stew arrives."

He pulled a chair out for his brother. Orlane and Rumpel sat at the table. The rest of us gathered around and took seats. I sat across from the brothers between Dex and Malleus.

The big goblin man scratched his grizzled black beard as he peered around the room, his other hand fisted on the shaft of his axe. Dex adjusted a dragon-shaped brooch on his shirt pinned beneath his cloak. With the rubies encrusting the piece, it was a wonder he hadn't gotten such an expensive trinket stolen by now.

Kier returned, followed by an older woman. She wore a bonnet that she kept low on her forehead, her eyes averted from ours, her shoulders hunched. In her arms, she carried a tray laden with tankards and steaming platters.

She placed the tray on the table and worked to set the tankards of ale and bowls of stew in front of us.

"Food." Orlane laughed.

I picked up my spoon and stirred the creamy white broth, chunks of potatoes, carrots, and tender lamb swirling in the sauce. I took a bite, the warmth of the broth melting in my mouth, the vegetables tender. Despite my aversion of this place, the food, at least, was edible.

"We've got three rooms available for the night. They'll cost you fifty silver apiece. If you want a hot bath, it'll be twenty extra."

Rumpel raised an eyebrow. "Do you charge all travelers such prices?"

"Yes, I do. No one gets a discount, no matter what their last name is."

Rumpel gave Kier a dark look as he pulled several coins from his pouch and slapped them on the table. "Enough for three rooms and a bath. I expect the water to be hot for such a price."

Kier bobbed his head as he plucked the coins from the table, counted them twice, and then placed them in his pocket. "Very well." He turned and slunk away, patting his pocket as he exited the room through a hallway at the back.

"He's robbed you," Malleus muttered as he took a bite of stew.

Rumpel crossed his arms, his biceps bulging under his shirt. "I daresay it's worth it. We all need the rest and a bath. You don't smell much better than the shite coming out my horse's backside."

Malleus chuckled at that. "I can't deny it. Reminds me of something your father would've said. He was never one to mince words, that one."

We grew quiet.

"I miss him," Malleus added.

"Do you really?" Dex asked, disbelief in his voice.

"Why wouldn't I? He was a brave man. A good ruler. Our land is suffering without him."

"But we're restoring it," Dex said.

"Are we? Is there anything left to save?"

"Of course there is," Dex scoffed. "You've got to believe in the good of our people."

"What I believed in is dead. The world I fought to save is dead. We're chasing after a life we'll never have again. The Sai-hadov know what we're up to. Do you really think they'll let us waltz into *their* city and take it from them?"

"Then why in the blazes did you agree to come on this quest?" Rumpel asked.

"Because Baelem asked me. Because I couldn't let you come alone. Because I'm a fool."

"Why are you a fool, Malleus?" I asked, my voice more accusatory than I'd intended. "And why do you believe the Sai-hadov are after us?"

He shook his head, then took a long drink from his tankard. My eyes met Rumpel's. I couldn't tell what he was thinking.

Malleus stood abruptly, then stomped away to stand by the fireplace.

"Well." Dex cleared his throat. "That could've gone worse."

"Or better," Rumpel mumbled.

Orlane slurped his last bite of stew, then plunked his spoon on the table. "More."

"Have mine." I slid my half-eaten stew toward him. I hadn't had much in the way of an appetite since I'd arrived in this world. My current company wasn't helping to make that situation any better.

I grabbed my bag and slung it over my shoulder, then I stood and wandered to the back of the room. Kier entered through a hallway. A smile stretched his face as he looked at me, his eyes lingering too long on my figure. His expression unnerved me, and I hugged my cloak around me as he crossed the room to stand nearby.

"Your room's ready, miss. I'll take you there if you like."

I glanced at Rumpel and the others who still sat eating. "I think I'll wait for my companions."

"Will you, then? What are they to you? Seems strange to have one lone lass traveling with a group of men." He raised an eyebrow, and I couldn't mistake his tone.

"I'm *not* what you're thinking," I snapped.

He propped his elbow on the fireplace mantel, unleashing the scent of his body odor. I wrinkled my nose as he leaned toward me.

"Pray tell, what is it you believe me to be thinking?"

I took a step away from him. "I'd rather not say."

"We don't get many travelers here. Rumor is there's a girl traveling with the prince. Elven girl." He reached out and pushed the hair away from my cheek to reveal my pointed ear. I swatted his hand away, but not before he got a look. "I thought so. You're the one we've been waiting for. You don't look so special to me. Is it true you're able to find the objects we've been trying to get all these years?"

"That's none of your business." I straightened my bag's

strap on my shoulder. "If you don't mind, I'm tired. I'd like to be shown to my room."

"Ready to go now, are you? I thought you were waiting for your companions."

I cast another pleading gaze to where Rumpel sat, but his back was turned as he was deep in conversation with his uncle.

It didn't matter.

If this lunatic wanted to make a move, I had my magic and a blade at my disposal. "I'm ready now."

"Very well." He drew out the words, then turned and led me to the staircase. Wood creaked as we stepped up. I held to the smooth banister as I paced to the second floor. Mounted on the wall, the head of the unicorn loomed above us, its eyes glassy and pleading.

"Interesting décor you have here," I muttered to Kier.

"Indeed. I slaughtered that beast myself."

Did he, then? My opinion of him dropped lower, if that were possible. I followed him to a room at the end of the hallway. He stuck a rusty key in the lock and turned it with a flick of his wrist. The heavy door creaked as he pushed it open, and he ushered me into a small space. A candle on a dusty writing desk illuminated the bed with a straw mattress. A fire burned in the room's hearth, and beside it sat a wooden tub filled with water. Soot smeared the room's window.

"I'll leave you to it." Kier squeezed my shoulder, unnerving me at his touch. I shot him a dark look. He cleared his throat, releasing his grip before stepping out of the room and shutting the door behind him.

A tarnished bronze rod served as a door lock, and I pushed it through the metal clasp, locking the door. It gave me a bit of relief to know the door was locked, although I was sure Kier had his ways of getting inside.

I walked to the tub and stood over it, but I hesitated before undressing. This place, and especially shifty-eyed Kier, had me on edge. The idea of taking a bath made me feel more vulnerable.

But the grime of the road stuck to my clothes and skin, and the tangles in my hair were proof that it needed a good washing and combing.

I placed my bag on the floor, pulled out a clean dressing gown, and removed a cake of soap which was wrapped in parchment paper.

After undressing and unbraiding my hair, I climbed into the tub. The tepid water made my skin immediately bristle with chills, but I bit my tongue against the chill and mustered my courage. After unwrapping the soap, I breathed in its scent of lavender and chamomile.

I used it generously, hoping to wipe away the stench lingering from Kier's presence. After dunking my head, I lathered my hair and rinsed the suds. Despite the cold, I sat shivering in the tub, trying to convince myself to get out and dry off. My eyes grew heavy, and exhaustion dragged me down, but I finally managed to climb out.

I grabbed a drying cloth that was placed near the fire, thankfully warm, and dried off quickly. After tossing the cloth aside, I picked up the white chemise nightgown and pulled it over my head.

A knock came at the door, startling me. Glancing down at my indecent appearance, I grabbed a robe from my pack and wrapped it around me, then picked up my knife.

If it was Kier, he'd better be prepared to turn around

and waltz himself away from my door unless he wanted my blade shoved through his middle.

I crept to the door and stood against it.

"Who's there?" I demanded.

"Me." Rumpel's voice.

Confused, I pushed the bolt aside to unlock it, then opened it a crack, keeping my body hidden behind the door.

"What do you want?" I asked.

"I came to see how you're doing. I saw the way that knave Kier was looking at you."

I sighed, secretly grateful he'd come to check on me. "I'm fine."

His eyes shown with concern. "Did he touch you?"

"Not for long."

"Are you sure?"

"Yes." I clutched my nightdress's collar. "I'm sorry, but I'm indecent, so I would appreciate if you left me alone so I could properly dress."

"Very well." He gave a bow of his head, then he took a step back. I pushed the door to close it but paused. My pattering heart was betraying me, and I didn't like feeling so alienated from him. I'd held my grudge long enough.

"Rumpel, wait," I said.

He turned, blue eyes intense as he met my gaze. I took a deep breath. Might as well get this over with.

"I'm sorry for being so cold toward you."

He raised an eyebrow, as if he were shocked that I'd confessed such a thing. "You what?"

"I'm sorry. You might as well accept my apology while I'm offering it."

"Why the sudden change of heart? This morning you

were accusing me of keeping you in the dark. You're an expert at reminding me that I'm your captor, which is true. It's what I will always be to you."

"That's not completely true."

He laughed. "Is that so? Then pray tell, what am I to you, Kardiya?"

I didn't know how to answer, so I said nothing.

He turned. "I'll go then."

"No, I'm not done."

I opened the door wider. He paused, turning to look at me again, and I took a deep breath. "The truth is, I don't like having a strained relationship with you, especially when we're so close to finding the final object and ridding your world of the Sai-hadov. I think it's best that we get along so we can get this quest over with as soon as possible, so I can get home and leave all this behind." My heart squeezed as I said the words, a feeling of emptiness creeping inside. I wanted to go home. I knew I did. But there were things in this world I would miss, too. People I would miss, if I were being honest with myself.

He didn't speak, just kept looking at me with that penetrating gaze, the one that sent warm tingles straight through me.

"Are you sure you want to apologize?" he asked. "What if I make you angry again?"

"I've no doubt it will happen. Sooner than I'd like, no doubt."

Someone passed in the hallway behind Rumpel, their footsteps making the floorboards creak. "I've got to go," he said. "Orlane is uneasy here. He doesn't like this place."

"I understand," I answered. I wanted to ask him to wait, but I'd already asked him once. I would be foolish to ask it again.

He didn't move from where he stood. My heart pattered so loud, I feared he would hear it.

"Kardiya," he said my name softly. He reached for my hand, which I kept on the door to keep it propped open. He brushed his fingers over mine. In his gaze, a storm brewed. It seemed as if he wanted to tell me something.

If he hadn't captured me. If my grandmother hadn't cursed him. If we had met as equals, what would we be to each other?

He leaned forward and pressed a gentle kiss to my forehead, then took a step back, and walked away without uttering a word.

What was I supposed to make of that?

I closed the door with a click, then slid the latch to lock it.

My hands were shaking, and I pressed them to my stomach. Why did I feel as if his kiss had been final? As if he never intended to kiss me again?

I climbed onto the straw mattress, pulled the blanket over me, and closed my eyes. When I did, all I saw was Rumpel and the hurricane brewing in his eyes.

I wasn't right for him. I never had been.

And he knew it just as well as me.

FIFTEEN

I WOKE TO THE OVERPOWERING scent of smoke. Screams came from outside my window, and an orange glow illuminated my room. Sleep fogged my mind as I sat up. Was the place on fire?

Stumbling out of bed, I grabbed my things and went to the door. As I grabbed the bolt, red hot pain scorched my flesh. Hissing, I pulled my hand away, clutching it to my chest. From the cracks surrounding my door, smoke snaked into the room. Its acrid scent burned my nostrils. Only now did I notice the latch glowing red.

I backed away from my door, keeping my burned hand pressed to my chest, holding my pack in my other.

Voices yelled outside my window.

I spun around and raced to it. Placing my bag by my feet, I searched for a latch to open it. Running my good hand around the edges, my fingers caught on a metal fastener. I pried at it, but the thing wouldn't budge. Rust caked under my fingernails. I tried again with no luck. Stupid thing was rusted shut. I'd have to break through the window, but what could I use to bust the glass?

Behind me, the door cracked. Smoke poured inside. Sparks shimmered as they burst through the ruined wood, followed by devouring flames.

I pulled my robe over my mouth and nose. Suffocating heat billowed inside. Tears streamed from my eyes from the pungency of the smoke.

I grabbed the chair by the writing desk, wincing as my burned palm touched the wooden slats. I dropped the chair. It thumped on the floor with a clatter. Picking it up again with my good hand, I sprinted to the window.

Using every ounce of my strength, I smashed it into the glass.

The panes broke into millions of shattered pieces. Fresh oxygen rushed inside the room. I gulped in stuttering breaths, wiping the tears from my sooty face.

"Here!" someone shouted below me.

In the haze, the form of Rumpel appeared below me, a black silhouette against the forest. Others crowded around him, though I couldn't count how many.

"Jump!" he called.

Shards of glass glittered like diamonds on the windowsill, sharp enough to slice through flesh. I grabbed the blanket off my bed and piled it on the window's edge. Behind me, the door burst open. Splintered wood exploded as flames consumed the doorframe.

An inhuman wail pierced through the roar of the fire. A bulky, humanoid form appeared in the doorway. It moved stiffly, one foot dragging behind the other.

Silver eyes glinted with madness. It wore the skin of a goblin man, stretched awkwardly over the shape, its nose flattened on its face, the eyes angled one above the other. Blood oozed from rips covering its body.

"Dark...elf..." it hissed. "Give us...what is ours..."

"Leave me alone," I yelled, backing toward the window.

"Give us…"

It lunged in a blur, moving faster than I thought possible. I scrambled away, but its unnaturally long fingers ending in glowing white claws grasped my hair, entwining in the strands. My head jerked backward with a snap. Pain shot from my neck down my spine.

I spun around, prying at the stiff, dead fingers. Its blood oozed onto my hands. The thing grabbed my neck, cold hands squeezing my windpipe. Its claws tore my skin. Warm blood seeped down my chest. I pried at its hands with no success, as if I were grasping fingers made of iron.

Panicked, I kicked the thing's midsection. A whoosh of air escaped its mouth as it fell back, releasing me.

I sprinted to the window, my heart racing like wildfire. Grasping the blanket-covered ledge, I propelled my body up and over. I hesitated a second as the two-story drop fell away from me.

"Jump!" Rumpel called.

Moaning came from behind me as I leapt down. Rumpel's arms cradled me, stopping my fall. He held me to his chest, his eyes wide as he took in the blood streaming from the punctures in my neck and soaking into my nightdress.

"What happened?" he asked.

"There…" Gasping, I pointed to the window. "Saihadov. Attacked me."

"What? How?"

"Wore the body of a… goblin. Probably one of the scouts. We've got to run. It was after the talismans."

Rumpel's eyes narrowed as he glanced up at the window. He held me in his arms in a protective gesture.

Though I had the urge to demand he release me, I couldn't make myself say the words. The strength of his arms cradled me to his muscular chest. Without fully realizing what I was doing, I placed my hand over his heart, feeling its steady beat under my fingertips. Concern filled his sapphire eyes. Concern for me? Dizziness made the world spin around me. How much blood was I losing?

I realized someone had wrapped a cloth around my neck and pressed it firmly to the punctures. With a few deep breaths, I regained my strength, and allowed a trickle of magic to flow through me, helping to stop the flow of blood.

A moment later, the world stopped spinning. I realized I stood by my horse, though I couldn't remember Rumpel putting me down, and part of me grew cold inside at not being near him.

"Is everyone here?" he shouted.

"We're all here now," his uncle answered, who stood holding the horses' bridles.

"Good. We're going. Now!"

We scrambled to mount the horses. Crooked Stripe's nostrils flared. She showed the whites of her eyes as she jerked her head back. Men yelling and carrying buckets of water rushed past us.

Crooked Stripe pranced, making it hard for me to get my bare foot in the stirrup.

"Steady!" I wasn't sure the beast could hear me over the yelling and roar of the flames. Rumpel and Orlane, atop their horse, rode to mine. Rumpel grabbed my mount's bridle, holding her still.

I didn't hesitate to stick my foot in the stirrup, grab the pommel, and mount the horse. Shrieks came from the burning building. I tried not to imagine the people dying inside, but the images came anyway.

My heart dropped. No matter how much I disliked Kier, I wouldn't wish being burned alive on anyone. But if we wanted to avoid being attacked by Sai-hadov again, we had no choice but to ride—and do it fast.

I kicked my horse to a gallop. We rode down a narrow trail. Malleus conjured baubles of red light—eerie in the dark forest, though the orbs served their purpose as they floated, moving fluidly and lighting the trees in a crimson glow.

My heart raced frantically. My breathing came out in shallow gasps as I held one hand to the reins, the other pressed to the cloth around my neck. Beads of sweat moistened my skin and soaked into my nightdress. My neck throbbed from where the Sai-hadov had attacked me, but my adrenaline dulled the pain. Cold wind slapped my face, helping me to stay conscious.

A shrill, inhuman wail echoed behind us. Fear ran like icy water through my veins. Behind us, a human-like form sprinted. Shadows blurred its outline. Silver eyes glowed from its twisted face. It ran unnaturally fast, as if its feet were being carried over the ground.

"*Faster,*" I breathed as I kicked my horse forward.

My hand burned where I gripped the reins, and my thigh muscles ached where I clamped the sides of the saddle. The others rode ahead of me. Tree branches slapped my arms as we galloped down the narrow trail. If it weren't for Malleus's red orbs, I would've gotten completely lost in the dark of the forest.

I kicked Crooked Stripe faster, her breathing heavy and labored. How much more could she take? She'd only last half an hour or less at this speed. But we had to out-run the Sai-hadov. I couldn't allow myself to think of the consequences if we didn't.

A shriek came from behind me, closer than it had been before.

I had to do something to stop it.

Balling my good hand, I urged my magic away from clotting my blood. When the majority of my power reached the focus of my consciousness, I conjured a fire-ball. It flared to life in an instant, so quickly I surprised myself.

I hurled the fireball over my shoulder.

It hit the ground and exploded.

Screams of pain shattered the still forest, followed by silence.

I glanced back briefly. A fiery form burned behind me, skin turning black, oozing blood, then melting like hot wax. My stomach roiled, and I turned to face forward, refusing to look back again.

We left the safety of the forest and traded it for hills dotted with boulders, finally able to slow our horses. The animals plodded along until Malleus's steed stopped, heaving for breath.

"I'll kill him if we go on any further," he called to us.

"Then we'll all stop," Rumpel called back.

I pulled back on my reins. Crooked Stripe hung her head, her sides rising and falling so quickly, I feared she'd fall over.

"Good girl." I patted her neck, never before so thank-ful for a trusty-footed steed to keep me out of the path of danger.

As I dismounted, my sore legs nearly buckled, and

I held my good hand to my neck, the cloth wet with my blood.

"Blasted creature nearly drove our horses to death," Malleus muttered as we gathered around.

"Did we lose it?" Dex asked.

"I think so," I answered. "I blasted it with a fireball. It didn't look like it would be after us anytime soon."

"What *was* that thing?" Dex asked. "I've never seen anything like it."

"A Sai-hadov," I answered. "It attacked me in my room. It was wearing goblin skin—most likely from one of the trackers we found on the road to the village."

"My goodness," Dex breathed. "Those creatures can *wear* our skin?"

"It's sickening," Malleus added.

"Agreed," Rumpel said. "But what's more troubling is that we found two dead trackers. One of them is still most likely after us."

"Then where do we go from here?" I asked. "We can't very well waltz into the Sai-hadov city knowing what they're after."

"Pray tell," Dex said. "What is it they're after?"

"The talismans," I answered. "That's what the Sai-hadov told me before he attacked me." With my adrenaline drained, my neck stung where the claws had torn through my skin.

Rumpel neared me, his face solemn. "Are you still bleeding?"

"I think so. I'd used my magic to stop the flow, but when I created the fireball, it took most of my strength."

"Let me see it."

My heart raced as he reached for the cloth. I knew it

must've been bad, but I wasn't expecting his face to pale so drastically.

"We've got to get you to a healer."

Orlane mumbled as he stood beside Rumpel. "Kardee. Hurt." He rubbed his hands, which I now noticed were red and blistered.

"Is he burned, too?" I asked.

"Yes, we all are," Rumpel said, moving his blackened sleeve up his wrist to reveal angry red marks. "Had to run through a burning doorway to make it outside.

"How bad is it?" I asked.

"Can't tell yet."

"We could go to the healer colony to the south," Dex suggested.

"There's a healer colony?" I asked.

"There is," he answered, though he pursed his lips, and a look of worry creased his brow.

"What's wrong?" I asked.

"The healers, like the Vallderwydth, practice old magic," Rumpel said. "There's no guarantee we'll be safe there."

"Are we safe anywhere?" I asked. "Seems like anywhere we go is dangerous."

"The elf is right," Malleus interjected, his voice gruff. "We're never safe. We won't have a chance of fighting off the Sai-hadov if we're all burned half to death."

Dex raised an eyebrow. "You think we should go to the healer? Are we actually agreeing for once?"

Malleus crossed his arms over his broad chest. "Only because we've got nowhere else to turn. Burns'll get infected if they aren't treated properly. Likely to kill you if they aren't tended."

"Fine," Rumpel said. "We ride south as soon as our

horses are rested."

A boulder lay near us, and I sat on it, the dizziness attacking me with vicious fury. Someone said something. The buzzing in my ears made it hard to make out the words. Using the last reserves of my magic, I fed it into healing my wounds, but the small trickle wouldn't be enough to save me.

Without another thought, I collapsed, and I heard Rumpel's voice.

"Help her…"

SIXTEEN

VOICES DRIFTED IN AND OUT of my consciousness. Whiteness surrounded me. Was I dead? I grabbed onto my first thoughts—my neck throbbing, my blistered hand, something soft covering me. Everything hurt. Pain throbbed through my nerve endings like blazing fire.

The voices came again.

"…wasn't alone."

"I know."

"Not much longer…"

I forced my eyes to open.

I lay in a bed, surrounded by white curtains that billowed in a warm breeze. My voice cracked as I tried to speak, my throat overly dry, my lips chapped. I searched for the source of the voices, wanting to call out to someone—anyone—that I was awake. But gathering my faculties took time.

Exhaustion hit me, so strong I wondered if I'd been drugged. My eyes closed once again, as if without my controlling them.

No… Wake up… I told myself, but sleep claimed me once more.

WHEN I WOKE NEXT, THE room was dark except for moonlight drifting through a hanging white sheet. The fog in my head dissipated as I sat up and touched my neck, wrapped in a clean gauze, no longer throbbing as it had been earlier.

As the pain subsided, my empty stomach grumbled. An open window let in the nighttime breeze, billowing the sheet.

I assumed this was the healer's camp, but where was everyone?

"Hello?" I asked, my voice a hoarse whisper.

Only the wind answered.

"Hello?" I called again, my voice stronger this time.

A young woman entered. Tattoos swirled over her milky white skin. She gave me a friendly smile as she placed a tray on a bedside table.

"Where... where am I?" I asked, my throat dry.

"The healers' village," she answered. "Here. Drink." She lifted a tankard off the tray and handed it to me. I took the warm mug from her, amber liquid swirling inside.

"What is it?"

"Lemon tea with honey. I added some healing herbs as well." She spoke with a soft, high-pitched voice. Wispy strands of hair fell from beneath her bonnet, surrounding her thin face. I wondered at her age. She couldn't be more than thirteen or fourteen.

"Thank you," I said as I took it from her, sipping it, its warmth helping to soothe my parched throat. I drained the cup faster than I intended, not realizing how thirsty I was, then handed her the empty vessel.

"Where are my companions?" I asked.

"They're resting. All but one. He hasn't left your side except to tend to his brother. Shall I call him?"

My heart squeezed. Rumpel had waited for me?

"Yes. Call him."

"Very well. There's food on the tray if you're hungry. I shall return soon." She gave me a quick nod, then turned and left through the curtain.

On the tray, I found a scone and some orange slices. I ate so fast I barely registered the flavors of dry pastry and citrus. When Rumpel entered, I chewed unladylike on an orange, and I wasn't sure why my appearance suddenly mattered to me.

I placed the half-eaten piece on the tray and sat up straight.

"Kardiya," he said my name quietly as he sat beside me.

I swallowed my food, then smoothed my hand over my hair, the braids undone. Untamed curls stuck out as usual. Sighing, I rested my hands in my lap. There was no use. Making a good impression on Rumpel was just as likely as a fairy godmother showing up and whisking me back to Malestasia.

"How are you feeling?" he asked.

"Better. My neck isn't throbbing anymore."

"That's good."

"Yes."

An awkward silence stretched between us.

"How is Orlane?" I asked.

"He's well enough. Shaken up, mostly."

"Understandable."

He ran his hand over the strip of hair running the length of his scalp. His eyes shifted around the makeshift room. His rugged, handsome features caught me off-guard.

"How long have I been asleep?" I asked.

"A day and a half."

A day and a half? "How much time have we lost?"

He shrugged. "That's not important."

"Not important? Aren't we trying to stop the Saihadov before they steal our talismans and take complete control?"

"Yes, we are. But it's more important that you're alive to do it. If we must wait for you to recover, we will."

I eyed him suspiciously. "That almost sounds like concern."

He sighed, eyes still focused on the curtain. Quiet, muffled voices came from outside the room.

"Kardiya, I feel I haven't been completely honest with you."

I groaned. Not this again. "What is it this time?"

He finally turned his gaze to meet mine. At the sight of his penetrating blue eyes, I had to catch my breath. "I can think of nothing but you. I think... I'm..." He shook his head. "Forgive me. I shouldn't be talking this way. Not after taking you from your home against your will. I know you'll never accept me. You shouldn't. You'd be a fool to consider it."

He left me speechless. My mouth grew dry. I wished I had more tea.

"What do you expect me to say?" I asked.

"Nothing. Please. You don't have to respond. I know I'm wrong. But as you already accused me of keeping things from you, I thought it best to admit..."

"Admit what? You've told me nothing."

"Isn't it obvious?" He reached out and tucked a curl behind my ear. "I'm falling in love with you."

I reminded myself to breathe.

I should've known it was coming. His words shouldn't have shocked me but hearing him admit it out loud confirmed it. Blast it all. Blast his rotten timing. Blast this stupid quest. And blast my grandmother and her stupid curse.

"I…" For once in my life, I had nothing to say.

"Would you like me to go?" he asked. "I don't want to upset you."

"I'm not upset."

His eyebrows rose. "You aren't?"

"No." Explaining my emotions was impossible, so I remained silent.

"I know my timing is horrible," he said. "But when you passed out after we escaped the Sai-hadov, the thought that you would die terrified me. I've never felt that way before. I knew then that if you survived, I had to tell you the truth. I couldn't lose you the way I lost Myrna."

I took a deep breath to calm my racing heart, but it didn't help. I'd never been so tongue-tied. More than anything, I wanted to tell him I felt the same way, but the words wouldn't come. What was stopping me?

The fact he'd kidnapped me? That he'd kept things from me? But those things didn't bother me now.

No. He'd been honest with me, and I would be a fool not to return the favor.

"Rumpel, I feel the same way."

"You do?"

I nodded.

"You're sure?"

"I'm positive." I winked. "I wouldn't have told you otherwise."

His smile softened the harsh edges of his eyes. "I thought for sure you would've turned me away the instant I told you."

I took his hand and squeezed it. "Why did you think that?"

"You have every reason to hate me. I wanted revenge because of what your grandmother did to me, so I stole you from your home. Never told you the extent of the prophecy. Your life is in danger because of me. By every right, you should loathe me."

"No, I don't. I may not agree with the way you took me from my home, but I'm coming to understand your reasons. I know in your heart, you're a noble person. You've done nothing but protect me since I arrived in this world. I thank you for that."

"I can't believe I'm hearing this. Is this really you, Kardiya?"

"It's me."

He leaned closer to me, cupping my face. He gently ran his thumb over my cheek. "You're the most beautiful person I've ever met."

My heart stuttered. Me, lying in this bed, my hair an unruly mess, wearing nightclothes caked in blood and mud and who knew what else, and he thought I was the most beautiful person he'd ever met.

I laughed. "Then you must be blind."

"I'm not blind. I'm in love, which may be the same thing." His teasing smile caught me off guard. He sighed. "What are we to do?"

"I don't know. I suspect we need to save the world

before anything is to be done."

"Good point."

I didn't bring up the looming prospect of my death at the hands of the Sai-hadov, or the fact that we came from different worlds. I was a princess who would be expected to marry a noble elf. I wanted to enjoy the moment and pretend nothing else existed.

He leaned in and brushed a kiss over my lips. Its briefness left me wanting more.

"I'll let you rest now." He stood and exited the room. I lay alone, my heart racing, my head spinning with his admission.

He's falling in love with me?

What an absurd notion! He was a goblin. I was an elf. We didn't mix. In fact, since my grandmother had cursed him, I was fairly certain we were mortal enemies. I closed my eyes and rested on the pillow, enjoying the comfort of the bed, the soft sheets against my skin, the warmth of the feather soft mattress.

I could stay here and never move again, but visions of the Sai-hadov danced in my vision, and a fear I couldn't shake plagued me.

If we didn't stop them, they'd take everyone the way they'd killed the trackers. It was only a matter of time before they gained more strength. When they did, it wouldn't be long before they spread through the entire land. They'd come to Malestasia and infect it with their poison the same way they were doing here.

No one was safe.

When I felt ready, I stood, my bare feet balancing on the cold wooden-planked floor. I made my way out of the room and through the maze of hanging sheets and sturdy wooden posts.

I entered an area larger than the rest, with a wide stone firepit at the center, and a layer of sheepskin pelts arranged on the floor. Rumpel and the others rested around the fire. Orlane lay sleeping by his brother. Dex chatted with the others, his face red and cheery as he held a flask. Malleus, as usual, stood away from the others in the corner of the room.

A few healers milled about, carrying trays filled with bowls or stacks of folded linens.

"Are you feeling better, miss?" someone asked behind me.

I turned to see the young woman who'd been in my room earlier. "Yes. Much better."

"Very good. Shall I bring you anything? Some more tea?"

"Tea would be lovely, thank you."

"Of course. My name is Abi. If you need anything else, just ask for me." She gave me a polite bow and walked away. Her gracious mannerisms reminded me of how the servants had treated me back home. They'd always been kind and generous to me, and I wondered if I'd taken them for granted.

I realized it was possible I'd taken many things for granted, including the love of my mother and brother. I prayed they believed I'd gone on my adventures to the mainland. If they knew where I really was, they would've both been worried sick.

"Kardiya," Rumpel said, interrupting his uncle's speech as he motioned for me to join them. I stepped with bare feet on the thick sheepskin rugs and made my way to them. Orlane shifted quietly as he lay beside his older brother.

I sat beside Rumpel. He wrapped his arm around my shoulder, and I leaned into his warmth. His show of affection came unexpectedly, but it felt natural to press my body to his, as if we were meant to be together. I couldn't remember a time I'd felt more content, a feeling that as I long as I stayed right here beside him, I would never worry about anything again. It was an inexplicable feeling, slightly confusing, yet so right, I breathed a sigh of contentment. His scent of wild amber surrounded me, and I couldn't hold back a smile as he glanced at me.

Dex gave us a subtle wink as he sipped from a flask. "It's good to see you revived, Miss Kardiya. May I assume that you're feeling better?"

"Yes. Much better."

"Very good." He took a sip from his flask, reminding me of my brother before he'd decided to give up the drink. I'd always hated that flask.

"May I also assume that you and my nephew are courting?"

Courting? What a stuffy word.

"I'm not sure that's any of your business, uncle," Rumpel said.

"Of course." He smiled. "I'm sorry to pry."

Orlane shifted on the floor, his face calm. It had been a while since I'd seen Orlane not worrying about something. With all the horrors we'd been through, it was surprising how easily he'd endured. He was stronger than I'd given him credit for—something else Rumpel had been right about.

Abi arrived with a mug of tea on a tray. I took the cup of steaming liquid from her. As I sipped its sweet flavor, I hoped there was a cauldron full of the stuff in this place somewhere.

Flames crackled from the fire pit, putting off the scent of wood smoke, reminding me of the incident at the inn. I closed my eyes, hoping to erase the images of the Sai-hadov burning alive.

Holding my mug of tea and leaning into Rumpel's warmth, I left my fear behind.

"What of our plans?" Dex asked. "Now that Kardiya is rested and well—thank the goddess—should we set off for Elevatia?"

"Yes. We'll leave at first light after we've gathered our supplies and allowed our horses enough time to recover," Rumpel said. "If we had the luxury of time, I'd give them at least a week to rest, but we haven't got it."

"I daresay I'm not looking forward to this final adventure." Dex pulled his cloak tighter around his shoulders. "We'll be lucky to make it out of the city alive."

"Agreed," Rumpel answered. "We'll have to be smart about it. Do you still remember the layout of the palace, uncle?"

"Yes, I remember it well enough. I lived there for the majority of my life. We'll have to pray the Sai-hadov haven't altered it too much."

"Let's hope. We'll have to draw up some maps, plan our route into the vaults. The best chance we have of surviving is to sneak inside, take the crown without notice, then escape."

"You make it sound simple," Malleus barked from his corner.

"If we have a smart plan of action, it will be."

"What of the spells surrounding the crown?" Malleus

asked, his voice sharp. "Have you thought of that?"

"Of course I have. We've got Kardiya with us, haven't we?"

"Don't be so confident, boy. Those spells are unlike any she's encountered before. This isn't like the other quests, I'll tell you that for sure. When your father placed a curse on the objects, he placed the strongest magic on the crown. He used the old language to place the spell, in a web so complicated, untangling could easily drain her magic before she realized what was happening."

"What are you saying?" I asked.

"I'm saying that the spell could kill you. It will steal your powers and leave you a corpse."

"Well, now I've been warned, I'll be sure not to use all my magic."

"Not that easy."

"Is anything easy?" I asked.

Dex chuckled. "Good point," he said under his breath.

I smiled at him, then faced Malleus. "How do you know all this about the crown anyway?" I demanded.

He shook his head and pursed his lips.

"How?" I repeated.

"Not important. What is important is that you know what you're getting yourselves into. A death trap. Saihadov lurking everywhere. Palace made of mirrors. The Inshadov, who'll slit your throat without hesitation. He hates mortals. He was one of us once. But he did something so evil in his lifetime, his soul got imprisoned in the Shadow Realm, to live forever in torment. Now, he wants nothing more than to make everyone as miserable as himself. He's little more than a depraved animal."

Malleus's words raised questions. How did he know

so much?

"If that's so," Dex said, "then why has he spent so much time in the palace having balls and parties? That doesn't sound like an animal to me."

"Then you know nothing. You've not seen what I have."

"What have you seen, Malleus?" Rumpel asked, a sharp edge to his voice.

Fear darkened Malleus's eyes. "Nothing I care to repeat. I've said it before, but I'll say it again. You're all fools for making this quest. Mark my words, this will *not* end well." He turned and marched out of the room.

I watched him go. Malleus knew something. Was there a chance I could get him to talk? I squeezed Rumpel's hand, then stood.

"Where are you going?" he asked.

"To talk to Malleus."

"Talk to him?" Dex questioned.

"Yes. He knows something. I think it best we find out before we set off for Elevatia."

"I'll come with you," Rumpel said.

"No. I'll go alone."

His eyebrows rose, but he remained seated. "You're sure?"

I nodded. "Wait for me."

"Is this wise?" Dex asked as I strode toward the door.

"I'll be fine. I just want to talk." Plus, I've got my magic and my blade if I needed it, but I didn't mention that to the others. I parted the curtains and exited the room, following a hallway that led to an open doorway.

I stepped outside. A chilly breeze gusted, carrying leaves that tumbled over the ground. Pulling my robe around me, I stared around the hilltop, searching for Malleus. The healer's hut loomed behind me, a large structure made of thatch and sturdy wooden beams. Beyond it stretched a forest. Leaves of red and gold clung to tree limbs, though most had fallen to the ground.

A dark shape moved by a tree. Malleus.

He leaned against the trunk, arms folded in his usual defensive gesture.

As I walked to him, my bare feet snapped over twigs, and he straightened. His hand hovered above the axe strapped to his belt. I stopped walking and held up my hands.

"I'm here to talk."

"Talk?" he laughed. "What bloody for?"

"I want to know more about the Sai-hadov. I thought you'd be the best one to ask."

He chuckled, a sound devoid of humor. "You're right about that." He pulled a pipe from his pocket, stuffed it with a wad of pipe weed, and lit it.

"Will you tell me what you know?" I asked, approaching him.

"I'm not in the habit of talking to elves—especially not *dark* elves."

"You've got a problem with dark elves?"

He took a draw from his pipe. "Your kind isn't to be trusted."

I took a deep breath to keep from snapping at him. "Why do you say that? I'm helping you on this quest, aren't I?"

"Look what your grandmother did to the prince." He waved his hand at me. "No, I don't trust you. I don't trust any of your kind."

"Do you trust anyone?" I asked.

"Not anymore."

I stood to face him. I'd had enough of his clipped words and innuendos. "Malleus, tell me what you know of the Sai-hadov."

"Can't do that."

"Why?"

"You'll not be able to sleep at night once I do."

"Fine." I crossed my arms. "I'll take that risk."

He shrugged. "Can't say I didn't warn you." He took another long draw from his pipe. "We call them the Shadow Lands, the place where the evil ones go. To get there, you can't be a common thief or criminal. You've got to do something so vile, you lose your soul. I won't speak of the deeds they've done. But those who get to the Shadow Lands are there for a reason.

"Trouble is, they never really died."

"What do you mean by that?"

"Traded their souls to live forever."

Chills prickled my skin. "Traded their souls to whom?"

He paused. Fear flashed across his eyes. "The Inshadov. I don't know his real name. He was the first. Found a way to drain his blood and replace it with a substance created from dark magic. Had to kill hundreds to accomplish it. Eventually turned others the same way he turned himself."

"Wait. I'm confused. I thought the Shadow Lands were a spirit place, like a hell or something."

"It is hell, sure enough, but not the one you might've imagined. You'll never kill the Sai-hadov. They can't die. Best you can do is send them to the Shadow Realm where they belong. We've tried before, more times than I can count. We couldn't bury all the soldiers we lost; there were too many, so we piled their bodies. Burned them."

He closed his eyes and took a deep breath, as if trying to get the images out of his mind. When he opened them again, he had a faraway look, as if reliving the past. "The wars happened after Rumpel left for your realm. He knows nothing of them. Dex, that bleedin' wimp, disappeared during the fighting. Neither of them has a clue what we're up against. They haven't seen what I have. Haven't seen what a Sai-hadov can *really* do to a person. That display in the forest with the monster who took the tracker was only a sampling of the torture they use." He took another draw from his pipe, as if the drug would take his memories, although his eyes remained haunted. I finally saw him for who he was—a person driven by fear.

"No one talks about the wars anymore. When Rumpel returned, we'd done our best to erase them from our memories. He's never been told the extent of what happened during the time he was gone. When he got back, we were nothing but a band of vagrants hiding scared in the caves.

"We'll never defeat the Sai-hadov. You can't trick them. Can't overpower them. Can't do anything but be killed and tortured at their hands. If you think you'll retrieve the items and send them into the Shadow Lands, you're wrong, although that's the last hope my people hold to. You're an outsider. Foolish. Young. Same as Rumpel. Neither of you understands what I've been through. I've been trying to convince you that we're doomed. Have been from the beginning. But I also understand you'll never believe me, so I stay."

My heart dropped. "Is there nothing we can do?"

"Nothing but die."

Full of optimism, wasn't he? "Couldn't we at least

take your people away from here? Back to my home on the Malestasian isles, maybe?"

"Wouldn't matter. The Sai-hadov will continue to spread until they cover all lands. There's nowhere to hide."

"I see," I said curtly. I wasn't sure he'd tell me anything more, but at least I'd gotten him to open up a little. Better to know what I was up against than be ignorant.

"Thank you for your honesty." I turned to go when he stopped me with a grunt. I turned around.

"One word of advice before we leave for Elevatia—make peace with whatever god you believe in."

"I'll keep that in mind."

SEVENTEEN

"YOU RETURNED UNSCATHED," DEX SAID as I walked inside the large room. He sat alone by the fire. The logs had turned to flickering coals that radiated heat throughout the room.

"Yeah," I mumbled in return.

"You didn't let him scare you, did you?"

I didn't answer as I sat across from him, staring into the flames, stories of bodies piled and burning seared into my memory.

"What do you know of the wars?" I asked Dex.

"Dark times," he answered. "Very dark times. Most of my people won't talk of them."

"You never told Rumpel what happened?"

"He knows a little. The rest…well. Why does he need to know? He'd lose all hope."

"But don't you think it's best he understands what we're up against?"

Dex took a drink from his flask. "He knows well enough."

"Why do you say that?"

He gave me a pointed stare, his eyes bloodshot. "Because he saw the Sai-hadov murder his parents."

"Oh." I swallowed uncomfortably. He saw it happen? No wonder he's so messed up.

"Trust me. If anyone understands the threat of the Sai-hadov, it's my nephew." He sighed. "I knew talking to Malleus was a bad idea. He's got a twisted soul. He fought the Sai-hadov so long, it's no wonder he's not one himself."

"That's a comforting thought," I mumbled, watching the flames as my stomach soured.

"Malleus would've been wise to never join the wars with those evil beings, but he was a different man then. He had hope. Thought we could defeat them. When we didn't, he gave up. I don't know that he'll ever find the same courage he once had."

"Do you think we'll be successful?" I asked.

Dex smiled, though it was an expression that reminded me of Rumpel, a look that didn't touch his eyes. "I wish I had a good answer for you. I can tell you this, my nephew is stronger than he realizes. He's like his father in many ways."

"I see." He hadn't answered my question. Did no one believe this quest would be successful? Sometimes I wondered why we were trying. "I should go," I said, standing.

"Of course. I believe Rumpel took his brother to a cot in a room at the back of the hut so he could rest more comfortably. You'll find him there. You're looking for him, I assume." He winked, and the expression annoyed me.

"I never said I was looking for him."

"No?"

"No," I answered. "And we're not courting, by the way."

"Well. You could've fooled me."

I bit my tongue, keeping my comments to myself. If we were all going to die on this quest, what did it matter if I *courted* Rumpel? *Still a stuffy word.*

I left the room. Walls made of sheets created passages. I passed by several rooms, some with goblins sleeping on cots, until I reached the end of the hallway. When I didn't see Rumpel or his brother, I turned around.

Abi walked toward me. In her arms, she carried a stack of folded clothes.

"Here you are," she said. "I've brought a change of clothing for you, plus some cleansing salts. The healers prepared a bath for you."

I brushed the clumps of dried mud from my night-dress.

"Fine," I said with a sigh. I'd had to leave my conversation with Rumpel for later. Besides, what would I say to him anyway?

I heard your parents died, and you watched it happen.

Yeah, probably best if I waited.

I followed Abi into an adjoining corridor, through a flap in the sheets that led to a bathing chamber. A wooden tub full of steaming water sat in the room's center. It looked half the size of the bathing spas back home, but it was better than nothing.

Abi placed the stack of clothes on a sideboard, gave me a polite bow, and left the room. I undressed and bathed quickly, scrubbing the matted blood from my hair, tinting the water pink.

A comb sat among the things on the side table, so I grabbed it and ran it through my hair until I worked through all the knots.

After climbing from the tub, I searched through the stack of clothes the healers had left for me. The satin of a green gown caught my attention. Picking it up, I inspected the fabric, and the coppery brocade decorating the collar. Slits up the side made it suitable for riding. I also grabbed a pair of soft breeches.

After dressing, I put on my grandmother's necklace and pulled on a pair of leather boots. Drying my hair with a cloth, I reflexively worked my fingers through the unruly strands. I'd have to braid it again to keep the knots from forming.

A glint caught my attention. Across from me stood a looking glass.

I stopped as I focused on my image, red hair hanging in soft waves to my waist, framing my feminine figure, made apparent by the riding gown fitted snugly to my torso.

If I didn't braid my hair this once, what would happen? Would I be letting down my defenses?

But it was only hair, after all. Maybe it meant nothing.

I gathered my things, found the room the healers had given me, and stuffed everything in my bag.

"I wondered where you went," Rumpel's deep voice said from behind me.

I turned around to face him. His eyebrows rose as he took me in, my hair falling in natural waves to my waist.

With his slack-jawed expression, I wondered if it had been a huge mistake not to braid my hair. Maybe I shouldn't have worn the dress either.

"Kardiya," he said my name with a deep voice. "You look…"

"I look…?"

"You look enchanting."

"Enchanting? That's an exaggeration."

"Not at all." He crossed to me in two strides and took

my hands. My heart melted at his touch, and my knees turned to jelly. Did he have any idea of the effect he had on me?

"Rumpel," I said his name softly. I knew there was something I wanted to talk to him about, but for the life of me, I couldn't remember what it was.

He sighed, his eyes a radiant blue that reminded me of the ocean. I couldn't pull my gaze from his, as if he held me spellbound. My heart thundered in my chest, and my breathing came in shallow gasps as he stood holding my hands.

By the goddess, all he had to do was stand there, and I completely melted like warm butter in his hands.

"Will you join me for a walk outside? There's something I'd like to show you."

"Of course."

He tugged on my hand and I followed him. We left the room, walked through the halls until we reached the opening leading outside, and stepped into the cool night-time air.

He guided me down a path that wound through the trees. Leaves and twigs snapped under our boots.

"Where are you taking me?" I asked

"You'll see."

The quiet of the forest surrounded us. Waning sunlight shone through the leaves. The air held a chill, although the broad tree trunks served to block the wind. Plus, the warmth of Rumpel's body close to mine kept me from shivering.

We rounded a bend, and a sunken pit came into view. At the bottom sat a fountain shaped as a mermaid. Water trickled from a conch shell she held in her hands, flowing down into a basin. The copper had oxidized, turning the metal a shade of emerald.

Fairies flitted around the open space, their periwinkle lights casting a soft glow over the leaves blanketing the ground.

The mermaid was such a startling reminder of home. We'd had a few who swam in the sea surrounding the island. Seeing one was supposed to bring good luck. Rumpel led me to the statue, and we sat on the edge of the basin.

The trickling water put me at ease. I reached out and touched the glassy surface, my fingers creating a rippling wake.

"This place reminds me of home," I said. "I would go down to the sea to collect seashells or coconuts. It gave me time to think. Sometimes I would spot the tailfins of mermaids. Everything seemed so perfect then."

"You miss your home?"

"I do. More than I imagined." My thoughts turned to my mother. Why did I always picture her with tears in her eyes? Her skin puffy and swollen from crying? She'd endured so much pain since losing my father and eldest brother, and I could only imagine losing me would completely break her.

I had to return to her.

But in order to do that, I had to make it out of this world alive.

"What are you thinking about?" he asked.

I rubbed my eyes, trying to drive away the prickle of tears forming. "My mother," I answered, my voice a whisper. "I miss her."

"I understand," was all he said, though his wistful tone

hinted at his empathy.

As I looked into his eyes, I realized he must've understood my pain more than I gave him credit for.

"You lost your parents?" I asked gently.

He nodded, casting his gaze toward the trees.

"Do you want to talk about it?"

He shrugged.

"I understand if you don't. I know it must be painful."

He looked at his clasped hands, so I grabbed them, pressing his palms between mine. "If you need to tell me, you can."

He sighed deeply, his fingers gripping mine in a desperate embrace, as if he needed something to hang onto.

"I was fourteen," he said in a hushed, haunted voice. "I'd been at the gateway, a warrior in my father's army, or so I'd like to think. Really, I was only a knight-in-training, put to work oiling saddles and polishing swords. After the Sai-hadov broke through the gateway, we did our best to fight them off, but they overpowered us and headed for the palace.

"I remember running after the Sai-hadov, knowing what they'd do to my parents once they entered the castle, feeling desperate to stop the demons. Pleading with the gods, if they'd just spare my parents." He stopped talking, his voice cracking. "But it wasn't to be. When I made it into my parents' chamber, I found Mother first."

He shook his head. "I'll never repeat what I saw on that day. Father was still alive. With his dying breaths, he told me to forgive Malleus, then he cast a spell around our city to keep the Sai-hadov inside. He used his magic to hide the three talismans in the corners of our kingdom. He knew if the Sai-hadov didn't possess them, they could never break through the walls and escape to take control of our lands. He died as the spell left his body. I didn't get the chance to tell him goodbye."

"I'm so sorry," I said, wishing I had more to offer, to say something to comfort him, but there were no words.

"Don't worry about me." His smile replaced the haunted look in his eyes. "It happened so long ago, my wounds have healed as best as they ever will. What of you?"

"What do you mean?"

"What of your family?"

I only shook my head. He knew very well I couldn't go back to them.

He released my hand, then removed the chain from his neck. The key dangled from the end. He grabbed it and held the talisman on his palm, which glowed with a faint white magic. "I've been giving some thought to this." He kept his eyes on the key as he spoke.

"Some thought to what?" I asked.

When he finally looked up, the fervent intensity of his eyes made my breath stutter.

"I was wrong to take you from your home. I was angry at your grandmother; I wanted revenge. I wanted to take it out on you. You carried her magic." He nodded toward my necklace. I clutched the wire-worked pattern. "I knew you were the one spoken of in prophecy, and those were the thoughts that drove me as I stole you from your home and took you to mine. I'll admit, in my eyes, you were less than a person. You were a means to an end."

"I know," I said drily. "Very well."

His smile lasted a second before it faded. "I was wrong about you. I thought you were like your grandmother, but you're different. Even though you might never see your family again, you agreed to save my people. You're a beautiful, graceful, noble person, and you don't deserve to be here. I refuse to be your captor any longer."

He grabbed my hand and pressed the key into my palm. "Go home, Kardiya."

I blinked. "What?"

"You were right all along. This isn't your world. It isn't your fight."

"But what about your people?"

"We'll find a way. We've already gotten the first two talismans. We only need the third, and then we'll defeat the Sai-hadov."

"Without me?"

He nodded.

"You really want me to leave?"

"Yes."

The finality in his voice made my heart drop. Leave? Could I really do it? We'd come so far.

I shook my head, those pesky tears prickling my eyes once again as I took his hand and placed the key in his palm. The image of my mother's pleading face would forever haunt my memory.

Forgive me, Mother.

"I can't leave," I whispered. "I've come too far to turn back now."

I looked from his hands clasping his key up to his face. Confusion clouded his features.

"Kardiya, think about what I'm offering you. Your life doesn't have to be like mine. You still have a mother who loves you. If you don't go back to your home now, you'll most likely die. What then?"

It doesn't matter, I wanted to say, but the words

wouldn't come.

Because seeing Mother again did matter.

But I couldn't walk away, leaving innocent people to die when I was the one who could defeat the Sai-hadov. I'd never be able to return to my mother with that guilt on my conscience. I swallowed the lump in my throat. "I won't quit until this quest is finished."

Surprise lit his eyes. "You can't mean that."

"I do."

He shook his head. "You never fail to amaze me." With a deep inhale, he took both my hands in his. "I suppose this means we're in this to the end."

"Yes. Together. We'll see the Sai-hadov driven from your world or die trying. I won't go home until we're done."

"Then you're a braver person than I am." With a glance at his key, he placed the chain back around his neck and tucked it under his shirt, out of sight. The finality of the gesture put me on edge. I'd made the right choice, and I wouldn't go back on my word to help him, but it didn't make the fear any easier to deal with.

"Will we survive this, Rumpel?" I asked. "Please. Tell me honestly."

He stared at the fountain before answering, as if grasping for something to say that wouldn't completely terrify me. "My father used to tell me to have faith. I'll admit, sometimes it's easier to believe what I see in front of my eyes than in mystical forces of good. When I see how powerful the Sai-hadov are, what they're capable of, what they've done to my people, reason tells me we don't have a chance of destroying them.

"But then, I remember Baelem's prophecy, that if we are to destroy them, you'll be the one to do so. It doesn't seem likely, but sometimes, it doesn't have to."

"So, it's possible?"

"Possible? Yes. Is it likely? Only if miracles truly happen, and let's pray they do."

EIGHTEEN

NIGHTFALL CLOAKED THE LAND WHEN we returned to the healer's camp. The moon rose, casting a silvery sheen over the trail leading to the thatch-roofed hut. Rumpel walked beside me. He kept his hand in mine, his strength giving me courage to chase away visions of the Sai-hadov lurking in my imagination.

After entering the hut, we followed the hallway to the main chamber.

I stopped as I took in Dex and Malleus hunched over a set of maps, working together, speaking in friendly tones.

"What's happening here?" Rumpel asked. His face must've mirrored the confusion I felt.

The two men looked up. "We're going over the maps of the tunnels beneath Elevatia," Malleus said. "Wasn't that the plan?"

"Yes, but… I didn't think you had agreed to do it. And you're working together?"

"Why wouldn't we be?" Malleus demanded.

"Because you've been avoiding helping us do anything productive for this entire quest," I answered. "And we're a little confused as to why you're helping us now."

"Kardiya, you of all people shouldn't have to ask,"

Malleus said. "Now, come here and help us. We're trying to remember the way through the vaults."

I wasn't sure, but that may've been the first time he'd used my actual name instead of calling me *Dark Elf* or *Elf Girl*, or some other ridiculous nickname.

Rumpel and I walked to where the two men sat. They'd placed a vellum scroll atop a low stone table. We knelt by them. Rumpel released my hand to straighten the scroll, and my fingers grew cold.

I suppressed an uncontrolled shiver.

"The healers have a library. I found a map of the old castle in the stacks," Malleus said. "It's outdated, of course. Probably drawn before you were born, Rumpel. But it's the best we've got."

"Should we rely on a scroll this old?" I asked. "Haven't the Sai-hadov reconstructed the palace?"

"Not necessarily," Malleus said. "They've covered the walls in mirrors, but we won't have to worry about that. The tunnels should be unchanged. They can't enter them."

"Why not?" I asked.

"My father's curse," Rumpel answered. "No one can get through the door leading inside the vaults where the crown is kept."

"Except you," Dex said with a smile, scrubbing a hand through his blond hair. "Hopefully."

"Aye," Malleus said, tugging at his grizzled beard. "But getting inside is only half the trick."

"Agreed," Rumpel said. "Those tunnels are mazes. Finding the crown won't be easy."

"But we have the map," I said.

"Yes," Rumpel answered. "But it was made before my father hid the crown. We're not sure where the crown is."

He sighed. "We'll have no choice but to wander through the tunnels and search for it, and once we break through the door, the Sai-hadov will be able to enter the tunnels."

"If they enter the tunnels, they'll catch us for sure," Dex said.

"Then we'll have to split up," Malleus said, dark eyes narrowed at the map. "Dex and I will stand guard at the door while Rumpel and Kardiya find the crown."

"What about Orlane?" I asked.

"He'll have to stay here," Rumpel said. "I can't risk taking him into the tunnels."

"Do you think he'll agree to that?" I asked.

"He will when I explain the danger. I would be a fool to take him into those tunnels with the Sai-hadov lurking."

Rumpel ran his hand over the map, his finger following a drawing of a tunnel where it intersected with the city's outer wall. "We can enter the tunnels here to avoid the Sai-hadov's detection."

"Do you think that entrance still exists?" I asked.

"Yes. The Sai-hadov don't take city defenses seriously. No one *wants* to enter the city. My people avoid going anywhere near it. The Sai-hadov have ignored the tunnels, which we'll use to our advantage."

"It's suicide going in there," Dex muttered.

"But we have no other choice," Rumpel said.

On the map, tunnels were drawn in curving lines to resemble a maze. "Once we find the crown, what then?" I asked.

"Then we use the three talismans to confront the In-shadov," Rumpel said. "We destroy him, drive the Sai-hadov out of the capital, and send them back to the Shadow Realm."

Confront them. The words rang in my head. Battling a being as evil the Inshadov was something I didn't want to contemplate. If we lost, what would a creature as malevolent as him do to us in retaliation? Would he do the same thing he'd done to Rumpel's parents? Something so horrific Rumpel refused to speak of it?

I shuddered, a cold presence lurking just behind me. Glancing behind, I saw nothing. Was it only my imagination?

"What happens if the Sai-hadov know we're coming?" I asked quietly.

"Then we're doomed." Dex removed his flask from his cloak's inner pocket, uncorked it, and took a sip. "Our only advantage is to take them by surprise."

"I agree," Malleus said, running his fingers through his beard. There was a time when I'd thought sure he was betraying us. But he'd remained with us. He'd helped fight off the Sai-hadov. He'd kept safe what he believed to be the first two talismans.

I rubbed my neck, stress and exhaustion catching up with me. Perhaps I'd never known Malleus.

"Let's get a good night's rest before our journey tomorrow," Rumpel said. "The gods willing, we'll reach Elevatia after dusk. We'll use the cover of darkness to sneak inside. Once we do, we'll take the last object. We'll defeat the Sai-hadov in time for our morning meal."

"Now who's the optimist, nephew?" Dex jabbed. "You sound more like me than you realize. You're certainly more positive about the outcome of this quest than you ought to be."

"I'd rather be hopeful than the alternative. Besides,

Kardiya obtained the first two talismans. We have to have faith that she'll get the last one as well."

Malleus grunted, crossing his arms. His bushy eyebrows lowered over his eyes. "We'll find out soon enough if you're right, Rumpel."

"Yes," Dex answered, casting a guarded look at his nephew, and then at me. "We will."

I couldn't mistake the doubt in his voice. I had to admit, I didn't share Rumpel's optimism, but what good would it do to bring up the danger we faced? We all knew what we were up against, yet we chose to move forward despite our misgivings.

Perhaps having hope was the only advantage we had.

NINETEEN

I PULLED MY CLOAK AROUND me as I stood near our saddled horses. Crooked Stripe whickered nervously beside me, and I stroked her neck, hoping she didn't sense the unease from my touch. The sky was gray, thick clouds hiding the rising sun. Tree limbs creaked in the wind that smelled of wood smoke.

Near the hut's door, Orlane sobbed as Rumpel told him he was leaving.

"You'll… come back?" Orlane managed between sobs.

"Of course I will," Rumpel answered, patting his brother's back. "Don't I always?"

"Don't die. Brother. Don't…" He caught his breath. "Die."

"Who said anything about dying? I'll be fine. We all will."

"Not this time. The Shadow know… know what we do. They kill us. All of us."

Orlane's words made a shiver of fear run like cold water through my veins. *They know what we do.*

"They won't kill us," Rumpel chided. "Don't talk that way, Orlane. I'll be fine. The healers will take good care of you while I'm away. You've got nothing to worry about."

TAMARA GRANTHAM

Orlane paused in his sobbing. "Don't die," he said pointedly, his tone serious. "Promise me?"

Rumpel gripped his brother's hands. "I won't die, Orlane. I give you my word." He spoke with resoluteness, though I wasn't sure why he'd promised such a thing. There was an overwhelming possibility he'd never be able to keep his word.

"Orlane," I asked gently. "Why do you say the Shadow knows what we do?"

"They watch us," he answered, his eyes wide and shining with tears.

"Do you know how they watch us?"

His eyes darted. He didn't answer.

"Orlane," Rumpel interjected. "Do you know?"

He tugged his hands from his brother's grasp and clapped them over his ears. "Don't. Talk."

"All right," Rumpel said. "We won't talk about it anymore."

Dex walked to his youngest nephew, purple cloak billowing behind him, and placed his arm around the boy's shoulder. He spoke softly to him. The boy released his hands from his ears, his eyes wide as he listened.

"You want to go inside?" Dex asked quietly.

Orlane nodded, and Dex looked back at Rumpel. "I'll help him get settled. I won't be gone long."

"We'll wait," Rumpel said, helplessness in his voice as his uncle guided Orlane through the doorway. Rumpel gazed after his uncle and brother, his face riddled with apprehension. I could only imagine what he was thinking. The responsibility of caring for a brother and restoring a kingdom must've been a heavy burden.

When Dex returned, he straightened his cloak's golden-embroidered collar.

"He'll be all right," Dex said. "He's worried is all."

"Should I go see him?" Rumpel asked.

"It would be better if you didn't, I'm afraid. It would only upset him more."

Rumpel stared at the closed doorway as if he would never see his brother again, and I imagined that was exactly what he was thinking as he stood with his hands clenched at his sides.

"May the gods be with you, Orlane," he said, his words lost in the wind. He turned from the healer's hut and stared toward the horizon.

"We ride east," he shouted. "To Elevatia. We finish this once and for all."

He grabbed his horse's reins, stuck his foot in the stirrup, and mounted. The rest of us followed his lead. We started off down the trail.

Branches formed a canopy overhead, blocking out the little bit of sunlight drifting through gaps in the heavy clouds. The damp air made the cold worse. No matter how many times I pulled my cloak tighter around me, it didn't help with the chill.

Wagon wheels had cut ruts in the mud. Our horses slipped over the uneven surface. Crooked Stripe jumped as a squirrel darted across our path.

A hush fell over our group, as if we sensed the eminence of our doomed future. Rumpel trotted his horse ahead of mine, his hand resting casually on his pack where he kept the scepter and ring. Malleus also kept his hand on his pack, with his false treasures inside.

Moss swayed from lichen-covered trees, and the croaking of frogs echoed in the distance. Pools of black stagnant water stood out amongst the protruding roots of cypress trees.

We stopped at a clearing and sat on a log for a quick midday meal of boiled eggs, and sandwiches made of pickled cabbage and roast lamb, food gifts from the healers. I kept my eyes on the forest as I sat on the log and ate, sensing something out there.

The others sat alongside me, not speaking, their eyes darting at every sound.

"Does it always feel so uneasy in this forest?" I asked.

"Not many people travel the road to Elevatia. Only a few brave merchants and the like," Rumpel answered. "I doubt we'll pass a single living soul on our way."

I took another bite of my sandwich, my gaze roving over the moss swaying in the branches.

"How much longer until we reach the city?" I asked.

"We'll be doing good to reach the gates before nightfall," Malleus answered, his dark eyes not meeting mine. He ran his fingers through the wiry strands of his beard in a nervous gesture.

Rumpel's gaze caught mine. I gave him a slight smile, but couldn't hold it, as images of the Sai-hadov haunted my imagination.

He finished his food and clasped his hands on his knees. The tendons and veins stood out beneath his golden, tanned skin. I reached out and gently touched his fingers, the warmth of his hands giving me strength.

"We'll get through this," I whispered gently.

He only nodded, and I wanted him to reply that yes, we would get through it. We had nothing to worry about. But the optimism he'd shared with us earlier had faded, replaced with the unsettling prospect of reality.

When we mounted our horses, a few raindrops fell, creating dark splotches on the packed dirt. By the time we made it away from the fallen tree, a steady drizzle dampened the earth.

I shielded my head with my cloak's hood, huddling under it as best as I could. My thoughts drifted to home. On rainy days, I would sit in front of the hearth, listening to the crackling fire, a book in hand, reading about journeys in faraway lands, daydreaming of my own adventures.

If only I'd realized what the future held.

I'd have never taken those days of lounging in front of the fire for granted.

Shivering, I clenched the reins with numb fingers. I'd put on my gloves, but they'd long since failed to keep my hands warm. When we finally rode out of the forest, the sun appeared as a hazy orb behind the clouds as it sank toward the horizon.

We stopped our horses atop a hill. Beyond us, tall patches of grass carpeted the rise and fall of the land. Far on the edge of the sky rose the towers of a city that glowed alabaster white against the hoary clouds.

"Is that Elevatia?" I asked.

"Yes." Rumpel tightened his horse's reins as she danced.

"It's beautiful," I said.

Dex nodded. "It was home."

"It will be again," Rumpel answered.

Malleus shook his head. "We're riding to our deaths."

"Not if we kill them first," Rumpel replied.

Malleus gave him a curious look. "Bold words, Prince."

"Don't call me that until we've chased the monsters out of our city and restored the throne. Until then, I'm no one."

Rumpel urged his horse forward. We followed him down the hill and out onto the open field. Swaying grass brushed our horses' legs. As the sun set, a single ray broke through a gap in the clouds. Hope swelled in my chest. We hadn't seen sunlight all day, yet here it was, waiting patiently to shine on us at the moment we needed it most.

As night drenched the land, the white towers of the city disappeared, replaced with torch lights, seemingly millions of them, glowing from the buildings and walls. We were left to travel in the gray hour before nightfall.

"We'll have to ride to the forest behind the city walls on the south side." Rumpel pointed ahead. "I don't know how much the forest has grown up since I was last there, but we'll find the entrance beneath the hollowstone."

"What's the hollowstone?" I asked.

"A stone entrance guarded by magic. Square stone, runes etched on it. Should be easy enough to spot."

"Not when it's dark," Dex said. "Should we use a spell for light?"

"Wait until we reach the forest," Rumpel answered. "We'd be wise not to alert the Sai-hadov of our presence. Riding out here in the open is risky enough."

The rain stopped, though the wind carried a biting chill as I scanned the path ahead. Treetops loomed against the darkening gray sky.

We rode into the forest. Stars and a silver-white moon glowed in the sky. I paused to glance up at the twinkling orbs, sending a silent prayer to the goddess, that she would protect us, that we would make it out of this quest alive. I considered praying that she would allow me to be with Rumpel, but I wasn't in the habit of asking for vain things.

Twigs snapping under my horse's hooves brought me out of my thoughts. Malleus whispered a spell. His red spheres hovered, casting a ghostly crimson light over the trees and scrubby plants growing along our trail.

"Do you see the stone?" Dex asked Rumpel.

"No. The forest is too overgrown. This might be more difficult to find than I thought."

We rode through the dense foliage. Even during the day, spotting any sort of stone would be difficult, but with only Malleus' red orbs to give us light, seeing it now was nearly impossible.

"Wait," Rumpel said. He stopped his horse, then pointed ahead. "What's that?" He dismounted, handed his reins off to his uncle, then stared up at a tree taller than the rest that leaned to the side. I also dismounted and walked to Rumpel.

"What are you doing?" I asked.

"This tree." He nodded at it. "It got blown to the side during a thunderstorm. I remember the stone was somewhere near it. Help me clear the brush."

I kept my gloves on as I aided Rumpel in clearing the sapling trees and shrubs. Malleus and Dex also dismounted their horses and hacked away at the bushes. We cleared out the area surrounding the tree when the hovering red lights highlighted a plane of smooth stone.

"Is this it?" I pointed.

"Yes," Rumpel said. "I think so." He knelt and ran his hands over the stone's surface. "Runes are etched on it. It's the hollowstone. Now we've just got to move it."

"What about the spell?" I asked.

"It's enchanted not to touch anyone with royal blood. The real trouble is moving it."

"I'll help with that." Malleus hefted his axe. "Past time I use my weapon for something." He knelt by the stone, then wedged the blade under the lid.

Rumpel grasped the stone's edges.

"On three," Rumpel said.

Malleus grunted in acknowledgment.

"One, two, *three*." Rumpel strained as he pushed against the lid. It glowed as it shifted an inch, magic lighting the woods around us as the stone's enchantment brightened.

Malleus and Rumpel grunted as they pushed the stone, inch by inch, until it revealed the opening beneath. Malleus straightened then snapped his fingers. An orb glided over the hole to illuminate a stairway cut into the stone tunneling beneath. Roots covered the steps, and the scent of damp earth wafted.

"Are we sure about going down there?" Dex asked, his nose wrinkled against the smell.

"Unless you'd rather stroll through the city gates and be attacked by a throng of Sai-hadov," Rumpel said. "I'm afraid this is the only way to get inside, Uncle."

"Ah, very well." Dex sighed, straightening the golden-embroidered collar of his cloak. "I suppose it's time I get used to crawling through caves and tunnels like a proper goblin." He chuckled, though no one laughed at his apparent joke. "Let's get on with it, then."

Rumpel nodded.

"What about the horses?" I asked.

"We'll have to leave them to roam," Rumpel answered. "We can't take them with us, and we don't know when we'll return. They'll make their way to safety. Hopefully."

I wasn't sure I agreed with him, but what other options did we have?

I sighed, looking up at Crooked Stripe who stood over me, chewing a mouthful of clover. Patting her nose, I spoke quietly to her. "I'll be back for you, you silly beast. Don't wander far." I removed her bridle, followed by her saddle, as the others did the same to their horses.

After we finished, we stood over the entrance to the tunnels once again. Rumpel slid into the tunnel first, and Malleus sent the hovering orbs to follow him. Rumpel's footsteps echoed as he took the narrow staircase. Splashing came from the hollow tunnel as he stepped to the bottom.

"I made it," he called up. "There's a few inches of water down here."

"Lovely," Dex murmured. "Let me go next. I'd rather get this over with." He grimaced as he lowered into the hole.

I straightened the straps of my pack on my shoulders. "I'll go."

Malleus nodded, his eyes meeting mine. He flexed his hands on the straps of his pack—the one he believed held the first two objects.

I glanced away from the big man, confused at his behavior, still unsure whether he was a traitor, or merely a man misunderstood.

After sitting on the damp ground, I slid my legs into the hole until my feet touched the staircase.

I kept my fingers pressed to the wall as I traversed the slippery steps. Rumpel held out his hand as I neared the bottom. I grasped his fingers. My feet splashed in the water, creating rippling waves, though my oiled leather boots kept my feet dry enough.

Above me, Malleus lowered into the hole, moving slowly as he climbed. The last of his red orbs followed him. Crooked Stripe's big head appeared in the hole. Her nostrils flared as she sniffed, snorted, then turned away.

"Horses would be smart to stay away from here." Malleus stepped to the floor, water splashing with an echo that reverberated around the cavernous tunnel.

I glanced up through the hole, seeing only tree branches against a dark sky. I wasn't sure why I worried so much about my horse as we turned away to follow the tunnel. Rumpel stayed back to walk next to me as Malleus and Dex led the way.

We walked a few paces behind the others. The two men talked quietly, though I couldn't hear their conversation. Rumpel grabbed my hand. The strength of his fingers in mine helped to quiet my unease. He leaned in and brushed a kiss over my forehead.

I looked at him, confused at his display of affection.

"What was that for?" I asked.

"You looked worried."

"It's that obvious, huh?"

He squeezed my fingers. "We'll get through this," he said, his voice firm and deep.

"I hope so," I answered.

The red light cast Rumpel's face in a crimson glow, deepening the color of the swirling tattoos on his cheekbone. I reached up and lightly ran my fingers over the symbols, their circular shapes reminding me of the pattern in my grandmother's necklace.

"Why do all goblins have tattoos?" I asked.

"They're not tattoos. We're born with the markings."

"Really? Do they have any meaning?"

"Most markings correlate with a person's magic. Markings on a person's face or head means their magic comes from their mind. Those born with the symbols on their chest use magic correlating with their heart."

"That's fascinating." I traced the symbol from his cheekbone to jaw, my fingers light on his skin. Warmth, like that created by magic, tingled beneath my fingertips. He sighed deeply, then placed his hand atop mine.

"You shouldn't do that."

"Why not?"

"The markings are especially sensitive to magic." He gave me a knowing, mischievous grin.

"Oh." I snapped my hand to my side, hand fisted, my cheeks burning red. "Sorry."

"No need to apologize. You didn't know."

Yes. I didn't know. I knew nothing about goblins or their ways, or their apparent magical markings with unexpected properties. What else about goblins did I not understand?

But there was no need to worry over those things now, not when we walked through a tunnel that could result in our deaths.

We reached a junction where passageways branched to either side.

"Which way to the vaults?" Dex asked.

Malleus pulled a folded piece of vellum from his vest pocket and unfolded it to reveal the map he'd gotten from the healers.

"The map doesn't say where the vaults are," Malleus said. "But if I remember, the king took the passageway through the south side of the castle to enter the vaults."

"So, we should go south," I said.

"Yes." Dex wrinkled his brow. "But which way is south?"

"Left," Rumpel answered. "The sun was setting on the western horizon as we entered the forest, and we've been traveling the same direction. We'll go left to travel south."

Malleus nodded, then folded the map and replaced it in his vest. We took the left tunnel and continued walking, the ground thankfully dry in this area of the passageway. Tendrils of roots hung from the low ceiling, and crumbling stones partially blocked our path in some places.

When we reached another junction, we repeated the process of scanning the map and following the tunnels in a southerly direction, all the while I walked with apprehension, realizing the Sai-hadov were lurking in the castle above us.

Ahead, the glint of metal appeared in the glow of Malleus's orbs.

"Is that the door to the vaults?" Dex walked faster.

We followed him until twin doors came into view. An onslaught of magic washed over me as we neared the bronze gateway. I bit my lip to distract myself from its intensity. Runes covered the doors, similar to the symbols on the hollowstone.

We stopped at the doors. Rumpel and I stood to face them.

"Here's where we'll part," Malleus said. "Once these doors are opened, there's a good chance the Sai-hadov will know. We'll have one advantage, as they don't know their way into the tunnels. Don't waste time finding the crown. When you return, we make our escape."

"And do it before those shadow demons catch up to us," Dex said.

"Easy," I said with a sigh, looking with apprehension at the etched runes.

"I wish you both the best of luck," Dex said.

"They'll need more than luck," Malleus replied. "I've already warned you about the crown's spell, so I won't bother doing it again. Take my words seriously."

"I will," I answered.

The big man nodded, shifting his leather pack on his shoulder. "Rumpel," he said. "The vault's doors, like the stone covering the tunnel's entrance, can be opened by anyone of noble blood. Use your magic and the doors will open."

"I understand."

Rumpel and I turned once again to face the doors. He took my hand and gave me a nod.

"You ready?"

"Yes." I breathed deeply. "Ready."

Rumpel closed his eyes, centering on his magic within. Calmness and strength came from the flow of his power, encircling me as he reached out and touched the door. The runes glowed with a periwinkle light, the hue of starlight, and it didn't escape my notice that his magic felt familiar, as if he drew from the magic of the star goddess the same as me.

Slowly, the doors swung inward. Rumpel opened his eyes, then glanced at me.

"You did it," I said.

"Yes, I did the easy part. The hard part of removing the crown is up to you. No pressure."

"Yeah, no pressure."

We glanced back at the two men before entering. Dex gave us a warm smile, but Malleus sneered.

"What are you bloody doing?" the big man said. "Hurry!"

Right. Without another glance behind us, Rumpel and I entered the vaults.

TWENTY

MALLEUS SENT HIS RED ORBS to follow us as we stepped inside. The doors boomed closed behind us. I jumped and spun around, staring at the sealed doors.

"Did you close the doors?" I asked Rumpel.

"It wasn't me. Must've been part of the spell."

"How are we supposed to open them?" I asked.

"My best guess is that we'll need the crown to do it."

"Of course. Easy. Why didn't I think of that?"

"Because we're in goblin lands. Everything here is convoluted and shrouded in secrets and magic. I'm surprised you haven't figured that out."

"Oh, I've figured it out quite well, thank you. Now, let's get this over with before Malleus throws a tantrum. Or the Sai-hadov attack. I'm not sure which is worse."

His lips quirked into a smile. "Agreed."

Our footsteps echoed through the hollow chamber. Square glass tiles covered the walls to form mosaics. Patterns of waves and sky ran alongside us as we hiked through the domed passageway. The moldy scent was absent, replaced with air that smelled fresher. I imagined there must've been vents somewhere.

Ahead, a set of wide steps led down to a circular

room. The tiled mosaics continued around the walls and wrapped the pillars in scenes of sea gods and dragons. On the ceiling was a depiction of a huge golden city with pearl-inlaid towers.

"Beautiful," I whispered, my voice echoing.

"Yes, the whole castle was like this once."

We took the stairs to the bottom. As we stepped to the floor, a surge of magic stung me, making my skin grow hot.

Magic engulfed us. Red sparks flowed up to create a barrier, snapping with the sound of electricity.

Rumpel cursed as he spun around, the enchanted shield encasing us. "I should've expected something like this."

"What is it?"

"Energy barrier. My father was fond of using them."

"How do we get out?"

He only shook his head.

"You don't know? He was your father, wasn't he?"

"Yes, but he never let me in on his secrets. I suspect he would've trained me in magic when I grew older, but his life was cut short." Rumpel sighed, as if trying to suppress the unwanted memories of his father's death.

I stared at the room, my heart beating wildly as I imagined the Sai-hadov searching through the castle to find us—to find our friends. On the floor, the mosaic pattern caught my eye. It depicted a crown encircled by a laurel wreath.

"Look." I tugged on Rumpel's sleeve and pointed to the image in the tiles. "It's a crown. Do you think it means something?"

"Possibly."

We walked to stand over the image. "We came here to find a crown, and here's the image of it." I knelt, then touched the glass squares.

Magic burst from the image. A bubble formed in the air, and inside it hovered a simple, wire-wrought crown.

I grasped my grandmother's necklace, the wire pattern pressing into my fingertips.

"They're the same," I said.

Rumpel raised an eyebrow. I glanced from my necklace, to Rumpel's key, to the crown, matching patterns wrought in each piece.

"That can't be a coincidence," I said.

"No," Rumpel said. "It's something I've suspected for quite some time. The necklace you wear is no ordinary magical talisman. It's goblin made."

"Goblin made? Then how did my grandmother come to be in possession of it?"

"I don't know. Right now, we've got bigger problems. Like how to get the crown."

I stood to inspect the bubble hovering before us. Like the shield, vein-like red sparks shot through the transparent orb trapping the crown.

"I wouldn't get too close," Rumpel said.

"Yes. I gathered that."

The crown's magic called to me. I reached out but didn't touch the shield, only observing its power. The spell held a heavy thickness, so strong it made my head pound with a throbbing headache, and I was forced to stand back.

Reminded of Malleus's warning, I took a deep breath and released its residual threads of magic.

"What's wrong?" Rumpel asked.

"The spell is very powerful. I have no idea how it

works or how to break it."

Rumpel's face fell. "But there's got to be something. Someway to undo it."

I shook my head. Despite stepping away from the orb, my skull throbbed. I clasped my hands to my head. Coldness settled deep inside me. With shock, I realized my magic was being syphoned away.

"It's taking my magic," I said.

"How?"

"I don't know. I didn't even use a spell."

My legs wobbled, and I sat on the floor, the stones cold beneath me. Dizziness made the room spin. I hugged my knees to my chest and closed my eyes, focusing on the last shreds of my magic.

Breathing deeply, I willed my magic to stay bound to me, yet my powers continued seeping away.

"What if we destroyed the shield?" Rumpel asked.

"How?"

He fisted his hands. "With my sword?"

"I doubt it would work. Enchantments must be fought with magic, except this spell is designed to absorb. The more I use, the more it takes."

I closed my eyes and rested my head on my knees. Even talking drained my energy.

"It hasn't taken my magic yet," he said.

"Because you haven't used it."

"What if I did? What if the spell works like the one in the hollowstone and in the doors?"

"What are you saying?"

"Maybe my father designed it so only a person with noble blood can break it?"

"Maybe." Confusion clouded my mind. Was the

room growing darker?

"I'll try it."

I wanted to warn him not to, but speaking was beyond me.

Maybe he's right. Maybe it won't take his magic.

He stood facing the crown. His magic left his fingertips in a burst of white magic. His spell collided with the bubble-like shield surrounding the crown. Sparks shot like lightning through the room, throwing Rumpel to the floor.

He landed with a gasp beside me. As he sat up, magic buzzed around him. Getting to his feet, he faced the crown. Breathing heavily, magic surrounded his fists, but the glow slowly faded.

I shivered. As the spell drained my magic, it took the warmth from my body.

Rumpel thrust his fist at the shield, hitting it with an impact that shook the room. A crack split the surface. Red sparks flying, the fissure sealed until the shield was whole once again.

With a groan, Rumpel sat beside me. His face had gone white. I placed my hand on his cheek, his frozen skin against mine.

"I... failed," he breathed.

No. I wanted to say, but the words wouldn't come.

My grandmother's necklace warmed my chest where it sat beneath my tunic. I grasped the chain and pulled it out, the wire-woven pendant swaying slightly as I held it.

Magic with magic.

Collecting the last reserves of my energy, I knelt, then slowly straightened to stand and face the crown.

After removing the necklace, I held the pendant with

shaking fingers.

I took one step, then another, until I reached the floating shield encasing the crown. Golden wire gleamed, taunting me.

Without overthinking it, I pressed my grandmother's necklace to the orb.

Static bit at my fingers, but it didn't blast me backward as it had done to Rumpel.

I kept the pendant pressed to the orb. The metal grew hot, but I ground my teeth and held it in place.

The metal glowed so hot it seared my fingertips. I cried out but didn't let go of the pendant.

By the goddess, I would get that crown, or I would die trying.

With a boom, the shield surrounding the crown and the shield trapping us both disappeared.

I fell back, landing beside Rumpel as the crown clattered to the ground.

Blisters covered my fingertips, but my adrenaline masked the pain. With a surge of energy, my magic returned, glowing to fill the empty spaces inside me.

I crawled to the crown and picked it up. Rumpel knelt beside me.

"You did it." Rumpel grabbed my hand and kissed my knuckles. "Kardiya, you're brilliant."

I pulled my hand away, wincing as he'd touched my burned fingers. "Ouch."

"Where are you hurt?"

"Just my fingers. They'll heal."

He took my hand again, cradling it in his so as not to touch my fingers. "You're burned."

"Yeah. It's not too bad."

"But we need to get this cleaned and bandaged."

"I agree, but that's not happening now, not until we use the three talismans to drive the Sai-hadov from the city. Still not sure how that works."

"We'll figure it out." He pressed a kiss to the palm of my hand, igniting a wildfire inside me as his cobalt blue eyes lingered on me. "I can't believe you did it. You never cease to amaze me."

"And I can't believe you're actually complimenting me." I gave him a quick kiss. "We should go. The Sai-hadov will be on our trail soon enough."

He nodded, then grabbed the crown and his bag before standing up. I also stood as Rumpel placed the final object in his pack.

Inside, I spotted the scepter and the glowing blue jewel of the ring. My stomach knotted with unease.

We'd claimed the three talismans, but that was easy compared to the final quest.

The prophecy surfaced in my memory.

The one who frees the talismans will be the one to destroy the Sai-hadov—or die trying.

TWENTY-ONE

SCREAMING CAME FROM AHEAD AS Rumpel and I crossed through the vault's tunnel. Rumpel gave me a dark look, and we started sprinting, the male voice echoing with a shriek of pain. My heart clenched with fear.

Were we too late?

As we neared the exit, the doors that had sealed behind us now stood open. I gasped as we reached the end of the hallway, my mind trying to process the scene of Dex lying dead on the floor, blood soaking his shirt and spilling over his purple cloak. Malleus stood over the dead man. A terrified Orlane cowered in front of the big brute, the warrior holding a knife to the boy's throat.

"*What*?" I gasped, my heart racing, my mind trying to catch up with the horror I saw before me.

Rumpel yanked the sword from his belt. "What's going on here, Malleus?"

Malleus tightened his grip on the knife he held at Orlane's throat. "Give me the crown or your brother dies."

"You bloody traitor," Rumpel spat. "I knew I shouldn't have trusted you."

"The crown." He kept the knife under Orlane's throat as he held out his other hand. "Give it to me."

Too much about this situation bothered me. How had Orlane gotten here? We'd left him at the healer's hut. Why had Malleus killed Dex? What reason did he have?

Something wasn't as it seemed, and I needed to figure out what before someone else ended up dead.

"Brother, stay calm," Rumpel said. He took a step forward, his sword pointed at Malleus.

"Stop there," Malleus barked, his voice booming. "Put your sword down."

Rumpel paused, unmoving.

"Do as I say," Malleus yelled. "Now!"

Rumpel's eyes narrowed at the traitor, but he placed his sword on the floor.

"Now give me the crown."

Rumpel shook his head.

"Give me the crown or your brother dies."

Orlane whimpered, his eyes wide and darting. Sweat beaded on the boy's brow.

"Orlane, listen to me. It will be all right," Rumpel said. "I promised it would be all right, didn't I?"

Orlane only sobbed.

"Give me the crown now!" Malleus shouted. "I won't ask again." His knuckles turned white as he gripped the knife's handle.

"You," Rumpel said, venom in his voice. "Will die for this." He reached for his pack and pulled out the crown. He took a step toward Malleus.

"Rumpel," I said calmly. "Don't give it to him."

His gaze darted between me and his brother. Fear flashed in his eyes—fear that he would lose his brother like he'd lost his parents.

I recognized that kind of fear.

226

It crippled a person's judgment.

Something glinted from Orlane's tunic. As I got a better look, the rubies of a dragon-shaped brooch gleamed.

Dex's brooch?

I glanced at the corpse on the floor. The man's shirt, though soaked with blood, was missing the brooch he'd always worn.

Why was Orlane wearing Dex's brooch?

My mind raced for a solution.

"Orlane, how did you get here?" I asked.

"Don't answer her," Malleus growled.

Orlane's face was so filled with panicked fear, he only managed a mumble for an answer.

"Orlane." Rumpel's eyes darted to mine, questioning, then he focused on his brother. "Is it really you?"

"It's him, all right," Malleus said. "He'll bleed just as well as anyone."

"But what if you're tricking me?" Rumpel held the crown closer to his body. "We left my brother at the healer's camp. How could he be here now? What if you're fooling us, Malleus?"

"Rum... pel," Orlane muttered.

"You don't believe me? You'd rather watch the boy bleed?"

Rumpel cast a pleading gaze at me. My heart pounding, I stepped toward the boy being held hostage by Malleus.

"Malleus," I said calmly. "There's no need to hurt Orlane. You know that, don't you?"

He cast me a lethal glare. "You hold your tongue, girl. You shouldn't be involved in this."

As I moved closer to Malleus and Orlane, the weight

of a spell tugged at me.

He's using a spell? Why?

"Malleus, tell me, why decide now to betray us when you've been so loyal?"

"I told you. Keep your mouth shut."

"No. I won't. Do you know why? Because I know who you are. Who you *really* are."

"What are you saying, Kardiya?" Rumpel asked.

I nodded at the big man. "That's not Malleus. You took his knife, didn't you? I'll bet you needed it as part of the transformation spell. Then you took Orlane inside the healer's hut. You pinned the dragon brooch on him then. It was a magical talisman, wasn't it? You were planning to use him as leverage as soon as you got close enough to the crown."

"Shut up," he spat. "Give me that bleedin' crown, Rumpel."

"Or what?" I demanded. "You'll kill your nephew? Your own flesh and blood? Drop the act. I know who you are. *Dex.*" I spoke the name with steel in my voice, releasing my magic to counteract the illusion spell.

The sparkling wave of my enchantment hit the man in the chest. He stumbled, his form shimmered as the spell encased him, tearing away his mask. The guise of Malleus evaporated, replaced with a startled Dex.

Rumpel drew in a sharp breath. "Uncle?"

Dex spat a curse and sliced his knife down Orlane's cheek. The boy cried out, clasping his hands to his face.

Rumpel rushed to his brother, but Dex leapt, his purple cape billowing, and kicked Rumpel in the mid-section.

The crown fell from Rumpel's grasp.

I dove for it, but Dex grabbed it first.

He turned and ripped the dragon brooch from Orlane's shirt. Rumpel slugged his uncle in the face.

He fell back with a muffled gasp, but before he hit the floor, his form faded, the brooch in one hand, the crown in the other.

"See you fools on the other side." His voice echoed as he disappeared completely.

Shock stunned me.

I tried to register what had just happened, but my mind had trouble wrapping around the loss—the crown was gone. Orlane injured. Malleus—who must've been the disguised Dex, dead on the floor.

I stumbled and knelt beside Rumpel, who crouched over his injured brother. Blood seeped from a cut in Orlane's cheek. Rumpel's hands shook as he pressed a handkerchief to the wound.

"How is he?" I asked.

"He's okay. The wound isn't deep. I don't think my uncle meant to... to..." Rumpel shook his head. "I don't even know my own family. How could he betray me? He was the closest thing to a father I had. Now I have no one."

Rumpel's pupils dilated, and his face had grown pale. He was clearly in shock. I rested my hand on his shoulder. Behind us came the sound of someone moaning. When I turned, I found the man on the floor who had appeared to be Dex; only now, magic shimmered around the body, revealing Malleus—the real Malleus.

He rubbed his forehead as he sat up, a knot forming on his temple, his busy eyebrows raised in confusion.

"What... happened?" he gasped.

"Dex betrayed us," I answered.

Malleus swore. "I knew it. I knew it the moment he

stole my knife."

"What do you remember?" I asked.

Malleus shook his head. "We waited at the doors for you. Dex used a spell to knock me out. Came out of nowhere. I didn't know what he was doing when I passed out. Couldn't move after that. Then... I woke up here. Bleedin' bloody bastard."

"He took the crown," Rumpel said over his shoulder. "He's probably been working with the Sai-hadov this whole time."

"He took my bag, too," Malleus said. "He's got all three objects now. He'll give it to the Sai-hadov, and they'll break free of the wall and take our lands. There's nothing to stop them. We're doomed."

I traded a glance with Rumpel.

"Not quite," I said.

"What do you mean?" Malleus asked.

"He's only got one object. The crown," I said. "The other two are replicas."

Malleus wrinkled his brow. "What?"

"Rumpel gave you fake objects," I explained.

Malleus surprised me by laughing. "Aye? Smart one then, Rumpel. At least someone's thinking in this group. You mean to tell me I've been carrying fake objects this whole time?"

I nodded.

"We couldn't trust you," Rumpel said. "Looks like we were mistrusting the wrong person, though."

Orlane sat up, keeping his brother's handkerchief to his face. "Bad... man," he said.

"Very bad man," I answered.

"I can't believe my own uncle would betray us like

that," Rumpel said. "What was that fool thinking?"

"He was thinking of himself," Malleus answered. "It's what he's always done. I'm not surprised."

"What do we do now?" I asked.

Rumpel shook his head. "I imagine Dex is taking the objects to the Sai-hadov. When they find out two of the objects are fake, they'll be after us."

"So, how do we get the crown now that the Sai-hadov have it?"

"I don't know." Rumpel rubbed his forehead. "I don't have any answers right now. Dex used that accursed brooch to transport my brother here, then he used it to transport himself out. If we knew where he went, that would be helpful..." He sighed, staring up at the ceiling, as if collecting his thoughts.

Weariness caught up with me. I sat on the floor beside Rumpel and Orlane, in shock at all that had happened. We'd come so close to having the three objects together only to have our victory ripped away from us.

"At least we still have these." Rumpel opened his pack, revealing the scepter and the ring.

"Can they help us get inside the Sai-hadov palace?" I asked.

"We can get inside with this," Rumpel said, holding up his key he wore around his neck. "The trouble is getting in undetected, then finding the crown and taking it."

He removed the two items from his pack. The gold and sapphires gleamed from the ring and matching scepter in the twinkling torch light. Malleus sat beside us. Orlane shied away from him.

"Bad... man?" he asked.

"No," Malleus answered, his voice surprisingly gentle.

"The bad man is your uncle Dex. He only looked like me so he could trick us. I'm on your side, Orlane, and I'll help you stop the bad men so we can go home. Now." He crossed his arms. "What's the plan?"

"We've got to get inside the palace and locate the crown," I said.

"Will this help?" Malleus pulled out the map and placed it on the ground. "We can take this passageway up to the first level. From there, we enter the palace. We've got one problem, and it might be a big one."

Rumpel raised an eyebrow. "What's that?"

"The three objects."

"What about them?" I asked.

"Prophecies, you see, they're always misleading," Malleus answered. "They're that way on purpose. They don't want just anyone figuring them out. Trouble is, we've only been searching for three objects, but the foretelling said something of a fourth."

"You've got to be joking," I said. "How're we ever going to find a fourth?"

He shrugged. "I'm only telling you what I've read— and I've read the prophecy a great deal."

"And you're waiting until now to tell us this?" Rumpel asked.

Malleus held up his hands in a defensive gesture. "I'm only telling you what I've read. The prophecy speaks of three objects your father hid—but then it speaks of four elements. Earth, air, fire, and water. In the past, it was the four elements that united our lands. I could be wrong, but in order for us to truly take back the throne, we'll need the fourth object."

I rubbed my neck where my muscles grew tight. "You

couldn't have told us this sooner?"

"What's the point?" Malleus said. "No way to find it. Unlike the first three objects, there aren't any clues to its location. My guess is that the king knew about it. Direct reference to it in the prophecy was left out for a reason."

My gut clenched at his implications. "So, even if we do manage to get all three objects together, we'll still not be able to send the Sai-hadov out of the city because we don't have the fourth object?"

Malleus shrugged. "Like I said, it was left out of the prophecy for a reason. Now, I'd say we not waste another minute. Not worth our time to worry about it now. Once Dex realizes the first two objects are fakes, he'll be down here in a hot second to get the real ones."

"He's got a point," Rumpel said. "We've got to get out of these tunnels. We're not safe here."

He placed the scepter and ring in his pack, and Malleus folded the map and slipped it into his coat's pocket. We stood and hiked through the tunnels until we reached a locked door. The rusted metal barrier had a knob and a lock.

"What now?" I asked.

"Now, we sneak inside," Rumpel answered with a mischievous grin.

He reached for the key around his neck. Metal chain links clinked as he removed it, then slid the key into the lock.

Memories surfaced of when he'd first taken me from my bedroom. He'd used the same key to take me from my home and into another world—a dark place filled with shadowy monsters and devious goblins.

But instead of the revulsion I'd felt toward him on

that day, my emotions had turned to admiration for a prince without a home, who was trying desperately to defeat an evil enemy and unite what remained of his people.

I couldn't hate him for that.

And I didn't.

Rumpel turned the key, and magic glowed from the lock. The mechanism clicked. The door swung inward on rusty hinges.

I wasn't sure what to expect of the Sai-hadov's castle. We walked into a place filled with light and mirrors, though to me, it reeked of darkness.

TWENTY-TWO

OUR FOOTSTEPS ECHOED, THE CEILING far above us. Despite the chandelier lights that hung suspended, a layer of dust covered the reflective glass, giving the place a grim appearance.

Faces of cherubs and grape leaves were carved into the gold-leaf frames surrounding the thousands of mirrors.

How could we expect to hide in such a place?

We made it to a circular foyer, a spherical couch at its center, covered in fleshy gray fabric that reminded me of a corpse's skin. Flames flickered from black wall sconces, the metal heavily embellished with the same patterns of cherubs and bunches of grapes.

I rubbed my arms as chills bristled. A shiver went down my spine while we waited in the foyer, turning in a full circle. The branching hallways seemed to go in every direction. After I focused more closely, I realized there were only two hallways, though the mirrors made it seem as if there were dozens.

"I recognize this one," Rumpel said quietly, pointing to the passageway branching to our left. "It leads to the stables. We're in the servants' quarters in the south wing.

I doubt many of the Sai-hadov use this area of the castle."

"Do you think the stables are still there?" Malleus asked. "Might be a good place to hide if the chance arises."

"Good point. There's only one way to find out," Rumpel said. "Follow me closely. We can't risk becoming separated."

We walked over thick rugs that covered the bare stone floor. Magic hung heavily in the air, tickling the exposed skin of my face and hands. I hugged my cloak around me, avoiding the image of our reflections in the mirror.

I had to fight back the impulse to run from the place and escape.

Minutes passed before we reached the next door, a simple wooden framework mounted on rusty hinges.

Rumpel pushed it open, and we stood looking out into the night, the looming shape of the dilapidated stables rising over us. The hooting of an owl was the only sound in the still of the darkness.

We didn't speak as we followed Rumpel out the door, down a narrow, cobbled footpath, and into the stables.

The scent of moldy hay hung in the air, making me wrinkle my nose against the damp smell.

Darkness made it impossible to see anything except the shapes of wooden beams creating stalls in front of us. Malleus conjured his red orbs, and they floated into the air, revealing a huge space empty of anything except moldy hay spread over the dirt-packed ground. Despite being inside a dilapidated barn, the tingle of fear that had coursed down my spine inside the palace was absent.

"We'll be safe enough here," Malleus said, turning to Rumpel. "Take the elf and go back inside," he said. "I'll stay here with the boy."

Rumpel gave him a sidelong glance. "You're not coming?"

"What's the point? My axe is no weapon against shadow, and my magic is nothing compared to yours or hers. Someone should look after the boy. I'll wait here for your return."

Rumpel took a deep breath. "You're sure about this?"

"Aye, as sure as I'll ever be." He clapped Rumpel on the shoulder. "When I was just coming to in the tunnel, you said something about not having a father. It isn't true. When your father assigned me to be head of his guard, that included protecting the two of you, and I did it without question, as if you were my kin, and that's never changed. I've always thought of you and Orlane as sons. I know I'm lousy at showing my emotions. I've never been good with words. I have no children of my own. I know I've made mistakes. Know I've done things that led to all this horror happening in our lands." He wiped at his eyes with the back of his hand. "But I'll have you know that I'm no traitor. Never have been.

"What happened at the gateway all those years ago, I can't explain it. It felt like... like something controlling me." He shook his head. "I know there's no excuse for my actions. But something wasn't right that day. I've paid the price ever since for opening the gateway and letting those monsters free to take our lands.

"But mark my words. It stops here." Malleus squeezed Rumpel's shoulder. "You." He looked at me. "Both of you, will be the ones to take our home back."

Rumpel grasped the man's arm. "We will not fail you, Malleus. We'll restore our kingdom. We'll avenge my father's death. That I promise."

"Aye, now go before you make a grown man cry. Accursed tears." He sniffed, then swiped his hand down his face.

Rumpel nodded and turned to his brother. Orlane stood resolutely, not crying as he had been earlier.

"I'm brave, brother," he said.

"You are. You always have been. Wait here for me?"

"I will."

Rumpel embraced his brother in a tight hug—the kind that didn't allow for any restraint, the kind that truly meant he cared deeply for him. When he turned to me, he took my hand and gave it a gentle squeeze. "You ready to defeat the Sai-hadov once and for all?"

"More than ready."

He smiled. "I like your attitude."

We walked out of the safety of the stables and into the chill night, taking the path toward the looming palace. Despite my tough act, deep inside, terror ate at me.

The last place I wanted to be was in that palace, where the mirrors held dark secrets and hid the truth, but I wasn't leaving this world until I killed the shadows, so I stayed at Rumpel's side, his hand in mine, and prayed the goddess allowed us to live.

When we entered, Rumpel took the ring from his bag and pressed it into my hand. "Put this on. It will disguise your image. Then we'll hold hands so it will do the same for me. As long as we're touching, the Sai-hadov won't see us."

"Why should I wear it?"

"Because if it comes to it, and they capture me, I want you to use it to escape."

"Me?"

He nodded.

"But what if you need it?"

"I'd feel safer if you had it."

I sighed, placing the ring on my finger. Holding out my hands, I watched as they faded. I grasped Rumpel's hand, and he faded as well, though neither of us completely disappeared.

"This is odd," I said, my voice sounding hollow.

"Yes."

"Where do we go from here?"

"The old throne room is my best guess. It's most likely where the Inshadov will be when Dex gives him the talismans."

"But we can't just waltz into the throne room. They'll find us for sure."

"True, but if the palace layout is anything like it used to be, there's a balcony surrounding it, and I know a secret passage to get inside."

"A secret passage?"

"Yes." He kissed my hand, his lips lingering. "I'm glad you're with me, Kardiya. This would have never been possible without you."

I gave him a smirking grin. "Not that I had any say in the matter."

"I apologized for that."

"I know." I gave him a quick kiss, though being so close to him made my heart throb, and I gently placed my hand on his chest. "I have to say, I'm glad you took me. My life was a complete bore until now."

"There's nothing like facing one's own death to keep the adrenaline flowing."

"Agreed."

Although he jested, I couldn't help but detect a darker meaning in his words.

But I'd made up my mind to keep going until the end. And I would.

TWENTY-THREE

WE CROSSED THROUGH ENDLESS HALLWAYS covered in mirrors.

Although our forms were nearly transparent, every glance at the reflective panels sent icy shivers down my spine.

I kept a tight grip on Rumpel's hand as we walked. We hadn't seen anyone, and the passageways remained eerily quiet, but I knew the Sai-hadov had to be somewhere.

"Everything is so different with these cursed mirrors everywhere," Rumpel mumbled. "But the throne room is in the east wing, which means the secret passage leading to it should be close. There was a panel in the wall..." he trailed off, looking from one mirror to the next. "The mirrors are covering it." He stepped to one of the heavy reflective panels and peeked behind it, then did the same to the next, and to the next.

I glanced behind a mirror and pried at the frame, looking behind it to see a paneled wall made of dark wood.

"One of the panels was lighter colored than the others," Rumpel said. "It's a hidden doorway."

We continued down the hall, looking behind each mirror, until I stopped.

"Here," I said. "Does it look lighter colored to you?"

He glanced behind the mirror where I stood. "Yes, that's it."

He grasped the edge of the frame. "Help me move it."

I stood on the opposite side and grabbed the heavy edge. We lifted it off the nail holding it in place, then lowered it to the ground.

We stood facing a paneled wall. Rumpel placed his hand on the wood and it clicked, then swung inward to reveal a dark hallway lined in stones.

We stepped inside, and Rumpel pulled the panel shut behind us. Only a little light drifted from the gaps around the doorway. As we started walking, the light disappeared completely. I kept my hand pressed to the wall, the stones cold under my fingertips, as I walked blindly through the passage.

"Father said these passageways were used by the servants centuries ago," Rumpel said. "The former kings didn't want the servants to be seen. But my father put an end to that—thought servants should be treated the same as everyone else. No one used these passageways when I was growing up. Well, except for me and Orlane. They made great places for games of dungeon catch."

The sound of Rumpel's voice kept me grounded. With complete darkness surrounding me, I could do nothing but listen and keep moving forward.

We walked until gray light came from ahead, illuminating the rough stone walls. I spotted a wooden panel like the one we'd entered through. We stepped to it, and Rumpel placed his ear against it.

"Can you hear anything?" I whispered.

"Music," he answered.

I also placed my ear to the wood. Sounds of violins drifted in a haunting melody. "Maybe they're having a ball?" I suggested.

"Yes. Maybe so."

He stepped back and carefully grasped the wood, swinging it inward. We looked out onto a balcony, but from this vantage point, we could see nothing below. A domed ceiling covered in mirrors rose above us.

With a deep breath, I grabbed Rumpel's hand, and we crept onto the balcony. We stepped to the ledge and looked down.

A multitude of people danced. Most wore ash-gray suits and gowns. Their jewels sparkled in the chandelier's light. On the edge of the dance floor stood a golden cage, resembling a giant bird cage. A man with a flamboyant purple robe sat inside.

I pointed. "Your uncle."

Rumpel nodded. "Yes, and I think I've also spotted the crown." He pointed to a raised dais at the head of the room. On a throne made of glass sat a man who wore a golden crown—*the* golden crown I'd recently found.

"Is that the Inshadov?" I asked, trying to get a better look at the man on the throne. From this distance, I could only make out a thin person wearing a white suit. His midnight black hair had a bluish sheen, and he sat with a straight back, unmoving as he looked out over the crowd.

"It's a mask," Rumpel said. "The image he wants everyone to see. He uses the magic of the mirrors to create the illusion."

"Is everyone down there a Sai-hadov?" I asked.

"Most likely."

"But they all look so... beautiful. I thought they were

supposed to be frightening."

"Yes. They're using the mirrors' spells to mask their appearance."

I studied the crown atop the king's head. "How are we supposed to get it? Ask politely?"

"That's one way. I don't know if it will be effective."

"Your uncle," I said. "Should we try to free him? Or does he deserve it?"

Rumpel clenched his jaw, his eyes hardened. "Goblins don't look kindly on traitors, but I can't allow him to die, either. The only reason he's alive now is because the Sai-hadov need his help in finding the two actual talismans he failed to give them. Once he's no longer of use to them, they'll kill him, and it will be a torturous death. I hate that he betrayed us, but I don't know if I can allow him to die in such a horrific manner."

"If we do free him, he'll have to be imprisoned."

"I agree."

As if conjured by our words, Dex looked up from his cage. His eyes focused on mine, though how he could've spotted us from this distance, I wasn't sure.

I grabbed Rumpel's arm and crept backward.

"What's the matter?" he whispered.

"I think he saw us."

"From down there?"

I nodded.

Whispering came from behind us. I spun around to face a person with unnaturally pale skin, gauzy white robes, and silver eyes. Startled, I looked into the eyes of the same phantom who'd lurked by my sleeping pallet, and who'd most likely taken the body of the other tracker.

The being moved so fast, its image blurred.

It held out a claw-like hand. White nails tipped its fingers, just like the talon we'd found on the tracker.

Magical bands encased me, stealing the air from my lungs. The world spinning around me, I sagged to the ground.

Rumpel, wrapped in lightning-blue cords of magic, fell beside me. His face contorted with pain, and he screamed out as welts formed on his skin. The stench of burned flesh pervaded the air.

The phantom-like being loomed over me, its eyes wide and silver, like mirrors.

I gasped as the being's hand wrapped my throat, its skin so cold it burned.

I struggled to breathe.

My lungs begged for air.

The hand compressed my windpipe so tight, stars spun in my vision.

Air...

The last thing I saw was the creature standing over me, removing the ring from my finger.

TWENTY-FOUR

I OPENED MY EYES TO a blur of whites and golds. As I focused, a high ceiling covered in mirrors rose over me. I turned my head and realized I lay on a marble floor at the foot of a glass throne. A man sat there. His hair midnight blue, his skin porcelain white, he looked down on me with eyes of mirrors, with no pupils or irises, as cold and detached as the glass surrounding us.

I couldn't shake the shiver running down my spine.

"Welcome to my home Kardiya Von Fiddlestrum, princess of Malestasia," he said, his voice smooth and controlled, as if he'd practiced the speech a thousand times.

"In… shadov," I rasped through a dry throat.

"Indeed, I am." He thrummed his fingers, which ended in claws, the same as the Sai-hadov phantom who'd captured me.

My stomach roiled. I squirmed, only to realize I was still encircled in magical cords.

"Release me," I said.

He smiled, a leering grin devoid of actual emotion. "If only I could, but as you were the one to retrieve the three talismans, you're still of use to me. I need your magic to aid me as I open the gate." I followed his gaze and focused on the phantom who'd captured us, eyes glowing with malice.

The Inshadov continued tapping his fingers on the throne's armrest. "Luckily, Zuriel was able to follow you without getting killed like his companion, and he was able to take the objects that rightfully belong to me. Now, we'll enter the world as we should have done all those years ago. With these, thanks to you."

He picked up the ring and scepter, which he held in his lap, something I didn't notice from my vantage point until now.

He had the ring and the scepter, which meant he'd taken them from me and Rumpel. Fear froze my heart.

Rumpel.

Where was he?

What had they done with him?

Bile burned my throat as the Inshadov slipped the ring on his finger. Magical blue fire ignited around him. His eyes transformed from flat mirrors to fiery blue flames. The power hit me with a wave so strong, my stomach lurched.

The king rose from his chair. He grabbed my collar with sickle claws that punctured through my cloak. He held me close, and his skin, white as bleached bone, stretched over his skull. Magic burned in his eyes from the power of the crown, scepter, and ring. I couldn't shake the enchantment's intensity as it crawled over my skin—a power stronger than any I'd felt before. With that kind of magic, what chance did I have of stopping him?

"Your magic will help me open the gate," he whispered, his voice melting through me as if he spoke a spell. "Then you will take me to your kingdom where I will do the same to your home as I will do here. I will transform our worlds in fire and blood. I will avenge the deaths of my people by the hands of mortals. I will kill you. I will kill every last one of you, and then I will enact an ancient spell, one that will cause you to be reborn as one of us."

The Inshadov traded glances with Zuriel, and the creature grabbed my arms and pulled me to his chest. His gauzy white robes tickled my cheeks, and his nails dug into my bicep.

I frantically searched the room for Rumpel, but only a few people wearing ballgowns or tailored suits stood watching me, as if I were a rare animal on display. They whispered quietly to one another as their mirrorlike eyes focused on me.

As I searched through the crowd, I didn't see Rumpel anywhere.

"Where is Rumpel Stiltskin?" I demanded.

"The prince?" The Inshadov cocked his head. "We punished him as was deserved, though you will see him soon enough. Come, the time has arrived for us to leave this city. The goblin traitor comes too." He snapped his fingers. Two Sai-hadov paced from the shadows of the room toward Dex's cage.

With the grating of metal gears, they opened the cage's door, grabbed Dex off the ground, and yanked him out.

Dark blood dried on Dex's forehead. Circles shadowed his eyes. He didn't acknowledge me. His haunted gaze focused straight ahead, as if he were in a trance. None of the humor and good-naturedness remained in his eyes, as if the Sai-hadov had taken his soul. He didn't speak as the Sai-hadov held him between them. Zuriel tightened his grip on my arm, moving me forward.

We followed the Inshadov, Dex, and several other Sai-hadov in a procession that led to the opposite end of the throne room until we reached a pair of ornate golden doors. Two Sai-hadov pulled them open, revealing a hallway lined in mirrors and black sconces. Fires flickered as we passed through the hall, moving silently, and I noted that only Dex and my footsteps made any sound.

My thoughts went to Rumpel.

What punishment had they given him?

The Inshadov said I would see him soon enough, but when, exactly? With the kind of torture the Sai-hadov were known for, would Rumpel be conscious? Would he recognize me?

We passed quickly through the hallways until we reached the doors leading out of the palace. After the doors were opened, we stepped into the cool night air. Crickets chirped in the distance, and stars glowed overhead, as if everything were right in the world, as if the Sai-hadov weren't about to infect the land.

Please, I prayed to the goddess. *Don't allow them to go free. Give me the strength to stop them.*

Nails dug into my skin, piercing my flesh, reminding me of my place. I was their prisoner, and after they took the goblin kingdom and my home, they would kill me. Becoming one of them was a thought that terrified me, and I tried not to ponder it.

It won't end this way. I will stop them.

Or I will die trying.

TWENTY-FIVE

WE STOPPED AT THE WALLS of the city in front of a gate that must've risen twenty stories tall. Etchings of a battle scene were carved into the oxidized bronze doors. A faint tingle of magic resonated from the gates—a spell that called to my primal senses, one laced with old magic, from a time when all races were one, when goblins and elves were equal.

I sucked in a sharp breath as two Sai-hadov moved forward, dragging a bloody Rumpel between them. His bottom lip was swollen where a cut split it open. His shirt was torn, revealing more cuts on his chest and torso. Dried blood darkened the fabric of his cloak.

The Inshadov moved toward Rumpel, his footsteps not making any sound, which unnerved me.

"Prince of the Goblins!" he said mockingly, a smug grin on his pallid face. "You've arrived in time to watch as I open the gates to your lands and take my place as the true ruler. I've been waiting a long time for this moment, and I've got you to thank for it. You, and her, of course."

Zuriel moved me forward to face the Inshadov and Rumpel. I wanted to break free and embrace Rumpel, to use my magic and heal his wounds, but I was stuck in the grasp of the Sai-hadov.

"Rumpel." I jerked my arm, though Zuriel held me with an iron grip.

Rumpel's eyes met mine.

Unlike the detached look I'd found in his uncle's eyes, Rumpel's gaze burned with defiance.

"We're getting away from here," I said. "We'll stop them."

The Inshadov shot me a dark glare. The magical bands, which had loosened while we walked, grew tight again. My magic drained from me, leaving me with barely enough energy to stay conscious.

"Bring them forward," the Inshadov said. Rumpel and I were forced to move, our feet dragging before we stopped in front of the imposing gateway.

The magical bands tightened around my ribs until I felt sure they would leave bruises. I gasped to catch my breath, dizziness making the doors seem to spin in my vision.

A line of Sai-hadov gathered on either side of us. They wore white, gauzy robes, the same as Zuriel, and had the same mirrorlike eyes. Some of them had dark hair like their king, others had white stringy strands, but others were hairless and resembled corpses.

Rumpel stood beside me, and I had the urge to reach out and grasp his fingers, though bands wrapped us both, keeping us apart.

I shifted my arms, trying to work my way out of them, but the more I moved, the more they constricted me.

Tears of frustration burned my eyes.

The Inshadov walked forward, standing between us and the gate.

My heart sank.

Was there nothing we could do to stop him?

His midnight blue hair glowed in the sputtering fire-light cast from the torches lining the giant wall. Breathing deeply, I tried calling on the magic within me, only to have it disappear, leaving an empty hole in the pit of my stomach.

The Inshadov gave me a slight nod as he held the scepter, and it was then I realized he was syphoning my magic the same way the shield around the crown had done. As blue fire glowed from the ring and scepter, my energy faded.

Stop! I wanted to yell as he turned to the gate, but with the cords constricting me, I only managed a pain-filled mumble.

He raised the scepter.

Blue fire ignited around him, burning to outline the giant doorway, shining around the battle scene that came into sharp focus. Bodies trampled beneath horses and chariots.

With a deep groan, the doors split open.

Rage burned deep in my chest.

All the work we'd gone through to get the three tal-ismans was for nothing. We hadn't stopped the Sai-hadov, we'd helped them.

Maybe Baelem had been a pawn of the Sai-hadov all along. Maybe she'd wanted us to get the items precisely so they would win.

But why would she do that? Why would she betray her people and curse them to die at the hands of the enemy?

It didn't make sense, but neither did Dex's betrayal.

As Rumpel had told me many times, goblins dealt in deceit and treachery, a fact I was fully realizing.

The gates opened wider.

Blue magical fire spread to engulf us, its heat warm on my skin, but not burning.

When the gates were fully open, they revealed a wide road paved in cobblestones leading away from the city to the rest of the outside world, where I spotted the jagged shapes of mountains against the star-filled sky.

"Finally," the Inshadov said, his voice filled with awe. "We will be free of this city, free of our cage."

He turned toward us. His smile curved into a wicked grin.

"Bring the prince," he called. "He will be the first sacrifice in my new reign over all goblin lands."

He flexed his hands to form fists, the jeweled ring glowing.

No, I wanted to scream as they dragged Rumpel forward.

My heart clenched painfully tight.

I couldn't lose him, couldn't watch him die. I flexed against the magical bands, willing them to loosen so I could save Rumpel, feeding what little I had left of my magic into the cords.

Slowly, my magic responded. The bands grew colder, but I still had no way of breaking through them.

The creatures carried Rumpel between them until they stood at the foot of the Inshadov. He circled the prince, then lifted the scepter and bashed Rumpel's face. The prince cried out where his skin split open along his temple. Blood oozed from the wound, dripping down his cheek.

I balled my hands into fists, rage burning like wildfire deep in my chest.

I would kill the Inshadov for this. He would suffer a thousand times over.

"The time for your death has come," the Inshadov said. "After your death, you will rise to become one of us, the first in our new army."

"No," Rumpel managed.

The Inshadov's eyes flared wide, burning with blue fire. "Yes!"

The ring glowed as he thrust his fisted hand into Rumpel's midsection. The prince gasped, falling hard to his knees.

The Inshadov knelt to be eye-level with Rumpel, then grasped the prince's face between his clawed hands.

"I will not give you the mercy I showed to your parents, allowing their souls to be free. After your death, you will be trapped like me, and understand the horror it is to live as a prisoner. You will come to understand us, as will all mortals who have never experienced true torment."

The Inshadov wrapped his hands around Rumpel's neck, strangling him.

Rumpel's lips went blue.

"Stop!" I managed a hoarse whisper. "Stop, now!"

Magic flowed out of me. My grandmother's necklace grew warm. The key around Rumpel's neck glowed. I looked down and saw the wire-crafted pattern of the pendant radiating pure white light the same as Rumpel's.

The Inshadov's eyes narrowed as he glanced from Rumpel's key to mine.

"What are you doing?" he demanded.

His smile turned to a grimace of pain.

The light glowing from both our necklaces became blinding. The Inshadov stood, grabbing the scepter and stumbling backward as he shielded his eyes.

"Stop doing that!"

He stumbled again, the ring and scepter's light turning from blue to fiery orange. He stepped across the gate's threshold, from the safety of the city and into the open world. The air shifted as he crossed, a spell come to life.

His skin turned to ash. He dropped the scepter. A clanging echo rang through the courtyard.

Gasping, he staggered back into the safety of the city's courtyard, though the wind gusted, breaking him apart.

His eyes burst from their sockets with the sound of shattering glass. He screamed, a primal roar that sounded more animal than human.

As his form evaporated, the doors began to close. By the time they were nearly sealed, the Inshadov lay wheezing on the ground, his body a deformed heap of ash.

The exposed muscles of his face twitched, then turned to ash, before he gave one last gasp, the booming of the closing doors echoing his final exhalation.

The Sai-hadov surrounding us panicked. Frantic screams broke out. Their forms shifted, from a humanlike appearance to ghosts. Howling with fear, they flew away from the gate to the safety of the castle. Their white robes flying, they left Rumpel, Dex, and I to stand over their king's remains.

Dex stood. The look of detachment I'd seen earlier in his eyes had been replaced with resolve. Tugging on the lapels of his purple cloak, he strode to the ash pile and removed the ring. He did the same with the crown, placing it on his head, and tucked the scepter under his arm.

I watched in utter confusion as the man moved.

What was he doing?

The Inshadov had nearly killed Rumpel, and now he lay as a pile of ash on the paving stones, the gate sealed once again, and Dex acting as if he'd expected it.

"Shame the Inshadov couldn't follow prophecy as well as me," Dex said smugly. He walked to me, then grabbed the chain around my neck and lifted it off. He went to Rumpel and did the same with the prince's key until he held it and my pendant in his hands.

"What... are you doing?" Rumpel gasped. He still knelt on the ground with the magical bands wrapped around him, his arms pinned at his sides just like mine.

"Four objects. Not three. Yes, you may be asking, why do I have five objects? A ring, a scepter, a crown, your key, and Kardiya's necklace. Ah, but I have a good answer, one I realized when I first spotted the elven girl's necklace hanging around her pretty neck when I met her in the goblin caves. This isn't one key and one pendant, they're part of the same, and in order to take the throne for one's own, they must be used as such.

"So, if you don't mind, I believe it's time for me to do what I started in motion all those years ago, when I placed a curse on that brute Malleus and placed the suggestion in his head to unseal the Sai-hadov's gateway."

"You... traitor," Rumpel breathed.

"Yes, I am. Have been for many years, except now it's finally paying off. Pardon me while I take my place as king of the goblins." He stepped past Rumpel and toward the gate.

Rumpel managed to reach out and grab the hem of

Dex's cloak. "Uncle. Why?"

"Why?" He rounded. His jaw clenched, and I'd never seen such hate in his eyes as I saw now. "Because I was always second best, the cheerful brother who would never amount to much. Nothing more than a dunce in your father's glorious empire. I know what it's like to be one's shadow more than those accursed Sai-hadov.

"Yes, I knew I would never defeat your father on my own. Had I killed him outright, I would've been imprisoned or sentenced to death. I tried other means—subvert ways of killing him. Poisoning. Hunting accidents. Every attempt failed. I knew if I were to truly take the throne, I needed help.

"So, I used that brute Malleus to free them. The creatures killed your father as I wanted, but then he had to go and hide the objects that controlled our land.

"Do you know how *bloody long* I've been waiting for this day?" he shouted, his voice enraged.

He stood straight, taking a deep breath to compose himself. "But I've waited patiently. I let events play out as they naturally should, using one thing to my advantage." He held up the pendant and the key. "Knowledge. I had the advantage of spending hours upon hours in the palace libraries, seeking out a way to retrieve the objects. It took months of continuous searching. I'd nearly given up when I stumbled upon the passage about a fourth object.

"'Maiden of the dark magic, keeper of the pendant, and the key of transformation in the hands of the unredeemed. Two forms united to open the heart of the kingdom,'" he quoted.

A breeze washed over us, carrying the scent of charred remains from the Inshadov's corpse.

"I nearly stole the pendant when I first met you, Kardiya. But then I realized I needed to allow you to find the three objects. So, I went on the quest with you. Supported you. Until I finally had my opportunity. But enough of that. It's time I do what I was meant for. Become the true ruler of our land."

He smiled as he held the key and pendant. Metal clicked as he pressed them together, the pendant forming the head of the key, as if they were meant to be one.

Radiant magic glowed around the final talisman.

Dex walked past Rumpel, not giving his nephew a second glance. Panic made sweat trickle down my face. I worked my arms back and forth, the bands beginning to loosen as the Sai-hadov's magic disappeared.

If I could just get one hand free!

As the cord's powers decreased, my magic returned, as did my energy. I worked faster, my wrists and forearms burning where the ropes dug into my flesh, but I couldn't let the pain distract me.

"Dex," I called.

He stepped to the gateway but turned to glance at me. "Don't open it!"

He laughed. "Don't open it? You must be madder than I thought. But you are a dark elf, after all. Shame. In a goblin's world, I doubt there will be a place for you. But we'll discuss matters of extermination after the gateway is opened, and the kingdom is mine."

He turned back to the gateway.

I grimaced against the pressure of the ropes as they tore through my skin.

The fibers snapped, and I released one arm, then the other.

As soon as I got to my feet, I went to Rumpel and knelt in front of him.

His swollen face was nearly unrecognizable. I cupped my hands to his cheeks, then gave him a soft kiss.

"Ouch," he moaned.

"Sorry."

"Don't apologize. Just get me free so I can stop my uncle."

I nodded, reaching for the bands encircling him. I pried at the knots until the cords fell with a thump to the cobbled ground.

Wind rushed around us as we stood and approached Dex.

"Uncle," Rumpel called, his voice laced with righteous anger as it carried through the empty courtyard.

Dex turned. His eyes went wide as he focused on me and his nephew.

"Rumpel," he shouted. "Stay back. You don't want to become the first traitor in my new empire."

"I'm no traitor, Uncle. You are!"

Dex scowled. He turned and placed his hand against the gateway. Rumpel raised his fist and blasted out a powerful burst of fiery magic that boomed as it hit his uncle's back. The man screamed and dropped to the ground.

"You..." Dex spat, breathing heavily. "Shouldn't have done that." He climbed to a standing position, dropping the key and scepter to pull a knife from his belt. "Now I've got no choice but to kill you."

He raced for Rumpel, moving with superhuman speed, though Rumpel managed to dodge the blow. Rumpel hit the man's jaw with a solid impact. Dex spat a mouthful of blood, then thrust his knife for Rumpel's heart, but the prince dodged, the blade nicking his shoulder.

As the men fought, I raced to the gateway and recovered the scepter, ring, and the united key. I had everything but the crown, which Dex still wore. I placed the ring on my finger. Unlike earlier, my form didn't become transparent. Instead, its power infused with my own in a burst of energy that filled me to the core. The colors in the courtyard stood out in sharp contrast. My hearing amplified.

As Rumpel hit his uncle's face, the man's head snapped back, its sound coming to my ears with loud clarity.

The crown fell from Dex's head and hit the ground, spinning before it came to stop by my feet, as if it wanted me to have it.

I grabbed it up, clutching the metal wire of the crown and the scepter to my chest. I backed to the gateway.

Dex spun around. His eyes went wide with madness. "Kardiya, stop!"

"No," I called to him. "You should've never allowed the Sai-hadov free on this world. Your treachery stops now." I spun around and placed my hand against the cold metal of the gateway.

Something knocked me from behind. I hit the ground, the wind stolen from my lungs. Stars spun in my vision.

Dex knelt over me and ripped the scepter from my hands. "You'll die for this!" he spat, ramming the scepter's sharp jewel into my stomach.

I cried out, clutching my midsection. Warm blood seeped from the deep wound.

Rumpel grabbed his uncle by the lapels of his fancy purple cloak and rammed him so hard into the gateway, the giant bronze doors rattled.

Dex's eyes rolled into the back of his head.

He went limp, and Rumpel dropped his uncle to the ground. He stepped over the body, then knelt at my side.

Grasping my hand in his, he gently kissed the back of my hand.

"Kardiya, you're hurt."

I managed a nod. I bit my lip against the radiating sting that burned like fire through my belly. We were too close for me to give into the pain.

"Help me stand," I gasped, grabbing up the scepter which was tipped in my blood. "We'll open the gateway… together."

"Are you sure?"

"Positive." I put as much determination in my voice as I could muster.

"But you're bleeding."

I touched his face gently. "So are you. We'll heal after we save the world."

He gave me the smile that showed his teeth, the one I'd only seen a number of times, and now I realized what that smile meant—it meant he loved me.

"All right," he said. "Let's finish this."

He took my hand. The pain stole my breath as I moved, but I clamped my hand to my wound, my other hand in Rumpel's, and we stepped past an unconscious Dex to face the gateway.

"Together?" he asked.

"Together." I nodded.

He held the scepter and key as I wore the ring and the crown. With hands touching, we pressed our palms to the gateway.

The world shuddered.

White light flared from the gate.

The power in the magic stole my breath—an ancient power, one that came from the universe, from the stars, a prehistoric enchantment that united us.

The gate parted, trembling as it moved. I shielded my eyes against the brilliant glow. Rumpel grabbed my fingers in his hand.

He gave me a brief smile as the gate opened completely, then stopped, revealing a sky beginning to lighten with the approaching morning.

Taking a deep breath, I looked out over the landscape of hills covered in swaying grass.

"We'll have to step over the threshold," Rumpel said. "If we don't have this right, we'll end up like the Inshadov."

"No need to warn me. I think we'll be okay." I reached up and stroked my finger along the swirling pattern covering his cheek. "Rumpel, I've never told you this, but…"

He pressed his finger to my lips. Smiling, he shook his head. "Tell me when we step over the threshold?"

I nodded.

Together, we took two steps forward and left the protection of the city gates. Sunrays streaked the sky above the mountains. I breathed in the fresh air, let it fill my lungs and fully renew my energy. Not even the pain from the scepter's wound bothered me.

"Okay," Rumpel said with a lopsided smile, his eyes twinkling with life and passion, as if his strength had also been renewed the same as mine. "Now, what were you saying?"

I stood on my tiptoes and pressed a kiss to his lips, then placed my hand on his chest, the beating of his heart warm under my palm. I didn't know the best way to tell him. I wanted to come up with something clever, something my brother would've spouted—in song, no less— to his gorgeous new bride. But I didn't have a way with words like him, so I decided to keep it simple.

"Rumpel." I took a deep breath, nervous butterflies stirring in my stomach. This wasn't as easy as I thought. "I love you."

"That's good." He said, kissing my cheek near my ear. "Because," he whispered, his breath tickling my neck. "We just opened the gateway together. You and I are the king and queen of the goblin lands."

TWENTY-SIX

WEDDINGS MADE ME NERVOUS.

My marriage terrified me.

I had one thing in my favor—I was head-over-heels in love with Rumpel, and that was the only thing that calmed my nerves as I stepped atop the dais in my home palace's ballroom and stood to face the man who I would spend the rest of my life with.

His genuine smile caught me by surprise. He looked regal in his dark blue, velvet doublet, a sword hanging from a belt at his side, and form-fitting black pants.

"You look stunning," he whispered.

I could only smile back. Words escaped me.

We stood in front of a crowd of hundreds of elves and goblins, yet to me, it seemed we were the only two people in the world.

"I love you," I mouthed to him.

"I love you more," he answered quietly, then he gave me a sly wink laced with mischief.

The officiator cleared his throat. We turned to him, and the elderly man, a dragon shifter—Odette's grandfather—gave us a gentle smile, the wrinkles around his eyes crinkling. His silver robes rustled as he wrapped a length of fabric around our hands and spoke the words of the ceremonial binding. His voice echoed around the tall pillars and domed ceiling. I had trouble concentrating on what he said, my stomach in knots and my heart fluttering.

The officiator's voice cut through my thoughts. "Will you, Kardiya Von Fiddlestrum, take this man, Rumpel Stiltskin, as your companion, your cherished friend, your bonded mate, and your husband, your companion for this life and for the rest of eternity?"

"I will." As I said the words, the magic inside me reacted, glowing so powerfully that tears sprang to my eyes. A vision came to me, of Rumpel and I together with children of our own, my brother and his wife with us as we visited the home of the witch Gothel and her husband, Raj. It lasted a brief moment, yet in that one scene, I saw a future of happiness. Perhaps not one of perfection or even of ease, but a future filled with laughter, love, and family, but most of all, a future of freedom for us all.

Freedom for a witch held captive in a tower.

Freedom for a dragon shifter held captive by a tyrant.

Freedom for a girl captured by a goblin in need of redemption.

I will... I repeated in my head. And I knew I would.

THE END

ACKNOWLEDGEMENTS

As I write the acknowledgments for my fourteenth published book/novella, it occurs to me that I may be stumbling into the pitfall of taking this publishing journey for granted.

But I refuse to do that.

There are too many people to thank who support me through the entire process, from coming up with those first few scenes that blossom into a story, bouncing off ideas (I thank my husband David for this) writing the first draft (I'm thanking my partner-in-crime and the best writing buddy in the world, Heather Cashman, for this one.)

Then to sending that unpolished draft to my beta readers: fellow fantasy author and true friend, Sabrina A. Fish, intuitive reader extraordinaire Kendra Forgey, and my husband David once again (the Alpha reader!) Their feedback is amazing and makes every book better.

The journey continues when I send my book baby into the capable hands of the crew at Clean Teen Publishing. Kelly A. Risser, what an amazing editor you are! Every book shines with your careful critiques.

To Marya Heidel: I'm stunned by your amazing

cover art.

To Rebecca Gober: For your knowledge into the world of marketing.

To Melanie Newton: Thank you for your support and guidance.

To Courtney Knight: For your dedication and hard work that goes into every book.

After the process of publishing, my book goes out to you, my readers, the most vital people in the entire process. Without you, I wouldn't get to call myself an author. I'm humbled by your support.

While they may not think they contribute much to my writing process, my kids are my inspiration, so I acknowledge them as well: Phoenix, Sequoia, Bridger, Gabriel, and Ronan.

And finally, my Heavenly Father, who gave me everything I have.

About The Author

Tamara Grantham is the award-winning author of more than a dozen books and novellas, including the Olive Kennedy: Fairy World MD series and the Shine novellas. Dreamthief, the first book of her Fairy World MD series, won first place for fantasy in Indiefab's Book of the Year Awards, a Rone award for best New Adult Romance of 2016, and is a #1 bestseller on Amazon with over 200 five-star reviews. She has recently signed with Clean Teen Publishing for a fairytale retelling trilogy.

Tamara holds a bachelor's degree in English. She has been a featured speaker at numerous writing conferences and a panelist at Comic Con Wizard World speaking on the topic of female leads. For her first published project, she collaborated with New York-Times bestselling author, William Bernhardt, in writing the Shine series.

Born and raised in Texas, Tamara now lives with her husband and five children in Wichita, Kansas. She rarely has any free time, but when the stars align, and she gets a moment to relax, she enjoys reading, taking nature walks, and watching every Star Wars or Star Trek movie ever made.